INTO THE QUIET

BETH C. GREENBERG

A NOVEL

ISOTOPIA
PUBLISHING

INTO THE QUIET

ISBN (paperback): 978-1-7359447-3-9
ISBN (hardcover): 978-1-7359447-4-6
ISBN (ebook): 978-1-7359447-5-3

Cover design, illustrations, and Isotopia logo by Betti Gefecht
Interior design by Domini Dragoone
Family tree background image © sabphoto/123RF.com

ISOTOPIA PUBLISHING
www.isotopiapublishing.com
www.bethcgreenberg.com

First Edition

For Larry,
who carried me over the threshold of our
first apartment many years ago
and has never once let me down.

BOOKS BY
BETH C. GREENBERG

THE CUPID'S FALL SERIES:
First Quiver
Into the Quiet

Isotopia, by Jeff Greenberg
(prepared for publication by Beth Greenberg)

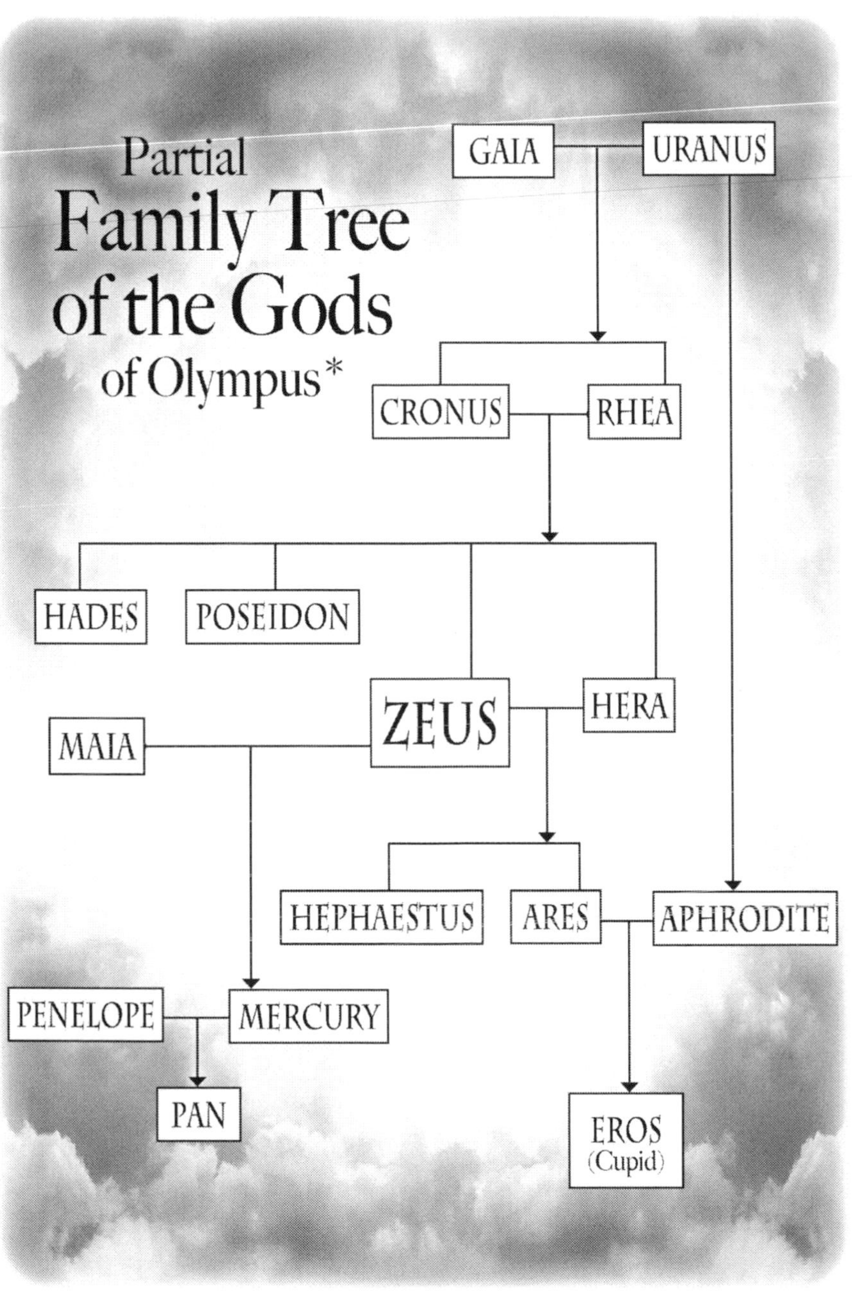

**Names chosen by gods in 480 C.E.*

A full listing of divine characters can be found immediately following the story.

Happy are those who dare courageously
to defend what they love.

—OVID

1

GODDESS

The second time Cupid's heart revved up should have been easier, and in some ways, it was. He recognized the stabbing pain in his chest right away, and he had a general idea what was expected of him.

But Cupid wasn't particularly eager to relive the Mia experience—except for that one exceptionally nice part just before he blurted out he loved her, realized her heart wasn't echoing his love beat, and vomited up his dinner. Also troubling, this signal was sharper than the first. The gods weren't messing around.

Cupid heaved his body off the barstool. His knees buckled from the alcohol swimming in his system—or perhaps from the grim understanding that his next trial was upon him—and he pitched forward. Pan thrust out his hand and steadied his best friend as he'd been doing in one way or another since Cupid fell to Earth twelve days ago.

"Easy," Pan said, his voice taut with concern.

Cupid dragged in a deep yoga breath, exhaled slowly, and nodded. "Okay, I'm ready." He sure hoped he sounded braver than he felt.

"Where's your shirt?"

Cupid's gaze dropped to his bare chest. *Right.* That pretty boy he'd been dancing with had tugged it off him. Cupid turned toward the dance floor, one giant, tangled organism pulsating under the purple lights. "It's buried somewhere in that pile of bodies."

Pan tapped his nose. Locating Cupid's scent would pose no challenge for the demigod of the wild even in human form. "I'll be right back. Don't move."

Cupid had nearly wrapped his head around the here-we-go-again when his shirt came flying at his face. Pan was not one to coddle.

"Lead on," said Pan.

"You're coming?"

"Of course. My ass is on the line, too, or have you forgotten already?" Truthfully, Cupid had been working quite hard to put Pan's ass out of his mind.

"Fine. This way." Off they went, Cupid's relentless heart-compass guiding the way with Pan trailing tight on his heels. Judging by the intensity of the churning in his chest, whatever Cupid was meant to find was right here at Versailles.

So intent was Cupid on following his heart, he nearly crashed into a raised platform that placed a dancer's gold-covered bulge exactly at eye level. An impressive set of white feathered wings fanned out from the dancer's shoulders and somehow fluttered gracefully while the lower half of his body popped and gyrated at his audience.

Pan licked his lips and stared, mouth agape. "*Wow.*"

"He's all yours," Cupid replied. "He's not my Worthy."

But Cupid was close; he could feel it. The signal pulled him along the edge of the stage and into a flock of wild women, screaming and stuffing money into the dancer's pouch. *Not this one, nope, nope . . . boom!* Cupid stopped short, and Pan—distracted by the slicked-up, writhing angel on the stage—slammed into Cupid's back, ramming him into the new love of his life just as she was tucking a bill inside the dancer's thong.

The woman grasped at the fabric to regain her balance, but the measly garment was no match for her downward velocity. The pouch gave way, spilling money and genitals, before Cupid could manage to grab the falling woman around the waist. A collective gasp went up around them—with Pan's enthusiastic, "Oh *hell*, yeah!" loudest of all—before the angel could tuck himself and his tips back inside.

"I'm so sorry," Cupid said, relaxing his grip around the goddess in his arms as she regained her footing. "Are you okay?"

She blinked up at him with a shocked pair of hazel eyes set into a deep blush. "I . . . I honestly don't know." But Cupid knew. The woman's racing pulse, dilated pupils, and dry mouth were dead giveaways, and he was feeling quite the same.

She shook her head, freeing a tendril of spun gold across her cheek. Without thinking, Cupid reached in and gingerly tucked the loose hair behind her ear. The two sets of eyes locked, and neither would let go, dazzle-*ee* meeting dazzle-*er* and vice versa. She melted his insides with every shaky breath passing between her lips.

"Take your time," Cupid said, finding himself in no rush to go anywhere or do anything except exactly this.

Need poured off this woman in hot, dangerous waves—waves that had already pulled Cupid under. She raised her hand to wipe the beads of sweat from her brow. Two rings dwarfed her left hand: a diamond the size of a robin's egg with a solid gold band below. Married.

"Hey, what's—" Pan stopped cold. "Oh boy. Q, we need to talk. *Now.*"

"Call me," Cupid answered Pan, barely registering his presence.

Fully prepared to sweep his precious love into his arms, carry her to bed, and pleasure her for the rest of his days, Cupid remembered his circumstances and the horrible ordeal he'd gone through with Mia. He couldn't draw another breath until he knew the truth.

Summoning as much focus as he was able, Cupid tuned in to the chorus of hearts beating all around him. He peeled them away one by one until he had distilled his beloved's from all the rest.

No echo.

Frantic, Cupid placed an ear to her chest and listened with all his might.

In that terrible moment, Cupid understood. The goddess in his grasp was not his Right Love after all; she was his next torment.

2

TORMENT

"C'mon, man. Get your face out of her tits. That shit is not dignified." Pan's fingers curled around Cupid's shoulder and pinched—hard.

Cupid turned his head as far as possible with the girl still locked in his arms and shot Pan the dirtiest glare he could muster. Pan's face was so close, the two men could have kissed. "Must you always be so crude? I was listening to her heart."

Pan's eyes worked back and forth between Cupid and his goddess. "She's the one, right?"

Not that he doubted it for a second, but Cupid focused on the wild thumping in his chest just to be sure. "Yes."

One of Pan's bushy, copper eyebrows quirked up. "And?"

And to the crows with you, Cupid wanted to say, because the truth hurt. Cupid's gaze dropped to the floor as he shook his head.

"Motherfucker." Pan's death grip relaxed into a gentle squeeze. "You best take your hands off her."

Sensation flooded back into Cupid's fingertips. Only a thin layer of fabric separated the pads of his fingers from the girl's warm skin.

Raising his gaze to her agonizingly beautiful face, Cupid asked, "Will you be okay if I let go?"

She blinked at him again, lacquered lashes opening and closing over eyes flecked with amber and emerald. Her lips formed the word, "Yes," as if trying to convince both of them—and failing. Her weight shifted away onto her own two feet but not before Cupid filled his lungs with all her delicious scents: vanilla and brown sugar, something fruity she'd been drinking, sweat and musk. He forced open his grasp and dropped empty hands to his sides, but he couldn't stop staring. And grinning. Just looking at her was making him downright giddy. Helen of Troy paled in comparison, but this woman seemed entirely unaware of her charms.

Pan clapped him on the back and placed his lips near Cupid's ear. "What's your next move, lover boy?"

"Who's *this*?" A dark-haired woman angled in beside Cupid's Worthy, took one look at Cupid, and grinned, causing a dimple to appear at the center of each of her full cheeks. "Well, well, well, Ruthie. Look what you found." Her brittle voice rattled Cupid's eardrums, but at least now he knew his goddess's name.

Ruthie. She blushed bright pink as she looked away.

A third woman, the tallest and skinniest and blondest of the group, looped her arm around Ruthie's waist and yelled over the music at Cupid. "Are you into girls, or what?"

The dark-haired lady reached across Ruthie and thwacked the tall woman on her arm. "Jesus effin' Christ, Wen. How about a little tact?"

"*Hellllo-oh*! It's a gay bar. The only straight guys in here are wearing G-strings stuffed with singles. Do you see a G-string?"

"Give the guy a chance, huh?" The brunette switched her smile on again and aimed it straight at Cupid.

Wen's gaze shifted over Cupid's shoulder, where Pan had been hovering with his arm around Cupid and taking in every word. "*Um*, can you not see the hot bear whispering sweet nothings in his ear? Hey there, Ginger." She twisted a clump of her blond hair around a bony finger. "What's your story?"

Ruthie covered her eyes and mumbled, "This is not happening."

Pan cleared his throat and greeted them with a tight, "Ladies." Somehow, he made it sound sweet for the women's ears, but Cupid heard his, "Get us the hell outta here," loud and clear.

"Hi. I'm Gail," said the one with dark hair, placing her hand over her chest, "and you'll have to excuse our friend Wendy over there. She doesn't get out much. I believe you've already met Ruthie." Gail jerked her chin toward Cupid and gave Ruthie a not-so-gentle nudge.

Cupid locked eyes with Ruthie, who looked as though she wanted to drop through the floor. He gave her an encouraging smile and shouted to make himself heard over the sex beat. "Hi, Ruthie. I'm Q!"

Ruthie's mouth curled up at the edges, and a series of deep creases rippled her cheeks like a pond making way for a pebble. *Ah, that's better.* "Nice to meet you, Hugh."

Cupid shook his head and chuckled. "That's 'Kyyyewww,' as in Quentin."

"Oh, sorry. It's a bit loud in here."

Cupid leaned in so she wouldn't have any trouble hearing his proposition. "Would you like to get out of here, Ruthie?"

The color drained from Ruthie's face. "Oh, no, I . . ."

Oh dear. Cupid reached out and placed his hand over hers. She gasped and drew back from his touch as if he'd stuck her with a hot poker. "I'm sorry," he shouted. "I just wanted to talk to you where it's a little quieter."

"I shouldn't. I mean, thank you and all. You're very sweet, but . . ." For a moment, she stopped protesting and met Cupid's gaze, and he thought she might reconsider. "No. I can't."

Good gods, this one was going to be a challenge. Cupid hadn't been rejected since the reinstatement of his charms. It's not that Ruthie was unaffected—she was shooting off pheromones like fireworks—but her willpower mastered her desire. What an unusual mortal she was.

The wise course would be to leave it for now, sober up, talk the situation out with Pan, strategize, and regroup. Cupid would have no trouble locating this woman again with or without her cooperation—the mechanism inside his chest would take care of that. Still, ego being what it was and Cupid's loins burning as they were, he wasn't ready to give up. After all, she was still standing here talking to him.

The music pounded away at Cupid's sensitive eardrums, one harsh line of electronic noise crashing into the next. Cupid had no love for the volume, but he couldn't deny the pull of that beat. His hips pumped in time with the music, drawing Ruthie's gaze directly to his center of gravity. As a gesture of goodwill, he clasped his hands behind his back; he'd learned his lesson with the unwelcome touch.

Ruthie stared—all three ladies did, but it was only Ruthie he cared about. Cupid made the most of his opportunity, copycatting that dancer Pan had his eye on. He wanted to unleash Ruth's inner tiger, the woman who'd stuffed all those bills into the stripper's thong. The hawkish friends on either side of her weren't helping his chances any, though Cupid had a feeling they were more likely to be bad influences on her than good.

Remembering his first time at the Stagecoach and how that woman named Rho had coaxed him ever so subtly out onto the dance floor, Cupid moved steadily backward, planting his heels behind instead of directly under his gyrating hips. Ruthie inched forward with him, taking tentative, wobbly steps on too-high heels. She followed him into the heart of the crowd, leaving her chaperones behind. Cupid stuck to the unwritten rules of their game, holding her in his orbit with his gaze, his smile, the *thoom, thoom, thoom* of his hips. She danced too, but Cupid would've bet she didn't know it. The bob of her head, the sway of her shoulders, the *tap, tap, tap* of her heel, and the glorious smile she finally released when she unclenched her teeth.

Cupid leaned in, taking full advantage of the excuse to place his lips next to her ear. "Having fun?"

She nodded enthusiastically.

He stole in closer yet, this time brushing the tip of his nose along the rim of her ear. "You're a good dancer."

"Nah." She blushed madly and dropped her gaze to the floor. Cupid didn't mind; she was still here, still dancing with him, and when she looked up at him again, they smiled at each other.

Oh, how he longed to gather her hips into his hands and hold her against his body. But this would have to do for now. The crowd jostled the two of them closer and closer together, and Ruthie didn't reclaim the distance. Her defenses were weakening. Another push, and she caught her balance with a hand on Cupid's arm. Braver and bolder his sweet goddess was getting—

"I need to go." She turned suddenly and fled, as much as one could flee in a wall of bodies. Ruthie picked her way through the crowd, and Cupid chased her to the sidelines. "I need to go," she repeated to her alarmed friends, who gawped at Cupid as if he'd violated her.

"Ruthie, please . . ."

She stared at him. *Please, what?* He really hadn't planned any further than that.

Figuring his chances were better if the others didn't overhear, Cupid leaned in one final time. "May I please have your number?"

"I shouldn't," she said, but she was still here, still clapping those eyelashes at him.

Seconds ticked away. Cupid could hardly believe his good fortune when Ruthie's hands moved to unclasp her little purse. She rummaged around inside, then pulled out a pen and a piece of tissue.

"This is all I have," she said with an apologetic shrug.

"It's fine."

She scratched out her phone number, folded the tissue twice, and placed it onto Cupid's outstretched palm. He curled his fingers around the flimsy sheet and clutched it to his heart.

"Thank you."

"I had a really nice time," Ruthie said.

3

SUMMONED BY ARES

Aphrodite's chariot required neither driver nor reins. Four white doves harnessed together under a gaily jeweled yoke cooed with pleasure at their beloved mistress's arrival. The goddess gathered the folds of her ankle-length chiton in one hand and mounted her sleek, golden carriage in a graceful swoosh. Setting her mind on the destination, Aphrodite reclined into the comfort of her luxurious coach, a present lovingly crafted by Hephaestus—the same husband whose sandals would be pacing the marble tiles of the palace floor until his wife returned from her late-night "strategy session" with the formidable God of War. The chariot rose into the sky, and Aphrodite left all thoughts of Hephaestus behind.

The doves soared higher and leveled off to an easy coast at an altitude reserved for the upper echelon. Aphrodite tried to synchronize her pulse to the smooth rhythm of the dappled wings, but it was no use. The closer her carriage to Ares, the more furiously her heart raced. By the time the chariot touched down outside the compound, Aphrodite's nerves were as twisted as a bag of angry snakes.

Pull yourself together, she admonished her frazzled self as the guard swung open the iron gate. The metal wall clamped shut behind her, sending a chill crawling down her spine. She marched toward the entrance with purposeful, measured steps. Holding her breath, she reached a fist to the thick maple door.

Before she could knock, the door swung open, and she was greeted by one of the foot soldiers. "Greetings, goddess," he said with a respectful tip of his chin.

"I was summoned by Ares." A fresh thrill ran through her at the singular "I."

"Yes, of course. He will receive you in his chamber."

Oh dear.

"Not the War Room?" she asked, but the guard had already taken off down the long passageway to the private residence. A litany of questions cycled through Aphrodite's brain, each one boiling down to the basic dilemma she'd been turning over and over since Cupid's fall: Would she risk it again?

The rumors were true, of course. The Goddess of Love enjoyed an abundance of paramours, both human and immortal, an embarrassment of riches—if she were the type to be embarrassed by such good fortune. The affair with Ares that had produced Cupid was ancient history by now, but Ares was only one lover in a long string. For a time, Aphrodite's seasonal trysts with the beautiful Adonis had provided her with the young, hard body missing from her marriage and the sort of sweet adulation one might expect from a puppy, but she hadn't had a decent lover since Adonis was taken from her all too soon by that wild boar.

Through the years, Ares had made it abundantly clear he would happily accommodate Aphrodite upon her say-so, which made resisting all the more difficult. At the same time, there was a definite wicked pleasure in keeping him burning for her.

Aphrodite's narrative had its own time-worn groove: she abstained for the sake of matrimonial harmony. Ares was the one lover Hephaestus absolutely could not tolerate. Truth be told, there was more to it than her husband's feelings; there was Zeus to consider. Having arranged Aphrodite's marriage to Hephaestus to discourage further infighting for the goddess's hand, Zeus would stop at nothing to preserve their union. He'd be none too keen to learn of this private meeting in Ares's lair.

The guard's knock on the chamber door was swiftly answered, and the final barrier gave way. Aphrodite's response could have been plucked from the romance novels in her private library: sweaty palms, heightened senses, the sudden flush of heat rising to the surface, a flock of butterflies beating their wings against her chest.

"The goddess Aphrodite is here—"

"Yes, I can see that." Ares sidestepped his soldier and flashed a grin at Aphrodite. "You're looking well."

Had he noticed the extra curl she'd worked into her hair tonight? Or the strategic dip of silk right there between her breasts—that spot Ares used to love to nuzzle with the tip of his nose? Perhaps he was picking up on the bright color flooding her cheeks, as scarlet as the chiton he wore over one shoulder.

"As are you." She cleared her throat. Her gaze feasted on the stunningly displayed masculine form, the hard lines of a body built to conquer enemy or lover. Those traits that defined Ares on the battlefield—passion, unpredictability, complete lack of apology for taking what he desired—also made for a most captivating sexual partner.

Ares smiled even wider. "Won't you make yourself comfortable inside?" The god could charm the fur off a bear.

He stood in the doorway, blocking the opening so Aphrodite had to brush against him to pass. Ares released a soft grunt as Aphrodite's bare shoulder caressed his chest. *Good.* All's fair in Love and War.

Aphrodite strode toward the lounge area near the window. Her steps sped past the four-poster bed occupying half the room but not quickly enough to avoid the distant but glorious memory of Ares, stretched out naked across its plush, gold quilt.

"Please, sit."

Aphrodite startled at the close voice and the hand that suddenly materialized at her lower back. She perched on the edge of the cowhide bench and arranged her skirts.

"You're nervous," he said with more delight than apology. "Here, have some wine." Ares filled the goblets on the table and handed one to Aphrodite. "To our son."

Our. His and mine. The walking, breathing embodiment of their mutual lust.

"To Cupid." She clinked her glass against Ares's and sipped at the wine.

"We did the right thing, you know," Ares said, observing her carefully. "The Council would have overruled the ascension. I'm only one vote of five."

"I know." She'd already faced the truth after shedding many a tear. Cupid's heart was in the right place, but his choices were questionable. He had more growing up to do before they could risk bringing him home.

Ares sat down beside her on the bench, not quite touching but close enough that she could feel his heat. "It's crucial for us to be firm now so they don't strip us of our power to control the situation."

Firm. Power. Control. And it was clear from the knowing twinkle in Ares's deep blue eyes that the "us" he kept referring to did not include Hephaestus.

"Yes, you're right, of course," Aphrodite said.

The Divine Council had already made an extraordinary exception in Cupid's case by allowing Aphrodite and Ares to preside over Cupid's reform. It was Athena who'd pointed out the Council's exposure in disciplining such a high-profile deity. And what situation had more potential for disaster than loosing a lovesick Cupid on the mortals at close range? After hearing her convincing argument, Dike, Apollo, and Themis unanimously agreed to assign primary responsibility to Aphrodite and Ares, while the Council, with Themis at the reins, would retain ultimate oversight.

Unless, of course, Hera chose to intervene. It hadn't happened in recent memory. Themis was one of few deities Hera actually respected and therefore left the goddess of divine justice to govern as she saw fit. But what if the aggrieved Hera became motivated to mete out her own idea of justice and set Cupid mooning over a chicken or . . . or a fish . . . or (gasp!) gods forbid, *Hera herself*? Aphrodite shuddered to imagine it. No, she couldn't allow that to happen.

"I trust your husband didn't give you a difficult time about meeting me alone?"

Hephaestus had been furious when the summons arrived. He'd never fully trust Ares alone with Aphrodite, but more than that, Heph hated being shut out of the discussion. He cared deeply for Cupid, and as the boy's de facto father, he felt entitled to weigh in on his punishment. Hephaestus knew how these things worked, though, and he was far too clever to complain, nor would Aphrodite give Ares the satisfaction.

"He trusts me."

"And why should he not?" Ares cocked an eyebrow.

"Exactly." Her sweet smile put Ares off the trail for the moment and onto the presumed reason for their meeting.

"I see you've chosen a married Worthy this time."

Aphrodite couldn't quite glean his opinion on her decision. "Yes."

"That's stirring the mortal pot a bit, isn't it? Breaking up a marriage?"

"Who says I'm breaking it up?"

Realization dawned, bringing with it a sly grin. "Her Right Love is the husband?"

"You know, it does happen occasionally."

A booming, easy laugh rolled out of Ares. "So I've heard."

"The institution of marriage does have its place."

"How very precious, goddess." And there it was; he thought her an idealistic fool.

"Don't forget the mortals only have to make it through seventy, eighty years, tops."

"Ah." Ares gulped his wine and gave Aphrodite a long, hard stare. "I suppose there are one or two lovers I could imagine committing to for that length of time."

His attention sent a thrill through her body. She finished off her wine, and he refilled both goblets. "What happened to them, this married couple?"

"They've lost their way, and now they're both being steered in dangerous directions."

"Did she cheat on him?" Ares favored Aphrodite with a leer that held all the torrid memories of their shared transgressions.

"Why would you assume it's the wife who cheated?"

Ares held up his hands in surrender. "Cupid did find her in a strip club. It's not outside the realm of possibility."

"Now who's being precious? Just because she was enjoying a night out doesn't make her a cheater."

Ares smirked. "Sweetheart, you're trying to sell me something I don't need to buy. Perhaps you should be delivering this impassioned speech to your *husband?*"

"Ugh, you're impossible," she said. And yet, something in her was stirred. She rather liked the idea of Ares thinking she'd been a little naughty.

Ares huffed. "So, the husband cheated."

"Honestly, must you be so black-and-white? There are other reasons marriages fail."

"Why go hunting for a unicorn when the stable is filled with horses?"

Aphrodite could lecture him on destructive habits and lack of emotional intimacy and poor boundaries, but what would she gain from arguing nuances of Love with the God of War?

"Whatever the reason for their strife," Aphrodite said, "Cupid will have to diagnose the problem and fan the flames of their Right Love past their Liminal Point."

Ares crossed his arms over his chest. "And you believe this challenge will satisfy the Council?"

"Reviving a twenty-three-year-old marriage is not so easy. A quarter-century's dust covers their first rush of passion. They've seen each other at their worst. They've lost faith. They take each other's gifts for granted, disappoint and hurt each other at every turn."

Ares tilted his head. "Are we still talking about the mortals?"

"Must you be such a tiresome cockroach?"

"Oh, love," Ares said with a chuckle, "you might be the only living soul who can call the God of War a roach and escape in one piece."

"I think you like it." What she'd meant to sound defiant came out far more intimate, taking them both aback.

"Maybe I do," he confessed. "Sounds like Cupid's got his hands full. He might be down there quite a while." Ares's evil grin found its mirror image in Aphrodite.

"He might indeed."

Well, here was a new kind of thrill. If not for her mischievous son, Aphrodite might have missed stumbling onto the most powerful aphrodisiac of all: the warm glow of Ares's respect. Now, the trick would be holding on to it.

Up to that moment, she might have convinced herself her motives were pure—what mother's conscience could bear to believe otherwise?—but that complicit smile destroyed all pretense of anything short of selling out her favorite son. Aphrodite was as disloyal a mother as she was a wife. Which was more egregious, she'd have to work out later.

She shot Ares a provocative glare. "The point is for Cupid to prove he can put Right Love before his own base needs."

"Base needs," Ares repeated with a half-lidded gaze, "can be quite compelling, don't you agree?" He lifted his hand to her shoulder and brushed his fingertips across her skin while the two of them sat rooted in place as if powerless to stop it. His caress raised a trail of gooseflesh up and down her arm.

"Indeed." Aphrodite's eyes fluttered closed for a brief, beautiful *what-if.*

Back to her senses, she shifted just beyond Ares's reach. "The boy is free to fulfill himself wherever he likes at this point, so there's no reason for him to taste the forbidden fruit."

Her would-be lover received the message with an understanding nod, retracting his hand agreeably enough. "No reason at all, goddess, except everyone knows which fruit is sweetest."

4

STRIPPED

Pan found Cupid outside, leaning against the wall of the nightclub, staring off into the distance. So much for his friend's respite.

Taking up a spot on the wall beside him, Pan asked, "You okay?"

"I'm in love again, so no, not really."

"That sucks."

"Yeah."

Something white flashed between Cupid's fingers. "Whatcha got there?"

"Oh, this?" Cupid looked at the paper as if seeing it for the first time. "Ruthie gave me her number."

"Q, you can't—"

Cupid shot him a look fraught with pain. "I have to."

Pan pivoted toward the building, whispered "Fuck!" into the brick wall, and stepped menacingly in front of Cupid. "There are rules you need to respect here."

"What kind of rules?"

"You can't go around fucking married people, for one."

"Who says I'm gonna fuck her? Who says she'd even let me?" Cupid's shoulders tightened into a stiff line. "You don't have to be so vulgar all the time, Pan."

"Okay, okay." Pan held up both hands in surrender. "Look, it's been a long night. This might not be the best time to hash this out. Why don't we sleep on it and talk in the morning?"

Cupid seemed to roll the quarrel around in his head for a minute before letting it go. "Fine. Let's go home."

Pan pressed his keys into Cupid's hand. "Take the truck."

"You're not coming home with me?"

"I'm gonna stay a while. I'm in the mood to dance." More accurately, Pan was in the mood for the dancer, but it wouldn't ease Cupid's mind to know Pan's designs. "Don't worry about me. I'll get a ride home."

Deep into his own misery, Cupid didn't have any fight left in him. "Fine. See you later."

Pan clapped his hand on his friend's shoulder. "Don't wait up."

Cupid's problems would still be there in the morning . . . and then some. Pan needed a hot body tonight, and he knew just the one. The stripper-angel greeted Pan from the stage with a *well-hello-again-hottie* smile. Pan took his place behind the greedy crowd thrusting their bodies and singles, content to wait until he could have the stripper to himself, not as some impersonal business transaction, but a true meeting of souls—or at least a private grinding of bodies.

Yes, this dancer was exactly the right boy to break Pan's all-female streak since Pablo. He could feel it in his bones. Pan bided his time, enduring dance partners who stepped in to fill the void in front of him. He pumped his hips and rode the music, but it was all for the angel on the stage. Pan barely saw the boys who interloped, and the angel broke eye contact with

Pan only to charm the patrons out of their money. Pan understood; the man was working.

The beat changed and brought with it the next shift of dancers. His angel thanked the audience, collected the scattered bills, located Pan in the crowd, and jutted his chin toward the Employees Only sign.

The angel hung back while his costumed coworkers filed through the swinging door. He held the door open for Pan, then followed him into the hallway. The door swung shut, blotting out the lights and techno music and carefully staged fantasies.

"You were watching me." Everyone was watching him, but Pan knew what he meant.

"Yes." Pan smiled with the ease of a man who knew he was watched right back—until he remembered it was the other man's job to attract attention. Indeed, the privilege normally involved compensation.

Shit. Might as well cut to the chase. Pan reached for his wallet. "What do you want? Twenty? Fifty?"

The man hung his head. "Oh. I thought . . . You know what? Never mind." He gave Pan a small wave. "My mistake. You have a nice night."

"Wait!" Pan grabbed the man's arm as he was turning away. "That was *my* mistake. I apologize."

The man scanned Pan's face, then shook his head with a dry chuckle. "Occupational hazard. Can we start over?"

"*Please.*" Pan slid his hand down the dancer's forearm, grasping him in a firm handshake. "My name's Pan, and you are . . .?"

"Jagger," he said with a sheepish grin. "Not very angelic, is it?"

Pan winked. "Who says I want an angel?"

Jagger's smile widened, not the stripper smile he'd flashed at his adoring audience but one that held real warmth without losing that touch of bad boy. "What *do* you want?"

"Anything not here."

"That's pretty broad."

"Let me narrow it down a bit for you." Pan took two big steps toward Jagger, forcing his back against the wall, bent forward, and pressed his lips to Jagger's mouth. Jagger yielded and responded in kind, reaching hungrily for Pan's mouth when he pulled back to catch a breath.

The waiting had worked Pan into a froth. Now that they were actually kissing, Pan was half-delirious.

"*Jesus.* Get a room, Jag," one of his coworkers teased as he rushed past them.

Jagger broke off the kiss, leaving Pan aching. He grinned up at Pan, light green eyes peeking out from behind dirty-blond bangs. "Damn."

Pan held his ground, lowering their joined hands to Jagger's scant costume. With a strategic backhanded brush, Pan confirmed that the other man's excitement matched his own. "Is that from our kiss or all those girls who had their fingers in your pouch tonight?"

Jagger shook his head. "I love my job, but I avoid Mix Night like the plague. Women are nuts. My boss messaged me this afternoon when one of the guys called out sick. I'm not great at saying no."

"Good to know," Pan said. "And *this*"—he thrust against Jagger's hand—"is entirely your fault."

A needy moan escaped Jagger. "Lemme just grab a quick shower. I reek of sweat and money."

Oh yes, Pan was acutely aware. He leaned forward, nicked his teeth along Jagger's shoulder, and tasted the salty skin at the base of his neck. "It's hot."

Jagger let out a soft grunt. His hand closed around Pan's head. "Screw the shower."

Pan chuckled, releasing a warm, breathy stream into Jagger's ear. It had been over a decade since Pablo, and Pan had all but forgotten the sweet pull of a hard body pressed against his chest. "Not that this isn't fun, but I want more than a dry hump in a dark hallway."

"Likewise," Jagger answered. "Mind if I put on some pants?"

Pan chuckled. "Seems counterproductive."

"Being arrested for public indecency would put a serious damper on the evening, don't you think?" Jagger set his palm against Pan's chest, forcing space between the two of them.

Pan replied with a loud sigh. "I suppose. Shake your tail, then. I'll wait here, *impatiently* . . . unless I can come back there with you and watch?"

"Sorry, friend. Management frowns on entertaining company in the back of the house. Besides, I don't want your eyes wandering. You're mine." Jagger sealed the deal with a hard kiss that left Pan breathless and thrilled.

He had to admit it felt pretty fucking fantastic to be singled out among the crowd, especially by the hottest guy in the room, not counting Cupid.

Fucking Q, get outta my head!

"Hurry!" Pan yelled down the hallway.

"Don't go anywhere," Jagger called back.

Wouldn't think of it.

5

WAITING FOR ZACH

Ruth's eight-year-old cockapoo greeted her with eager, chirpy barks and full-on body wagging, the sheer joy in the dog's entire body tempered only by desperation to go out. *Zach hasn't come home yet.*

"Hang on, Pookiedoo. Mama's feet are killing her." Ruth kicked off her ridiculous heels with a groan and sank her feet into the woolly mules she kept by the door. "Okay, little marshmallow. Let's get you outside."

Pookie loped across the yard to her favorite tree and squatted. Every floppy white hair quaked as Pookie emptied her bladder. She pushed her front legs forward and arched her back in a luxurious stretch before trotting to the nearest bush to investigate. Ruth followed her all around the yard, conjuring the beautiful boy at the club to keep her company under the cover of the black night.

Away from Quentin, Ruth could think again. Her head shook by itself, remembering how she'd accidentally torn off that stripper's G-string. *Gawd*, the mortification and then the giddiness when Quentin broke her fall—a fall he'd caused, and not just by banging into her. A girl didn't stand a chance against sex personified, certainly not an old married lady like Ruth Margolis Miller. Her silly self could hardly be blamed for mentally undressing the boy. They were in a strip club, for goodness' sake.

Still, Ruth could've shrugged off the attraction to yet another of the hardbodies lining the room (albeit one with a dazzling smile and dreamy bedroom eyes) if he hadn't gone to all the trouble of noticing her, too. How did it make any sense that someone so young and sexy was looking at *Ruth* with actual hunger in his eyes? Or was that her overly active imagination at work again? This certainly wouldn't be the first time Ruth's fantasy life intruded on reality, as Zach would have been quick to point out with a subtle arch of eyebrow. But dancing with Quentin was no illusion, and neither was his request for her number.

Could she have ever summoned the courage to give it to him? *No, that would not be courage. The word you're searching for is "infidelity." You did the right thing—the only thing.*

A slippery tongue at Ruth's ankles snapped her out of her musings. "Ready for bed, girl?"

She left the mules by the door and plucked up her stupid sandals by the straps. Her friends seemed to manage their impractical heels without complaint. Why was Ruth such a fuddy-duddy?

The kitchen was a detour that would cost her precious minutes—who was she kidding, at least an hour—of sleep, yet Ruth couldn't resist the pull of her internet world, the universe of her own making, where she could be bold and sexy and exciting and anyone. *I need to hydrate,* she told herself.

She jiggled the mouse as she sank into her desk chair. The monitor sprang to life at her touch, the way Ruth had responded to Quentin's, she remembered with a giggle and a sigh. She typed "male stripper g-strings" into the search bar and scanned the results. *A picture's worth a thousand hits*, even if the image falls far short of reality. This one would have to do unless she could happen upon a Quentin selfie stash. Maybe he had an Instagram account. *Be still my heart.*

Ruth tapped out her vignette, not too long or she'd lose her audience. She still had enough alcohol in her system to tease out the embarrassing highlights—the sexy stripper she'd accidentally stripped and the real-life god who'd asked for her number.

Facebook friends of her "ShouldKnowBetter" alias would "You go, girl!" all over her night-on-the-town post. They'd surely have some LOLs and crude remarks to share over her grab at the dancer's package. But it would be the encounter with Quentin that would earn her the most social currency because the more dangerously Ruth put herself out there, the more vicarious pleasure she provided. And if old, past-her-prime Ruth could catch the eye of a hot, young stud, there was hope for everyone.

Post.

When her excuse for staying awake expired at the bottom of the tall glass of water, Ruth pulled out the big guns: *I'll wait up for Zach.*

The initial responses flew in. Her night owls and friends on the West Coast jumped all over it, bringing a predictable but comforting smile to Ruth's face. She felt a little less silly for all of it. Hey, whatever doesn't kill you makes a good story, right?

When her eyelids started to droop, Ruth made a liar out of herself again. Rather, Zach made a liar out of her by not coming home before she started up the stairs. 2:07 a.m. *Wow.*

She filed away her impractical shoes into their individual drawstring bags, where they would stay until her blistered feet lost their power over her memory. The black sequins scraped her cheeks as she peeled off her tank top. She tossed it onto the pile for the dry cleaner, quickly followed by the trying-too-hard skirt.

An audible moan of relief accompanied the unhooking of her strapless bra. For one unselfconscious millisecond, Ruth imagined Quentin standing there in her dressing room, watching her take off her clothes. The titillation lasted only long enough for reality to crush her fantasy. *Boy, did I do that kid a favor sparing him this spectacle.*

Focusing on Quentin's body was a far better plan. She felt only slightly guilty fantasizing about licking her way up—no, down—those washboard abs beneath the surface of his skintight tee. After all, what did it matter where her mind traveled as long as her body stayed inside the marriage?

And could her husband say the same? Ruth could only imagine the details of Zach's late nights at the office with his lusty associate. Unfortunately for all involved, Ruth's imagination left no blank unfilled.

She blamed herself. If not for her passion for those kids at the Brighter Tomorrows playspaces, she and Zach never would have donated a sponsorship-level gift to the organization, never would have attended the annual gala, and never would have stimulated the salivary glands of the VP of Development.

Of *course* Joan would seek out this "generous couple" among the crowd of twelve hundred to thank them in person. Her persistence didn't surprise Ruth; Lord knows she and Zach had been shaken down by too many fundraiser types to count. Ruth couldn't even fault the woman for skewing her attention toward Zach. His business acumen deserved every word of praise Joan heaped upon him, even if her delivery was about as subtle as a tub of glitter. Joan would have been a fool not to offer Zach a board position, and Joan was no fool.

No, what set off Ruth's *Oh shit!* alarm was Joan's too-intimate, "I'd just love to set up a time to learn more about your philanthropic priorities." She didn't fool Ruth with her offhand, "Both of you, of course."

Joan didn't relent till all three of them had pulled out their phones and calendared their get-to-know-you lunch for the following week. Ruth called her bluff and joined them at Bistro Le Coeur—*really?*—though Joan seemed completely uninhibited by Ruth's presence. Anything Zach said that was even remotely funny earned him a big, horsey laugh and a squeeze on his arm. Ruth had started to wonder if she'd become invisible when Joan rounded on her and asked, "And what kind of work do you do?"

Oh, she would've loved to have clipped the bitch's superior attitude with, "I'm a stay-at-home mom." How delicious it could have been to lay claim to the issue of Zach's loins—and by extension, the rest of his body—but that childbearing gig hadn't quite worked out. "Stay-at-home nothing" described her better, a barren nest where their dreams of raising a family together had gone to die.

"Homemaker" worked for the town census, but the title wasn't exactly a big fluffy feather to stick in her cap. Besides, Ruth was more general contractor to the hired homemakers—housekeeper, gardener, architect, and interior designer—than someone who produced anything herself.

Sure, she could have reached back to what she used to be, a highly capable accountant, sought after by the partners at her firm. That opening, though, would only steer the conversation to the "indefinite leave" to start a family, which became permanent after several failed attempts at IVF and Ruth not being well enough physically or emotionally to keep up appearances. "Professional volunteer" described Ruthie best, but twisting the lid off that jar would only set Joan gushing over how she and Zach were going to make beautiful organizational magic together. Zach didn't help Ruth's confidence any with his hangdog expression and unspoken, *Sorry, hon, I know you hate this question.*

Flashing her brightest, tightest smile at the woman spewing competence and confidence all over her husband, Ruth had settled on, "I'm a kept woman."

"Well, aren't you the lucky one?" Joan had volleyed back, her tone and phony smile a dozen shades of condescension.

"Yes, I sure am." Ruth had squeezed Zach's hand under the table, lest he forgot to which woman he was connected by ketubah, moral obligation, and the state of Indiana.

Two years later, Zach was still bouncing back and forth between the women—Joan by day, Ruth by night, and the weekends a wrestling match between the two.

There he was now, the quiet purr of his engine rolling into the garage bay before cutting out. Zach would sit in the car for a few minutes, Ruth knew, transitioning as well as he could, attempting to leave his professional half outside but failing as usual. The work permeated his being, and how could she complain? He was a good man working to repair the world.

If the work were his only mistress, Ruth could've lived with that. She would've been lonely, but she didn't depend on Zach to fulfill her every need. That's where her friends and her volunteer work and her writing came in, not to mention the whole world of intimate strangers who lived inside her computer. Problem was, Ruth couldn't quite set aside her suspicions about the woman who cheered Zach on and worshiped him with slavish devotion.

Of course, Joan didn't have to overcome the daily ho-hum of managing a household, of slogging through unsexy discussions about the ravages of ice dams and clogged septic lines. Nor did she share the burden of failure and loss of the hopes and dreams a man had every right to: a son or daughter to follow in his footsteps, a precious toddler to twirl around.

And lest Ruth forget, Joan was glamorous (something Ruth would never be), a big-city girl with perfect posture and high cheekbones. Flawless skin expertly made up nonetheless with just the right shades of concealer and blush and lipstick and eyeliner, the professional but also miraculously sexy drape of auburn hair decades from graying, and the ideal figure in—and no doubt, out of—her wardrobe of expensive business suits. The effortless wearing of stockings and high-heeled pumps, showcasing what Ruth's father would've called "a great set of gams," toned from early morning treadmill runs while boning up on the day's headlines. God, Ruth hated her.

Zach had perfected the art of climbing the back stairs without making a sound. A muffled jangle could be heard as he set his keys into the leather tray on his bureau. The belt whooshed through its loops, and he hung it on the first peg with all the other black belts, she knew without seeing. He let out a sigh while loosening his "noose," an activity Zach relished as much as Ruth appreciated shedding her bra, and unfastened his cuffs and the buttons lining his chest. Twist right, twist left, he shrugged out of his jacket and shirt.

Ruth followed him in her mind's eye to the dressing room bench, which let out a soft squeal as he sat. He untied his shoes and set them down on the carpeting too quietly for her to hear. He stood again, unzipped his trousers, and let them hit the floor. If society would allow it, Zach would walk around like this all day, in just his white briefs. Wouldn't have bothered Ruth any; he was nicely built from tip to tail, and their generous travel schedule allowed for a year-round tan despite the harsh change of seasons in Indiana. Sturdy on top with a nice smattering of hair on his chest and not too much on his back, Zach had just enough flesh to grab hold of where other men his age had a serious pair of love handles. Years of personal training sessions afforded Zach pleasingly muscled arms and lean runner's legs. As for the parts concealed by his briefs, Ruthie had no complaints there.

Just as he'd done every work night regardless of the hour, Zach painstakingly matched up the creases of his trouser legs, folded them over the hanger, and filed them with the matching jacket into their color-appropriate slot in the closet. Finally, he freed himself of the last of the trappings of his indentured servitude by stepping out of his briefs and tossing them into the wire laundry cart. After a particularly long day, he'd scratch his balls for a few distracted minutes, a pleasure Ruth never begrudged him.

The one noise he couldn't stifle was the whir of his electric toothbrush. He emptied his bladder and saved the flush for the morning so as not to disturb his sleeping wife. He washed his hands and tiptoed into the bedroom.

Her side of their king bed barely registered his weight as he sat on the edge to set his alarm for tomorrow's rise-and-shine. With minimal jostling, Zach scooted between the sheets, stretched out, and pulled the covers neatly across his chest. He was a back sleeper and a sound one at that.

Any second now, Zach would reach over, run an experimental fingertip along Ruth's arm to see if she was awake. They might have a pillow-talk version of "How was your day, dear?" and if he had the energy and the optimism, he might even see if she was game for a little action. Tonight, thanks to Quentin, Ruth just might give in.

She waited in the dark for a sign, any sign at all that Zach wanted her. She inhaled and exhaled in measured breaths, waiting for the touch that never came. She trained her ears extra hard for his usual whispered, "G'night," but the only sound that penetrated the silence was Zach's soft snore.

6

STRATEGIZING

A tightness in his chest woke Cupid from a fitful sleep. *Ruthie. Versailles. Love. Married. Not a dream.* "Wonderful," he muttered to himself and whoever happened to be listening in from above.

The heart message compelled Cupid out of bed to the conversation he needed to have with Pan. Cupid hopped into his sweatpants and shuffled into the kitchen. In just two weeks on Earth, he'd already developed a strong appreciation for the dark brew worshiped by mortals. He filled the water reservoir to the top and poured the ground coffee into the filter; he had a sinking feeling this was going to be a full-pot day.

Cupid trudged to the cabinet where the cereal boxes stood in a row. Too many choices stared back at him. With no patience for decisions, Cupid grabbed the box of Lucky Charms, not that he placed stock in luck, but the colorful box at least promised a high sugar content. He poured a mound of cereal into a bowl, floated the colorful shapes in a sea of milk, and sliced a banana over the top. The coffeemaker stopped churning just as Pan lumbered into the kitchen wearing a pair of tight black boxers and a huge grin.

"You smell like sex," Cupid declared with a wrinkle of his nose. "A lot of sex."

Pan chuckled as he pulled two mugs down from the shelf. "Good morning to you too, sunshine."

"That's not Cheri's scent."

"Nope." Pan offered nothing further but filled the two mugs with coffee, set them down on the table, and plopped down into his regular seat. He closed his eyes and sucked down half the mug before glancing up at Cupid again. "What?"

Cupid tipped his chin toward Pan's room. "Is someone here?"

"Just you, me, and the lamppost."

Cupid set his bowl onto the table and sank into the chair opposite Pan. Fine. If Pan didn't want to tell him who he'd—

"I made a new friend last night, too," said Pan.

Cupid scooped up a spoonful of cereal while his mind replayed the events of the night: catching Ruthie's fall with his body, their all-too-brief chat, the crushing blow when he discovered the resounding absence of the echo beat. The winged dancer.

"You had sex with *that stripper*?"

"I did. Is that a problem for you?"

"No. Why would it be?" Cupid hurried another spoonful of cereal to his mouth while Pan stared him down.

"I don't know, Q. Why would it be?"

"It's not."

"Good, because I distinctly recall your saying, 'You can have him.' Remember that?"

"Yes, but I didn't think you'd go and *have* him." Cupid released a heavy breath. "Never mind. I'm being a jerk."

Pan kicked Cupid's foot under the table. "Yeah, a little bit."

Cupid kicked him back, and they sipped their coffee in silence while Cupid gathered his emotions. Could he help it if he was being irrational? It hadn't bothered Cupid in the least when Pan slept with Cheri, but this was . . . well, *obviously* this was different. But hadn't they gone to Versailles so Pan could hook up with a guy? That didn't mean Cupid had to like it.

"What was he like?"

Pan's head jerked up, and he gave his friend a soft smile before answering. "You really wanna know?"

He did and he didn't. Cupid rolled his eyes. "I asked, didn't I?"

Pan studied him a few seconds longer before delivering his answer with an unnecessary swagger. "He's quite limber."

"How nice for you." Under different circumstances, Cupid would have been more than pleased to show Pan exactly how limber he could be.

"You're being a jerk again. Just sayin'."

"And you're not?" Cupid slapped his spoon at the soupy rainbow before shoving the bowl into the middle of the table. He crossed his arms and shot daggers at Pan though he was angrier with himself for getting so damn upset. Was falling for a married mortal not enough to occupy Cupid's heart?

Pan stood with a force that scraped his chair along the floorboards. "Shit."

He strode past Cupid toward the coffee machine, jammed his mug down on the counter, leaned forward onto his palms, and swore again. Pan's freckled skin strained across his massive shoulders like Cupid's bowstring, the intimidating might of the hunter barely contained by his mortal form.

When Pan finally spoke, his voice sounded strangled and weak. "Do I honestly need to tell you I wished it was you instead of Jagger?"

Cupid's indignation was momentarily interrupted by a swell of pleasure he was quick to tamp down. "Jagger? What kind of name is that?"

"How the hell should I know? Maybe his parents are Stones fans."

"Stones?"

"Ugh!" Pan grabbed his head with both hands and growled. He spun around, his cheeks redder than the bushy beard surrounding them. "Are you trying to be difficult, or is this yet another of your many divine gifts?"

Was he? "I can't stand it when you're mad at me."

Pan's head arced like the sun crossing the sky. He scrubbed his face with both hands, blew out a thick sigh, and braced himself against the edge of the counter behind him. "I'm not mad at you."

Cupid wanted to believe him, and Pan's tone did sound more frustrated than angry. "Good," Cupid said. "I'm not mad at you either."

Pan unclenched his jaw and gave Cupid a tight nod. "Good."

Cupid tracked Pan's movement to the refrigerator. Remembering his hunger, Cupid dragged his bowl within striking range and tucked in. The cereal had gone soggy while the two men were arguing.

They spooned their respective breakfasts into their respective mouths in wary silence until Pan tested their careful truce. "Even if I had risked making the most colossal mistake of my life last night, it's not as if you were available."

They'd gone around and around on this, agreeing on a powerful mutual desire and a stronger commitment not to act on it. "You weren't really considering it, were you?"

Pan huffed as he reached for his coffee. "Not more than once every five minutes." He raised the mug toward Cupid, gave him a wink, and brought the coffee to his lips.

"Silly goat," Cupid said, his smile cutting hard into both cheeks.

"Whatever. Let's talk about you for a while."

Me. Right. Cupid stirred the spoon around the dregs of the bowl. The so-called rainbow had melded into a color that matched Cupid's outlook, a grayish sludge most unworthy of the goddess Iris. As much as he hated arguing with Pan, at least the skirmish had temporarily taken his mind off the real problem.

"I wouldn't have thought it was possible, but I love Ruthie even more than Mia. Last night when she drove off and left me standing there . . ." The ache tore at his chest from the inside out. "I don't see how I can bear to go through that whole dating routine with Ruthie. I'm not sure how I survived the first time around."

"Something tells me you won't have to. That rock on her finger isn't just decoration. She already has a husband."

"You think he's the one?"

"You're the expert. All I know is the first murder suspect is always the spouse."

"You think her husband wants to murder her?"

"My point is, you have to rule out the husband first. You certainly can't go around introducing a married lady to other men if her Right Love is already married to her."

"Okay, that makes sense, but what if he's not the one? What about your rules?"

"Hmm." Pan's bushy eyebrows drew together.

Cupid's heart sank. He really hated it when Pan didn't have the answers. Of course, that hadn't stopped Pan yet from voicing his opinions.

"If your punishment requires violating the matrimonial laws of man, we can only assume the gods will back you up."

"That's a horrible assumption," Cupid replied. If anything, the exact opposite was far more likely.

Pan sighed. "Honestly, Q, I think it would be best to focus

on first things first. Your Worthy is still wearing her ring, so that's a good sign. She didn't jump at your offer to take her outside, another plus."

"Not from my perspective," Cupid said.

As usual, Pan ignored Cupid's misery and plowed ahead. "For some reason, she gave you her number, which means you might have an opening without resorting to that stalking system in your chest."

Cupid heaved out a humorless chuckle. "Tell that to my chest, why don't you?"

"I guess that can't be helped," Pan answered sympathetically. "Do we agree that job number one is checking for an echo beat with the husband?"

"Yes."

Cupid's gut was so twisted up, he no longer knew what to hope for. He didn't relish that moment of hearing his beloved's heart beat for another. Could there be a more crushing blow for the God of Love? Of course not, which is exactly why this evil punishment had been concocted for him. As long as he lived, Cupid would never forget the hideous twisting of his heart when he recognized the perfect echo beat between Mia and Lieutenant Goode and knew for certain he'd lost her.

Not that this state of uncertainty was the slightest bit more pleasant. No, Cupid had no stomach for hurting Ruthie as he'd unintentionally hurt Mia by stumbling through the process of locating her Right Love and mucking everything up with his own selfish desires. In all likelihood, Ruthie's husband represented the cleanest, quickest solution for all concerned. That's what Cupid would hope for, then.

No sooner had Cupid finished his deliberations than the challenge jumped out at him. A husband and wife were obviously well acquainted already and had, presumably, experienced the thrum of love at least long enough to decide to get married. Much more would be required than simply giving the two parties a nudge in each other's direction. Cupid would have chosen the relatively fertile ground of a clean slate like Mia and Patrick's any day over a Right Love gone fallow.

"Okay, this can't be too difficult," Pan said, "assuming they still live together, that is."

"Another assumption."

"You know, it would be helpful if you tried a little positivity here."

"Easy for you to say." Pan had spent his night rolling around with a limber angel while Cupid tossed and turned with a broken heart.

"I believe your stay here on this planet would go much easier for you and me both if you'd kindly retain one minor detail about your situation: *you're* the one who shot your magic arrow into the hellhound's ass. I'm just a guy doing his day job."

Cupid sank against the back of his chair and harrumphed as sourly as a person who knows he's in the wrong can do. "Fine."

"Moving on. What's your range?"

Cupid sifted through his readings of Mia's heart: all those restaurant dates he'd chaperoned, the tragic one-way beat when that awful Reese had shown up at Mia's door, the unmistakable echo when Lieutenant Goode and Mia first made contact at the accident scene.

"About five meters."

"What if you were standing in their yard? Could you hear inside the house?"

"Through the wall? I doubt it."

"Hmm, okay, we've got to get you inside while they're both in there too. Breaking and entering is a no-no. Speaking of laws, don't forget you cannot sleep with her. Wait, let me be more specific. You cannot touch each other's happy parts. No kissing, no dry humping, no 'making her feel good,' no whatever else your little head comes up with for a justification. Just don't. Understand?"

"Yes." Cupid fought the urge to stick out his tongue. He'd had enough lectures for one day, and it was barely eight o'clock.

7

WRONG NUMBER

The engine inside Cupid's chest revved to life before he finished his second cup of coffee. Probably for the best—he had a phone call to make, and he needed to calm down first. As he had discovered with Mia, his erotic superpowers did not transmit through the phone. If Cupid didn't win an invitation to meet Ruthie in person with this conversation, he would have to resort to stalking Ruthie with his heart system. How would he ever earn her trust after such a violation?

Nerves jangling, Cupid retreated to his room and slumped onto his unmade bed. Lying among his tousled sheets to call Ruthie felt wrong on every level. He sprang up and strode to the windows, where the sun filtered in and warmed his skin. *Deep breaths.* The pleasant memory of dancing with Ruthie washed over him until a stab to the heart set him sharply back on task.

"Okay, okay," he mumbled to the impatient gods. With shaky fingers, he tapped the number Ruthie had given him, held the phone to his cheek, and closed his eyes for maximum concentration. As the phone rang in his ear, he realized that he should've rehearsed.

"Hello?" That brittle voice . . . *Gail.*

Disappointment came at him like a crashing wave, but Cupid had a job to do. Wallowing was not an option. "Hello," he said.

"Who is this?"

"It's Quentin."

"I think you have the wrong number."

Yes, did he ever. "Wait, don't hang up. Ruthie gave me your number last night."

"*Oh my god!* You're that gorgeous hunk from the club."

Cringing, he tipped the phone away from his ear. "Yes, that's me."

"Wait, you asked Ruthie for my number?"

A lie might have served him better, but Cupid still hadn't gotten the hang of it. "Um . . ."

"Oh. Got it." Gail sounded as disillusioned as Cupid felt. "She pulled the ol' bait and switch on ya, huh?"

"I guess."

"I'm sorry you got stuck with me."

"It's not like that, Gail."

"Sure it is. Look, I'm sure she was just trying to help out a friend. I've been kind of a mess since my divorce. They took me to the club to cheer me up. I guess Ruthie thought I needed a little bit more help. You got caught in the crossfire."

No, Gail. *You* did.

A loud, dramatic sigh filled Cupid's ear. "I suppose the graceful thing to do would be to let you off the hook," she offered half-heartedly. "Unless, of course, you had any interest in getting together?"

No, Cupid had zero interest in Gail. But then, Ruth seemed not to want anything to do with him. A god had to do what a god had to do. "Sure, that'd be great."

"Really?"

Cupid forced out a chuckle. "You sound surprised."

"I didn't fall off the turnip truck yesterday, pal. I saw the way you were looking at Ruthie."

"Yeah." He should probably work on that. "Well, I guess she wasn't looking back. In any case, she gave me your phone number, not hers. I know how to take a hint."

"The only hint you got is that Ruthie doesn't know what's good for her."

"You think I'm good for her?" Cupid's spirits lifted only long enough to remind himself there was no echo. It didn't matter what this woman thought. It didn't matter what Cupid thought. It didn't even matter what Ruthie thought.

"Sure, honey. Absent the marital vows, Jewish guilt, and I'm guessing about a twenty-year age difference, you're the best thing that's ever happened to her."

Right. Rub my nose in it. "Those things don't matter to you?" he asked.

"I'm a divorced, agnostic cougar, so hell no." The lady had spunk, at least.

"I'm sorry about your divorce." Cupid had watched the ordeal play out far too many times from his vantage point on the Mount, and it was rarely anything short of horrific. Standing here now with his own two feet on the planet, Cupid couldn't even imagine the depth of emotional pain involved in the dissolution of a marriage. From the little Mia had shared, Cupid had to wonder if the gods didn't have it right after all: keep the marriage and sleep wherever you want.

"Don't be," Gail answered. "*I'm* not. The bastard cheated on me with his hygienist. Can you believe it?"

"Uh . . ." Having no clue what a hygienist was, Cupid could hardly be expected to form an opinion. He didn't know what *agnostic* meant either. He might need a dictionary to keep up with this woman.

"Oh." Gail laughed. "I should probably have mentioned my ex is a dentist. The hygienist was his assistant, not some random person he saw twice a year though I wouldn't put it past Angelo to work that quickly."

"Sorry," Cupid repeated. What else was there to say? He doubted he could have named one Olympian who *hadn't* cheated. Awesome powers did not equate to self-control. In fact, in Cupid's experience, the opposite was usually true.

"Eh, I'm over it. I mean, it sucks for the kids, especially our son because *poof*! There goes his role model, right?"

"I guess." Cupid was reminded of Mia's sweet son Jonah, the oldest of the three boys. So trusting, so innocent, so thirsty for a good man in his life. Cupid missed the little guy something fierce, missed them all so much, but Mia and the boys needed space to let Patrick into their lives.

He preferred to dwell on Gail's problems. "How many kids do you have?"

"Three. My son is fourteen, sandwiched between two sisters, seventeen and twelve."

"How did the girls handle the divorce?"

Gail's voice took on a wistful quality. "The older one, not too well. Her teenage years have been a horror show. This was just the latest excuse for her to act out, and she's not one to let an opportunity slide. The younger one still thinks her daddy walks on water. I have no idea how he spun it for her, but she punched the ticket for the whole show. You can imagine she's been a joy to live with."

Cupid was tempted to apologize again but held his tongue before a third "sorry" slipped out. "Sounds rough."

"Let's just say we've had our fill of 'teachable moments.' You want to hear the worst part?"

Fairly certain he didn't, Cupid walked back over to his bed, straightened the comforter over the messy sheets, and sat down on the edge. "Sure, if you'd like to tell me."

"I have to pay for all my dental work now." She dissolved into a fit of laughter. "Enough about me. If I don't save a few secrets, we won't have anything to talk about on our date. Tell me about yourself, Quentin."

Danger prickled at Cupid's skin like a blast of cool air after a hot shower. "What about me?" He hoped his lame stall tactic would hold her while he scrambled to gather up the scraps of his invented backstory.

"Oh, I don't know," she said with a chuckle. "Do *you* have any slutty exes running around town you want to tell me about?"

"No." Mia was not a slut, and he most certainly did not want to tell Gail about her under any circumstances.

"Any slutty exes you *don't* want to tell me about?" She laughed at her own joke, but Cupid didn't find it any more amusing the second time around.

"No again."

"Lucky you."

Luckily charmed, just like his cereal. "I guess."

"Hey, you mind if I ask you a serious question?"

Probably. "Okay."

"What do you want with a couple of ladies old enough to be your . . . *aunts*?"

The answer spilled out as easily as milk from a carton because it was the truth, at least where Ruthie was concerned. "Honestly, I hadn't noticed."

Gail snorted into the phone. "Seriously? That's what you're going with?"

For an honest guy, Cupid constantly seemed to find himself at the receiving end of a whole lot of mistrust. Was it his fault he shared a gender with the bums who had deceived the women he'd met on Earth? "I'm actually a terrible liar."

"Well, I think that's an excellent quality in a man."

"I just find that sticking to the truth is safer."

"Huh." A few seconds of silence stretched out between them before Gail spoke again. "Since we're being all sincere here, may I be very honest with you, too?"

"Of course." Cupid braced himself again. Gail seemed to say exactly what was on her mind, which was both extremely helpful and utterly terrifying.

"You seem like a nice boy, and lord knows, you're handsome enough. Okay, understatement of the century there . . ." She trailed off with a giggle. "Thing is, if you're looking to get a sugar mama out of this deal, you can pack up those big blue eyes and that come-hither smile and every last one of those delicious muscles, and just go on looking somewhere else. Feel me?"

Crap. There she went again, speaking a language Cupid most definitely was not taught at the academy. *Sugar mama?* Whatever that meant, Cupid felt comfortable the term did not describe his goal of uniting Ruthie with her Right Love.

"That's not at all what I want," he answered.

"Good, because every penny my lawyer squeezed out of my sleazeball ex is going to my kids' education, and if you think you're gonna prey on Ruthie, you better just think again."

Cupid found himself grinning into the phone. "Good."

"I beg your pardon?"

"I'm glad Ruthie has a friend like you to protect her from sleazeballs. And by the way, I am not one of those, I promise you." A twinge of guilt reminded him of the mistakes he'd made with Mia and how he'd hurt her, despite all his honorable intentions.

"I didn't really think you were, but I felt it was worth mentioning before we go any further."

Cupid picked up the thread where she'd left it hanging for him. "Does that mean you'll go out with me?"

"You only go around once, right? Might as well get good 'n' dizzy."

Relief brought a smile to Cupid's face. "Excellent. Are you free Friday night?"

8

STALKER

It wouldn't do for Cupid to materialize in Ruthie's life again before his date with Gail, yet the mechanism inside his chest didn't wait for Friday night. The gods roused Cupid early Monday morning, barely allowing him time for a shower before compelling him to his car.

Cupid had no address to type into the car's GPS, but he needed no external guidance. His heart signal yanked him this way and that with zero regard for the paved roadways of Tarra. He held his breath and sped up through the worst of the mismatched navigation, relaxing only when road and heart set him on the same path.

The arduous journey led Cupid in a different direction than he'd traveled to Mia's, away from the billboards and concrete and restaurants and banks—so many banks. Cupid noted the exit sign for Tarra Heights as his heart-motor steered him off the highway and spun his car in a tight loop before spitting it and its occupant onto Newcastle Parkway.

The homes in this part of town spread their elbows wider and wider. Magnificent fences did the talking for their owners: *Everything on this side belongs to me.* Even the street accessorized like its wealthy occupants, clothed with broad swaths of tailored grass and dripping with stylish overhead lamps.

The force pulled Cupid into a right turn onto Bridle Lane. He searched the fenced-in properties for barns or horses roaming the vast yards, but the only beast with a bit between his teeth turned out to be Cupid. This highly sobering realization struck Cupid at the exact moment his unseen rider tugged at the reins. *Ho!*

He slowed the Prius to a crawl and coasted past a mailbox decorated with the face, feet, and tail of a fluffy dog. Cupid smiled to himself. *Yes, that feels like my Ruthie.*

The driveway offered a welcoming cobblestone entry at the curb but twisted out of sight behind a forest of mature trees just a few meters from the street. Cupid thought better of taking the brazen route to the house in the light of the breaking day. He continued around a slight curve in the road and parked near the next mailbox.

Planning to study Ruthie's activity from the safe vantage point of his car, Cupid was once again proven wrong by the throbbing in his chest. He shored up his courage, gripped the door handle, and opened the latch. Just then, the menacing growl of an approaching car pinned Cupid in place. A sleek, black car sped past him, nearly shearing off the door of the Prius.

Double-checking his side mirror this time, Cupid stepped out of his car and backtracked to the doggy mailbox. A subtle but effective octagonal sign planted in the corner of the yard let Cupid know he was approaching a home protected by a security system. These mortals and their elaborate machinery designed to keep out danger while doing little to hold in everything they purported to cherish most: love, family, loyalty, honesty.

He lacked Pan's stealth, but Cupid's heightened Earth senses allowed him to travel unseen through the natural camouflage of the woods lining the winding cobblestone driveway. At the top sat a massive, pink brick home, a house designed with a big family in mind. Two rectangular garden plots framed the front door with artfully arranged symmetry to welcome invited guests, which Cupid was not.

Mother would love the brightly colored flowers. Cupid checked himself for the nostalgic indulgence. Aphrodite's preferences were no longer his concern.

On the upper floor, a light switched on. Cupid stole behind a row of tall rosebushes at the side of the house, watching and waiting while the occupants stirred to life. A parade of lights illuminated a figure, *definitely Ruthie,* moving downstairs to the first floor and across the house toward the garage.

He slipped behind the hedge as the side door opened. Out flew a ball of fluff approximating the size and color of the mailbox. The dog's tiny nose lifted and twitched. Its head turned toward the exact spot where Cupid was hiding. *Skatá!*

Cupid shot across the yard to the cover of a broad maple. His heart was hammering so hard, he half expected to see his chest punching against the tree trunk supporting him. He gained control of his breathing before chancing a glance. There she was, *sigh,* the object of his deepest affection and cruelest affliction. He feasted his eyes on her effortless elegance though it twisted his gut to stand this close to what he could not touch, let alone possess.

The little dog yipped, and Ruthie traipsed after, tying the belt of her knitted sweater over a pair of plaid lounging pants. "What is it, Pookie? Did you find another bunny, silly girl?"

Cupid had thought her beautiful on Saturday night, but the natural look appealed to him even more. Unaware of the eyes following her every move, Ruthie didn't carry the burden of worrying how she looked. No creams or artificial coloring marred her skin. Cupid felt jealous of the sunrays kissing her cheeks.

Hmm, he'd thought her taller. Hadn't her hips lined up just below his when Cupid grabbed her from behind? The puffy height on top of Ruthie's head last night was absent now, but could it really just be the hair lying flat? *Ah, of course.* She'd traded in her high heels for the low slip-on shoes now shuffling toward him.

Surely, it was wrong to wish she'd discover him here; no good could come of that, especially with Cupid's inability to weave a lie. As the driveway sign and window stickers attested, these mortals were serious about trespassing. Pan would be furious if Cupid entangled himself with the authorities again. Still, Cupid registered disappointment when a passing squirrel stole the dog's interest and steered Ruthie toward the backyard instead.

He didn't realize it then, but that moment of near discovery would be the closest Cupid would come to Ruthie all day. Except for brief outdoor jaunts with the dog, Ruthie spent her whole day inside the house. Cupid's heart signal kept him tethered within visual range until well after sundown, when that growling car that had nearly hit him returned to Ruthie's garage. At least one of Pan's assumptions appeared to be true.

Cupid spent the next three days observing Ruthie's routines: dog walking, grocery shopping, meeting friends for coffees and meals, visiting the town library, spending several hours on two different days at a place called "Brighter Tomorrows," and doing whatever it was she did alone inside her house. Each day, he extended his hours with the aim of tracking Ruthie and her husband outside their home, where he'd be able to read their heartbeats.

In four days, the couple never once left together.

9

DAY JOBS

After four days of fruitless stalking, Cupid returned to Pan's late Thursday night with nothing but sleep on his mind. Judging by the wild ruckus coming from Pan's bedroom, his friend had other ideas. The two had barely spoken all week beyond Cupid answering Pan's texts with progressively sadder emojis until Pan had finally sent, *Write back when you have an update.*

Cupid climbed under the covers and curled the pillow tight against his ears, but there was no blocking out the carnal activity. *That is definitely a man in there.* Most likely, Pan had brought home the stripper again, but Cupid was too exhausted to bother sniffing out the scent. He tried to be happy for Pan—at least someone was getting some action—but the lack of sleep piled on top of the lack of sex left Cupid seriously grumpy on Friday morning when chest pains dragged him out of bed just after six. At least the house was finally quiet. Either Pan's partner had left, or they were still asleep. Pan wouldn't have let an opportunity go to waste.

Cupid stumbled into the kitchen with his eyes half closed. A man sat at the counter, his back to Cupid. "Morning," Cupid mumbled.

The man spun around on his stool. Blond hair, nice smile. It was him all right, *Jagger.* "Hey. Hope it's okay I grabbed a yogurt. I have to go straight to work."

"The club's open now?" Cupid held the coffeepot under the faucet. "You want some coffee?"

"Coffee would be great, and no, I have a day job."

Cupid glanced up from the sink and took in the logo on Jagger's navy T-shirt, a cartoon refrigerator with little white legs running past the words "Speedy Appliance Service."

"Ah." Cupid busied himself with coffee grinds and cereal boxes and silverware while the other man watched him move around the kitchen. "Pan still sleeping?"

"Yep. I finally wore him out." The stripper shot Cupid a brazen grin.

Cupid's spoon clanged to the counter. "So I heard."

The accusation was met with an unapologetic shrug. "Maybe you should join us next time."

"I don't think that's a very good idea." In fact, Cupid could hardly think of a worse idea than a three-way with the hot stripper Pan was sleeping with to get Cupid out of his system.

Another shrug. "Can't blame a guy for trying."

"I don't," Cupid replied, knowing full well the blame was his own.

The coffeepot beeped. Cupid filled two mugs and set one down in front of Jagger.

"Thanks," said Jagger. "So, what kind of work has you up at the butt crack of dawn?"

"Oh, I, uh . . ." Surely, what Cupid had been doing all week counted for work. It certainly wasn't fun. "Surveillance." The word popped into Cupid's head, courtesy of the police shows he'd binge-watched after fixing up Mia with Lieutenant Goode.

Jagger glanced up from his coffee. "You a cop?"

Pan's deep guffaw preceded him into the kitchen. The skimpy, white underwear barely concealed Pan's morning wood, a fact that did not go unnoticed by any of them as Pan strode immodestly over to Jagger and slipped a possessive arm around his shoulders. "No, babe. Q is most definitely not a cop."

If Pan's aren't-you-jealous-of-my-new-toy smugness left any doubt as to what the two had been doing all night, the pungent air plugged in the gaps. Cupid bit his tongue and battled the urge to jump them both.

Jagger shrugged out from under Pan's arm, slid off the stool, and patted Pan on his belly. "You trying to make me late for work, hot stuff?"

"Maybe. Is it working?"

Jagger shook his head and grinned. "You're what my momma calls a bad influence."

"Said the stripper," Pan replied with a chuckle.

"Whatever, dude." Walking steadily toward the front door, Jagger called back, "Thanks for the coffee and the nice visual." The door closed behind him, leaving the two gods alone together in the awkward aftermath.

Cupid avoided eye contact, focusing all his available concentration on mixing his cereals and slicing his banana. "I guess I don't have to ask what you've been up to this week while I've been gathering information on Ruthie."

Pan pivoted around, mug in hand, and leaned back nonchalantly against the counter. "Well, for starters, Euphrosyne fell yesterday."

"*Our* Euphrosyne, the goddess of merriment and mirth?"

Pan chuckled. "Yeah, it's not a real common name down here."

"Wow. I didn't even know the Graces could fall."

"I guess if you live long enough, there's a first time for everything," Pan said with a pointed look.

"I suppose. What could she have done to earn her punishment?"

"I don't know yet," Pan said. "I intercepted her and got her settled in over on the South Side, but I haven't had a chance to loop back and check on her."

"Yes, you've been quite the busy boy." Cupid's sarcasm was meant to sting, but Pan shrugged it off.

"Speaking of getting busy, you have that date tonight with Ruthie's friend, right?"

"Yes."

"Time to get back on the horse, eh?"

Cupid's glance rode down Pan's bare chest and lingered a beat too long below the coffee mug. It wasn't a stretch to picture Jagger all saddled up between Pan's legs. *Not helpful.*

"It's not really about that, Pan."

Pan shrugged and sipped his coffee, leaving unsaid what Cupid heard loud and clear: *Better do it while you can.*

10

DATING GAIL

Gail looped her arm around Cupid's bent elbow as they strolled together toward his car. "Thanks for dinner. That was surprisingly nice."

"Surprising, huh?" Cupid grinned at her. "I'm not quite sure how to take that." Though if asked right then, he might have answered exactly the same way. This Gail was different from the version he'd met at the club—still the brutally honest, fierce woman he'd spoken to on the phone a few times now, but more relaxed, not trying so hard. He liked her.

She was no Ruthie, but then, Cupid couldn't have Ruthie. *Ever.* Unless the gods had another nasty surprise in store for Cupid, Gail did not appear to be off-limits. There was something to be said for Pan's suggestion. Why shouldn't Cupid have a little fun?

"Take it as a compliment," she answered.

He teased her without a trace of malice. "Why would you agree to go out with me if your expectations were that low?"

She slowed and turned to face him. "I wasn't sure we'd have

anything to talk about over dinner, so *that part* was a nice surprise." Gail reached up to cup Cupid's cheek. "Just so you're aware, my bar for the rest of the evening is extremely high."

"In that case," Cupid said with a breaking smile, "we better get out of here."

"You read my mind."

Truth be told, he'd read her scent, but that was the kind of detail Cupid had learned to keep to himself. "Home it is," he said, tucking her into the passenger side.

"No." Her hand blocked the door from closing. "I can't bring you home. My kids . . . they're teenagers. I have to set a good example."

"I understand. Hmm . . ." Cupid leaned on the roof of the car as he contemplated their options. He'd picked up Gail for their date; he knew how she lived. Pan's bachelor pad was no place for a lady like Gail. "I don't think you'd appreciate the ambience at my place."

Gail giggled. "That's why god invented hotels."

"They did?"

With a tilt of her head, she asked, "How much wine did you have?"

He'd been careful. He knew better than to drink more than he could handle. "About a glass and a half. Why?"

"Never mind. Get your hot little bod inside this car, and I'll direct you."

Direct him she did, and her instruction didn't stop once they reached the Hickory Hotel. Gail knew exactly what she wanted and how and where she wanted it, and Cupid was more than eager to deliver—multiple times. What Gail lacked in elasticity, she more than made up for in experience.

He'd had enough sexual encounters by now to appreciate Gail's intimate knowledge of erogenous zones—his and hers.

Even more exciting was her enthusiasm. Every inch of Cupid's body thrilled her, and she was delighted to return the favor. After nearly two weeks of self-imposed celibacy, Cupid made up for lost time with a stamina that leapt Gail's high bar with plenty of room to spare, and she wasn't shy about letting him know.

Flopped onto his back next to her, Cupid chuckled. "Well, I'm so glad to hear that."

"Would you mind foraging for some protein in the minibar?" she asked.

"Sure." He hopped out of bed without the slightest clue what he was looking for. *Minibar?* He needn't have worried. Gail turned on the bedside lamp and pointed him to the spot below the TV.

He crouched down and read aloud the contents of the cabinet. "What would you like?" he asked, craning his neck around to the bed.

Gail had scooted to a sitting position against the headboard and gathered the sheets up to her chin. "Trail mix, I guess. And a water bottle?"

Cupid grabbed the provisions. Her eyes locked on his midsection as he stood, and he stirred to life. Feeling playful, Cupid gripped the cellophane bag between his teeth and crawled up the bed like a tiger stalking its prey. Gail giggled as he dropped the bag into her lap and leaned in for a kiss. While their tongues danced, Cupid curled a finger around the edge of the sheet and tried to slide it downward, but Gail held on tight.

He pulled away from the kiss. "Why are you all covered up?"

"It's bright in here." It was the first he'd seen of her confidence flagging.

Cupid rolled off to her side and propped up his head in his hand. "Okay," he said softly, "as long as you know you're beautiful."

"*Please.* Let's not go overboard here." She tore open the bag with her teeth. "Want some?"

"Sure."

She filled his hand, and they watched each other while they snacked. Cupid had yet to encounter modesty from a partner, and it made him curious. "Mind if I ask you something?"

Gail tipped the water bottle away from her lips. "Not sure. Ask me, and I'll tell you if I mind."

"Fair enough. Have you been with many men since your divorce?"

"A few," she answered carefully.

"Were you shy like this with them?"

"I've never been a fan of keeping the lights on."

"Would you like me to turn the lamp off?" He rolled over and reached for the switch, but Gail grabbed his wrist.

"No. Please—" Startled, he pulled back. She released his hand. "I want to see you." She cringed as the words left her mouth. "Is that creepy?"

Cupid smiled and traced a finger along her shoulder. "No, it's sweet." He wanted to see her, too, but not if it made her uncomfortable.

"I've never been with anyone like you before." Her confession made her blush. "I mean, even when I was young, I *never* . . ." She waved a hand in front of her face as if to erase the babbling. "I just want to enjoy this while it lasts, as long as you don't mind."

No, Cupid didn't mind being the object of pretty much everyone's desire. Perhaps at some point, the novelty would wear off, but for now, the attention was a definite aphrodisiac, as evidenced by the erection resting against his thigh.

"Not at all, *but*"—Cupid slid his hand lazily down his body while Gail watched every move he made—"I'm sure we can think of better things to do than just looking."

"Oh, good god!" Gail closed up the water bottle and tossed it and the leftover trail mix onto the floor.

Cupid rolled on top of her and made Gail forget to worry about covering up. When their energy had left them for good, Gail staggered out of bed, gathered up her clothes, and took them into the bathroom. Cupid followed his cue and pulled on his clothes as well.

By the time Gail emerged, Cupid was lacing up his boots, yet another human inconvenience he performed under protest. She sat down next to him on the bench at the foot of the bed.

"Thank you," she said. "That was the most fun I've had in years."

Cupid tightened the bow and shifted to face her. "Thank *you*," he said, leaning in to give her a tender kiss. "I had a great time, too."

"Please. You can be with anyone you want."

The sharp blade of Cupid's predicament sliced into him. "You'd be surprised."

Gail couldn't possibly understand how wrong she was, but she did seem to recognize the pain in his eyes. "Sorry."

Cupid leaned back on his hands. He didn't want to hurt Gail, but they were here for a reason. "How is Ruth?"

Gail gave him a hard stare. "Ruth."

He shrugged. He was being a jerk, but what choice did he have?

"Of course." Gail blew out a heavy breath. "You know what? I wish Ruthie could experience something like this. It might make her feel alive again."

"What do you mean?"

"She's been sleepwalking through her life, going through the motions for months, possibly years. Nobody's paying attention."

"But she's married."

"Technically." Gail grimaced but didn't elaborate.

"Surely her husband is paying attention." Cupid would never take his eyes off Ruthie were she his wife.

"This isn't my story to tell." Gail stood, an air of finality in her tone.

"Okay—"

"*But* I strongly suspect he's stepping out."

"Stepping out where?"

"You know, dipping his pen in the company ink, if you get my drift."

"Sorry, I don't."

Gail sighed and folded her arms across her chest. "He's screwing his business associate."

"Why?"

"*Why?*" Gail repeated Cupid's question, as if asking it made no sense. "She probably '*gets him*,' sees how clever he is. What man doesn't love feeling smart and successful and adored?"

"And Ruthie doesn't do that?"

"*Pshhh.* Ruthie is married to the guy. Zach isn't bad looking, but let's face it, we're all a little older than when we wore those rose-colored glasses. He's got less hair on top, and maybe that 'distinguished' patch around the temples feels a bit more like plain old gray. He snores and farts—excuse my French—and a wife sees these things. It's not our fault, but it's just hard to see the superhero sometimes when you're the one washing the skid marks out of his tights. Feel me?"

Cupid didn't know a damn thing about aging, but Gail wasn't making it sound very pleasant. "If all that's so bad, why does anyone ever stay married?"

Gail slumped back down next to Cupid on the bench. She seemed to be answering him from a long-ago place. "When you love each other, you let those things slide. There's a shared history. His crow's feet come from laughing through the bad times. His roll of pudge . . . maybe I put it there with my biscuits and gravy. Our gray hairs sprouted while worrying about our kids together. He visits my mother every week in the nursing home, held my hand at my father's funeral. You wear grooves into each other after a while; the needle fits into the slot."

Cupid nodded even though much of what she'd described was beyond his life experiences.

"But then the lying bastard cheats, and you hire the most vicious lawyer his money can buy."

"Are we still talking about Ruthie?"

"Same song, different verse."

Gail had slipped into another realm. She seemed convinced of what she was saying, but that didn't mean Cupid was. "Are you absolutely sure Ruthie's husband is cheating on her?"

She rounded on him with narrowed eyes. "Just like a man to defend him."

"I'm not defending anyone. I'm just asking if you're sure."

"Never mind, I know how the bro code works."

There she went again. "Bro code?"

"You just naturally take his side because he's a guy."

"Why would I take his side? I've never even met him." Well, not unless he counted the near miss with the car.

Gail's tirade barreled down its own track without regard for Cupid's responses. "Whatever. Look, I love Ruthie, but she refuses to see what's happening. One very sad day, she's gonna pull her head out of her books and realize her marriage is in shambles."

That explained the frequent visits to the library. "She likes to read?"

"She *lives* to read—her escape from reality. That and chatting online with her so-called friends all over the world."

"That doesn't sound so bad."

"She never leaves her computer."

"But she was at that dance club when I met you . . ." *and in and out of her house all day*, but Cupid wasn't supposed to know about that.

"You have no idea how long Wendy and I had to work on her to get her to come out with us the other night. *Weeks*. And once she builds this little sanctuary she keeps talking about, I'm afraid she'll never come out again."

"What sanctuary?"

"A reading nook, she calls it. She's been planning on converting the nursery for years. I don't know that she'll ever pull the trigger. That would put the final nail in the coffin."

"Whose coffin?"

Gail paused and bit her lip before answering. "The babies she could never have."

"Oh." Cupid had seen his share of infertile deities on the Mount, and their stories usually ended very badly for all concerned. He couldn't bear it if Ruthie turned into a child-stealing monster or sprouted snakes for hair.

"That's good they're redoing the nursery, then. Is she building it herself?"

"Hell no." Gail smirked. "Please. Nobody in Tarra Heights actually builds anything. We hire people."

Finally—an opening. "Maybe she'd hire me."

"You're a builder?"

"Sort of."

Gail gave Cupid another of those disbelieving frowns he was really growing to dislike. "Mmhmm. Okay, look. You like her. Ruthie sends out this vibe—I get it. But I have to tell you, Quentin, you are barking up the wrong tree. Ruthie just ain't that kinda girl. She's very brave online, basically a different person, from what I gather, but that is the closest Ruthie Miller will ever come to unfaithfulness in her marriage. I love Ruthie, but I don't want to see you get hurt either."

Gail had turned out to be more complicated than Cupid had bargained for, but her heart was in the right place. He set his hand on top of hers and curled his fingers into the spaces. "Thank you for your concern, Gail. If there's a job to be had at Ruthie's, I could really use the work. I'm new in town, so I don't know a lot of people. If you can put in a good word for me, I'd appreciate it."

She regarded him gravely. "You know I will."

11

GETTING HANDY

"You told this Gail you're a builder?"

"More or less."

Pan allowed himself a mental pat on the back. It seemed his protégé was catching on to the fine art of truth-bending.

"One doesn't grow up in the palace of Hephaestus without learning a thing or two about crafting."

"No offense, Q, but you always seemed more the Mother-will-provide type than a do-it-yourselfer." At the mention of Aphrodite, Cupid's mouth edged downward at the corners, and Pan instantly felt like a shit for invoking her.

"Just because I chose not to doesn't mean I can't."

"I have no doubt you are capable enough if you set your mind to the task. You really believe she'll convince Ruth to hire you for the job?"

"I told her I need the work."

"Oh boy. I'll bet you gave her that sad puppy look you're giving me right now, too."

Cupid shrugged. "Ruthie pushed me away, and I need to stay close. I have to make this happen."

"Well then, my friend, we better get you some tools and some practice."

"What kind of practice?"

"Hmm, I don't know. I suppose you could build a new entertainment center for my great room."

Cupid's eyes narrowed a bit. "Oh, can I now?"

"Hey, you should be thanking me. You remember all those cars you crashed on your phone while you were learning to drive? I'm giving you the chance to work out the kinks before you make a fool of yourself with your new girlfriend."

"She's not my—"

"Get in the truck, Q. You are about to experience Home Warehouse."

The bright yellow awning drew Pan's truck like a giant magnet. *Come hither. I have lumber and macho tools and muscle-bound men inside, waiting for you.*

"Where on earth do we begin?" Cupid asked, his voice filled with awe as he spun a 360 inside the store.

Pan surveyed the signs suspended over the aisles by thick chains. "Power tools. C'mon."

"Wow. Daedalus would lose his mind in here."

It had been years since Pan had purchased any tools, and he didn't have time right now to sort through all the new technology on his own. "Yeah, uh, I should probably find someone to help us. Don't touch anything while I'm gone."

Now, where were all those aggressive sales associates who would never leave him alone when he wanted them to? Pan slipped from one aisle to the next, scouting for a yellow apron. Huh. Must be celebrating a birthday in the break room or some damn thing.

Whatever. How hard could it be to choose a nail gun?

He returned to Cupid, speeding his steps when he picked

up a chorus of voices. How could Pan have missed the obvious? Open a jar of honey, the flies will come. Chuckling out loud now, Pan rounded the endcap and took in the sight: five Home Warehouse employees waving power drills in Cupid's face.

"The impact driver is going to get you more speed and better control. This Ryobi P1891 has 1600 inch-pounds of torque and one-handed loading—"

"If you've got a tight space, you're going to want a right-angle drill. This baby right here has a sweet three-eighth-inch, single-sleeve ratcheting chuck—"

"You can't beat this variable speed reversible hammer drill with a 6.2-amp motor—"

The only one to notice Pan's entrance was Cupid, who telegraphed a desperate *Help!* from the bullseye of a tight circle of bodies. Pan parted the yellow sea with two firm arms and struck a protective stance at Cupid's side. Several of the drills were running, the bits spinning a whole lot closer to Cupid's body than Pan could stomach.

"Could we have a little breathing room, please? If you could all take a couple steps backward? Thank you." Pan shot an eye roll at Cupid though they both knew full well this wasn't his fault. "Now, who here has actually *used* one of these things?"

Pan narrowed the field to two qualified associates, then chose the more fuckable. *Rayne.* It took Pan less than three seconds to mentally strip down the silver fox to his hypothetical Scruff profile picture—warm, wise eyes set off by salt-and-pepper hair and sideburns, a tuft of matching chest hairs subtly highlighting hard-won pecs, just barely visible in the modest head shot. *Yum, and let it Rayne down on me.*

The three of them set off on a treasure hunt through the warehouse with Cupid walking alongside Rayne and Pan wheeling the yellow plastic cart behind them. Pan half listened as

Rayne rattled off an impressive collection of know-how while Cupid absorbed every word. That Rayne only had eyes for Cupid didn't trouble Pan. If Cupid had the hots for anything, it was whatever tool Rayne was holding—and only because he needed to equip himself for Ruthie's sake.

Pan followed them dutifully to the register and emptied the cart while Rayne made his big play for Cupid, a cell number printed on his business card and delivered with a wink and a corny line: "Call me if anything comes up." Before the chip reader had finished with Pan's Amex, he had a plan to capitalize on the horny haze Cupid had so generously cast.

At home, Cupid and Pan unloaded the truck, neatly piling the precut plywood along the wall of the garage and arranging the new tools on a makeshift table. For the next several hours, Cupid threw himself into the task of learning carpentry with that same determination he'd brought to learning to drive. He wielded his T-square like a pro and created an impressive set of preliminary drawings. Whatever instruction he failed to glean from his detailed interrogation of Rayne, Cupid located and devoured on YouTube. Watching from a distance, Pan couldn't help but wonder what Cupid might have made of himself if he'd attacked his academics with such rigor. Surely, he would've been way less fun.

Still, everything about this industrious Cupid stirred Pan. The humble way Cupid approached the unfamiliar task, still very much a stranger in a strange land yet somehow radiating complete confidence that he could and would master every new challenge. The absent-minded tuck of the drafting pencil behind his ear. The intensity of Cupid's focus as he absorbed the expert advice with his whole being. And holy hell, the power tools humming in his hands as he practiced. Pan had to get the hell out of there.

"Hey, I really should go check on Euphrosyne. Do you have everything you need?"

"Huh? Oh, let me see . . ." Cupid's fingers traced over the lines on his paper. "I'm good. Just waiting for your decision on the finish color."

Exactly. "I'll pick up the stain on my way home. Try not to bring down the roof while I'm gone."

Cupid turned right back to the computer screen without registering Pan's remark. If he kept this up, Q would be winging his way home in no time flat, which would truly suck for Pan. No time like the present to start consoling himself.

Pan tapped out a quick text to Rayne:

Remember the 2 guys who bought out the store this a.m.? Coming back for stain. Will need help loading truck ;)

Rayne's message lit up Pan's phone seconds later.

At your service :)

Pan considered hinting he'd be alone but thought better of it. If Rayne didn't seem into it, Pan would play innocent and let the guy off the hook. There were plenty of fish in that yellow sea.

It turned out Rayne was more than happy to see Pan. They each carried two cans of stain to the truck, which Pan had conveniently parked at the far end of the parking lot.

"Is there anything else I can do for you?" Rayne asked with a definite twinkle in his eye.

"Not with your clothes on," Pan answered.

Rayne required little coaxing into the cab, where he proceeded to service Pan with a smile. Afterward, as Rayne was straightening his apron, he inquired about Cupid. "I got the impression your friend had never so much as hammered in a nail. That circular saw has a vicious kickback. You sure he's safe going from zero to sixty?"

"Q's a quick study," Pan answered, to which Rayne waggled his eyebrows and said, "Lucky you."

Yeah, as if we would have just done that if I could have had Q.

Pan's tension eased for the moment, he drove across town to do some actual concierging. The goddess of mirth had fallen two days ago, and Pan had done little more than settle her into the South Side Apartments with a promise to return soon. He hadn't known Euphrosyne well on Olympus—the Graces kept mostly to the Underworld and held little sway over the beasts of the hunt. Still, Pan recognized that the fragile creature weeping outside her apartment building was not her usual self.

Euphrosyne rose and wrapped her arms around Pan, melting his heart with her desperate embrace. He took one look at her bleary, bloodshot eyes, set deep into flawless porcelain skin, and spirited her off to the nearest bar.

He passed her two tequila shots, which she downed like a champ while sobbing through her story. Zeus had summoned Euphrosyne to cheer Hera from one of her famous sulks. Euphrosyne had pulled every trick in the book, including enlisting the help of her two sister-Graces and all the Muses, but each attempt had only dragged Hera further into her foul mood. Hera had become more and more irritated with Euphrosyne's increasingly frantic ploys. Next thing she knew, Euphrosyne found herself tumbling through the clouds.

"You have to help me get home, Pan. I'm not meant to be separated from my sisters. There is no singular 'Grace.' *Please.*"

She was right. Aglaia and Thalia could hardly be expected to continue producing splendor and good cheer while their triplet sister suffered her punishment. Pan could only imagine the bleakness on Olympus right now. A shiver tore down his spine.

"Of course I'll help. That's what I'm here for." Pan covered Euphrosyne's delicate, marble-white fingers with his own craggy hand. "Now, tell me everything you remember about your judgment."

Euphrosyne lifted her napkin to the corners of her eyes and dabbed at her tears. "It was all Hera. She waved her arm as if shooing away one of her gadflies and yelled, 'Go now, and amuse someone else for a while, why don't you?'"

"Oh. I see."

"You do?" She looked up at him with too much hope in her eyes.

Damn, sometimes Pan really hated being the bearer of bad news. "I think so. I think you're meant to spread your mirth down here."

An ugly laugh came out of Euphrosyne. "What mirth?" *Right.*

The idea hit Pan like a neon sign—the one hanging off the comedy club across the street, to be precise. "The Episode hosts an open mic night once a week. Maybe you could pull together a routine?"

"What? How? I'm a goddess, not a comedian."

Pan shook his head and chuckled. "And I'm a hunter, not a . . . well, not everything I've become in the last two thousand years. We do what we have to do."

"I don't have a clue what earthlings would find amusing."

"You could start with that line about not being a comedian." At least the *Star Trek* fans would have a chuckle. "Watch some TV. Use that laptop in your apartment to study earth culture. You'll figure it out." Pan gave her an encouraging smile she did not return. "I have to run. You have my number if you need me."

There was no need for Pan to feel guilty for rushing home to Cupid. After all, he was a job, too. Yep, just another active file demanding Pan's attention.

The garage door screeched its way up the tracks, revealing Cupid's brand-new work boots first, followed by his dust-covered overalls and safety goggles. Pan was much relieved to see Cupid adhering to the precautions they'd discussed. Bent over the sawhorse, tightening a clamp as if his life depended on it, Cupid didn't even flinch as Pan's truck approached.

Pan hopped out of his truck and delivered the containers of stain to the supply shelf. He had been gone less than two hours, and Cupid had already assembled the outer casing.

"Wow, you work fast."

"As do you," Cupid shot back without taking his eyes off his work. "I can smell that salesman on you."

Pan hardly needed to apologize for blowing off a little Cupid-induced steam. He could have brought up Cupid's roll in the hay with Ruthie's BFF but dismissed the accusation with a light chuckle instead. "Rayne was quite passionate about his stain colors."

Cupid lifted his eyes past the clamp to give Pan a harsh glower. "Can't wait to see what you two decided on."

With an irritated huff he immediately regretted, Pan acknowledged the obvious, at least to himself. *We decided we'd both rather have been with you.*

12

LADIES' LUNCH

I'm happy for my friend. I'm happy for my friend. Repetition wasn't helping all that much, and Ruth feared that Gail would see right through her fake smile. Why hadn't she bowed out of this ladies' lunch when she had the chance? Surely she could've faked a cough.

"Don't ever turn to a life of crime," Zach loved to tease his wife. "You'd be caught in a heartbeat." Up until quite recently, Ruth's inability to fib hadn't held her back in life; she was a woman with nothing to hide. Honest and fair in her dealings with friends and the legion of subcontractors they employed, Ruth laid her head on the pillow each night with a clear conscience.

But lately, there had been a shift, it was only fair to acknowledge, a mental meandering she wouldn't go so far as to classify as infidelity—nothing nearly that drastic—but Ruth was, at a minimum, skating a slippery slope. Conversations had occurred around topics more appropriately discussed with her husband than the men she'd "met" online. *They're just words:* the biggest treason for a woman enamored with words. Her lame excuse held up less and less as the frequency of those intimate chats increased, and the subject matter spiraled deeper into taboo.

In her heart of hearts, Ruth felt guilty of coveting many things she could not have—babies, obviously, but at least that longing was justifiable. The other yearnings were not just unreasonable; they were downright reckless—the firm body of her youth, the excruciatingly tantalizing boys that filled her newsfeed, the spark of outrageously romantic new beginnings. Life would be so much easier if she'd just stop wanting those things, but there was an undeniable thrill in the fantasy she knew she'd never act on.

Thus far, the banter alone had been enough to sustain her, the hot fudge topping drizzled over her vanilla ice cream. The problem was, this Quentin was no virtual acquaintance; he was real, and he was here in Tarra. Worse yet, he seemed to want her, too. *Why*, she could not fathom, but even Ruth had to admit there was a definite something in the way he'd looked at her. She'd been wise to toss him to Gail; it was the right thing to do.

Doing the right thing sucked sometimes.

With Gail's post-date text Friday night—*I owe you BIG time!*—Ruth could no longer lie to herself. She cared way too much about this Quentin, and not in an altruistic way.

She'd achieved exactly what she'd set out to do, pawning off her own little problem while helping out a friend. Ruth had no business being angry with Gail, and she hated herself for her uncharitable reaction, but there it was. And there Gail sat, waiting for her.

Of course Gail was already seated when Ruth arrived. She'd be champing at the bit to "share." Wendy would be her typical fifteen minutes, can-you-*buh-LEEVE*-the-traffic late. In the meantime, it would be up to Ruth to put on her best performance. She plastered on a smile and prayed Gail wouldn't see what a shit friend she truly was.

Gail turned toward Ruth's approaching footsteps. *Jesus*, the woman was glowing. For real.

Could've been you.

Gail popped out of her seat and wrapped Ruth in a giant, swaying hug. "Thank you, thank you, thank you!" Fortunately, Gail couldn't see Ruth rolling her eyes.

"Welcome," Ruth mumbled, carefully rearranging her features.

Ruth's ass had barely touched the chair when Gail took off like a horse out of the gate. "Ohmygod, Ruthie, he's positively divine. You'd think someone so young and so *hot* would be callous or conceited, but he was just so . . . *gah*!" Gail fell back into her chair with a dramatic sigh. "I cannot thank you enough."

Ruth bit her tongue and forced her lips into a smile though she imagined it had to be twisted and ugly. "Actually, you have." *Now please, for the love of all that is holy, stop.*

"Well, I insist on buying lunch today. It's the least I can do."

"Fine. I'll have the"—Ruth perused her menu and slapped it closed with a flourish—"twin lobster plate."

Gail was undeterred. "Deal."

Wendy floated in on a wave of apologies and slid into the chair on Ruth's other side. "What did I miss? What deal?"

Here we go again.

"Ruthie's hot, young suitor from the other night asked her for her number."

Wendy's jaw dropped open, and she punched Ruth in the arm. "Look at you go, cougar mama."

Ruth blew out an exasperated breath while Gail plowed ahead with the punch line. "And she, being *married* and all, much like *yourself*, slipped him *my* number instead. By the way, Ruthie, that was kind of a cruel trick you played on the boy. But damn, girl, I love you to the moon for it."

Wendy turned her astonished face to Ruth. "Wow. You did that?"

Ruth shrugged. She could have just turned him down, she supposed, but then he would've been lost forever. At least this way, there was a chance of . . . *Of what, exactly? Oh Ruth, there you go again, mistaking yourself for one of the heroines in your romance stories.* How was that fair to any of them? A twinge of guilt clouded Ruth's envy as she imagined Quentin's face at the instant of discovery. But then, he'd gone right ahead and arranged a date with Gail, hadn't he? Probably never wanted Ruth in the first place, just picked off the most vulnerable sheep in the flock like any smart wolf would do.

Impatient for more dish, Wendy turned to Gail. "So how was he?"

"Exactly how you'd think." Delighted to have an appreciative audience, Gail oozed and gushed anew. "The boy is seriously gifted. And his *stamina . . .*"

"Lordy, Gail. How many times have you two gone out?"

"Just one."

Wendy's jaw dropped. "You fuck strange men on the first date now?"

Gail turned bright red at the waitress's untimely arrival. A sweet girl around Quentin's age, she had the good sense to pretend she hadn't heard. "May I get you ladies something to drink?"

"Yes," Ruth answered swiftly. "A glass of your most expensive prosecco." She flashed a smile at Gail, who ordered the same.

"Make it three," Wendy said, waiting for the girl to scurry away before chastising Gail again. "What if he was an ax murderer?"

Gail choked out a laugh. "Honey, if that was murder, please let me die a thousand more deaths. At a minimum, give me assault with that deadly tongue."

Ruth could taste the bile licking at the back of her throat. There was only so much she could take. "Okay, I think we can do without the details."

"Speak for yourself there, missy," Wendy interjected. "I want *all* the details."

Gail shot Ruth a sheepish smile. "He'd like to have that job at your house."

"What job?"

"Your building project."

The nursery. A prickle rushed across Ruth's skin. She could have her nook and a little eye candy, too. "How does he even know about my building project?"

"Please. You didn't think your name would come up in conversation?"

Wendy leaned into the center of the table and grabbed each of her friends' hands. "Of course it did, in the heat of the moment . . . '*Oh, Ruthie, oh, oh,* come *with me . . .*'"

Ruth yanked her hand away. "Ugh, Wen. Could you be any tackier?"

Wendy glanced at Gail for encouragement but found herself at the business end of an evil glare. "Oh, fine. Whatever. *She's* the one who reads that crap," Wendy said, jutting her chin at Ruth. If they knew she wrote "that crap" too, Ruth would never hear the end of it.

Pivoting toward Gail, she asked, "He brought me up?" For the first time since she'd walked through the door of the bistro, Ruth's smile was genuine.

"Come on, honey," Gail answered quietly, "we both know it's you he really wanted, not me."

Ruth had a dozen follow-up questions, but she couldn't figure a way to ask without sounding like a teenager with a crush. "He's a builder?"

Made sense, the sculpted body, muscles swollen from a day's hard labor. Ruth swooned a bit as she inserted Quentin's face and body into the hot, horny handyman story she'd written last year. Yes, Quentin would make a very fine Henry, sawing and nailing things down in a pair of worn jeans, sweating through his ribbed, white tank.

Wendy snapped her out of her daydream. "Who cares what he is? Honey, if that man showed up at my house with a tool belt strapped around his waist, I'd let him pound whatever the hell he wanted."

"Classy," Gail said, sharing a giggle with Wendy. "Look, Ruthie, I promised Quentin I'd give you his number, so I will honor that promise. The rest is up to you. You can finally get your study built." Gail dug her phone out of her purse and tapped on it for a minute before stuffing it back inside. "Just call him."

Ruth had been talking about the project for almost a year now. Her phone buzzed with the incoming text message. There it was, Quentin's phone number waiting for her.

"You really think I should call him?"

Surely one of her friends should talk her out of this, and it certainly wouldn't be anyone from Ruth's online community. No, they'd be shaking their pompoms and cheering her on. Quentin was the brass ring, the living, breathing fairy tale knight in tight denim, and one didn't throw away that once-in-a-lifetime chance when it slammed into you in a nightclub.

Gail leaned into the table and used her "confidential" voice. "Look, I was hoping not to have to mention this, but Quentin said he could really use the work. You'd be doing a mitzvah."

"Oh." Ruth was all in favor of providing jobs. She gazed into the smiling, nodding faces of her two closest friends and realized she was doing the same.

Their prosecco arrived, and the waitress took their lunch orders. Wendy offered a toast before Ruth had a chance to head her off at the pass. "To Quentin!"

Ruth's gaze shifted to Gail as she tipped back her wine. Did

Gail honestly want Ruth horning in on her little arrangement with her new young stud? An ugly thought followed—the kind that would fill Ruth with deep shame when she reflected on this moment later: *Misery loves company.*

Gail had been hinting not too subtly for weeks now about Zach and Joan, but Ruth wasn't biting, at least not to any of the people who inhabited her "real life." Had she voiced a suspicion or two to her online friends? Maybe. There was no harm in venting; they all did it. Ruth's marriage was Morticia and Gomez Addams compared to most. Still, Ruth had been cautious about expressing even the slightest doubt to Gail.

Ruth took a gulp of her prosecco, reorganizing all the dialogue in her head until she could configure something that made sense. There was only one possible course of action to pursue, and it seemed both extraordinarily simple and exasperatingly unlikely. Her marriage being the unbreakable bond she willed it to be, she would hire Quentin to do the work in her home, and he would complete said work without receiving more than the occasional appreciative glance from Ruth. At the end of the day, she would have both the reading nook she always wanted and the conviction that her commitment to Zach surpassed any inappropriate urge that might have briefly tempted her.

With each sip of boozy insight, this decision earned more and more merit. By the time she'd reached the bottom of her glass, she'd even managed to attribute only positive motives to her BFF: Gail had called Ruth's bluff to help her move past her dithering on the nursery project and to help Ruth see that her marriage was strong enough to handle the temptation.

"It's settled." Two pairs of eyebrows lifted in response to Ruth's announcement. "I'll call him tomorrow."

13

GETTING HIRED

Cupid wanted to snap something in half. Pan's neck would have been his first choice, but with murder possibly permanent down here, he'd settle for the shelving he'd assembled while Pan was out screwing the tool salesman. Pan hadn't even made up an excuse when he left to meet Rayne for a repeat performance on Sunday. Luckily, the clamps prevented Cupid from harming both himself and his project. He would have hated to waste three solid days of work.

The buzzing phone in his pocket provided Cupid a much-needed distraction. He didn't recognize the caller's number, but the skip of his heart told him it was Ruthie. "Hello?"

"Hi. Uh, hello . . . Quentin?" Her voice sounded as shaky as Cupid felt. It made him want to wrap his arms around her and tell her everything would be okay even if he hadn't worked out the *how* part yet.

"Yes," he answered. "It's me."

"Right. This is Ruth. From the club?"

"I know." Cupid cradled the phone against his neck.

"Oh. I wasn't sure . . ."

He closed his eyes to sharpen his fuzzy memories of lips and eyes and hair into a vivid picture. "How are you, Ruthie?"

"I'm all right. Actually, to be honest, I'm a little nervous. I owe you an apology."

Cupid couldn't read her body language through the phone, but he could certainly hear the apprehension. "Please, don't worry about it. I totally understand. The last thing on Earth I meant to do was make you uncomfortable."

"Thank you, but it wasn't your fault. I think I was probably sending out signals."

Signals. If she only knew her heartbeat was bouncing off Mount Olympus and straight into Cupid's chest!

"You're fine, Ruthie." Her name was a torture he could not stop inflicting on himself, and so were the questions begging to be answered: Why had she called? What had Gail told her about their date? Was Ruthie completely disgusted by him now?

Ruthie had worked up the nerve to call; Cupid needed to trust her to finish the job. Waiting, as Cupid had learned with Mia, was not his strong suit.

He sank into the couch, throwing off puffs of sawdust all around him. At least the image of Pan dragging out his long vacuum hose and cursing at Cupid all the while provided some measure of pleasure. Cupid pressed the phone against his head so as not to miss a syllable. Ruthie's next words were like sweetly plucked harp strings to Cupid's ears.

"Gail tells me you might be interested in converting our, uh, spare room to an office?"

"Yes!" Cupid answered with all the enthusiasm coursing through him. Too late, he remembered how that dancing girl, Rho, had played hard to get and nearly driven Cupid insane with desire. He'd already tried the direct approach with Ruthie, only to end up in a hotel room with her best friend. A new tactic couldn't hurt. "I mean, yes, I might be interested."

Ruthie kept him waiting again, heart pounding in his throat, wondering if this game-playing strategy was all wrong, too. Must every girl be so different and confusing? Perhaps his perspective was skewed because he'd only recently begun this falling in love business, but it seemed that the deities were far less complicated than these Earth dwellers.

"Maybe we could meet somewhere to discuss it," she said, then hastily added, "for coffee?"

At least she'd given him a fighting chance. This time, Cupid settled on a middle-of-the-road tone, a sort of impassive interest in earning a little money. "Sure, that would be great."

"Would you, by chance, be free today?" She backpedaled so quickly, Cupid began to believe she was as confused and flustered by all this as he was. "I mean, Gail mentioned you were probably not in the middle of, uh . . ."

"No problem. Today is fine. I just need to take a shower."

"Oh, sure, that's fine. Obviously. I mean, I wouldn't want to interfere with your shower." Ruthie ended her word-tripping with a nervous laugh that made Cupid rethink his shower reference. It didn't bode well for his mission if the two of them couldn't manage a conversation without dying of awkwardness.

"Do you know the diner out on Route 58?" he asked.

"The one with the great pie?"

"Yes. How about meeting me there in, say, thirty minutes?"

"Okay. And while you're, um, getting ready, I'll pull together my drawings."

"Looking forward to it, Ruthie."

Her name lingered on Cupid's tongue, the delicious flavor of it following him into the shower stall. He worked a generous dollop of gel into a lather along his arms and chest, massaging his fatigued muscles, spent in the best possible way, bettering himself for Ruthie.

His sweet, shy Ruthie. He pictured her standing in her future study, gazing out the elegant French doors onto her garden. Would she let go, just a little, enough to feel the heat of Cupid's body pressing against her from behind? Imagine his lips grazing her shoulder or a "careless" bump of their hips?

How Ruthie would blush right now if she knew what he was doing to himself at the thought of her. Would she see the evidence in his eyes as they sat across from each other inside the safe, well-lit diner?

For all his worry over Ruthie's response, Cupid could barely endure his own wild chest-banging when she pulled into the diner's parking lot.

She stepped out of her car. He fought the urge to pounce.

Ruthie turned toward him with that same google-eyed swoon Cupid had chalked up to drunkenness the night they met. He tested the air around her with a subtle sniff, but there was no alcohol on Ruthie's breath. She was under the influence of Cupid as he was very much under hers.

He took her shaky hand between his. "Hello again." Cupid didn't trust himself to say her name out loud. "Thank you for giving me this chance."

She blinked back at him as if surprised to find herself there. Her hand fell away as she reached into her back seat. "I'll just grab my bag."

Cupid fumbled behind her, attempting to open and close doors Ruthie seemed determined to manage on her own. He tried to relieve her of the tote bag, but when she insisted on carrying everything, Cupid stuffed his useless hands into his pockets and followed her inside the diner.

One nod from the owner's daughter told Cupid she

remembered him though her obvious attraction seemed to confuse her. Last time, it was Pan she'd desired.

Ruthie wielded her laminated menu like a shield, studying the offerings for several long minutes before ordering a decaf, black.

Cupid peered over his menu. "That's it? No pie?"

"I shouldn't," Ruthie said, pushing the menu into the waitress's hand as if she'd gain five pounds just from reading it. Cupid wasn't sure he'd met anyone quite as good at denying herself, certainly nobody he knew on Mount Olympus.

"I'll have a regular coffee and slice of key lime pie with two forks, please."

Ruthie gave Cupid a reluctant smile that reminded him of Mia's "maybe," which lifted his spirits. Perhaps Ruthie could be persuaded to let down her guard after all.

Ruthie dashed that hope soon enough, with anxious eyes darting around the diner until their coffees and pie arrived. Cupid slid the plate to the middle of the table, stabbed the fork into the stiff meringue, and brought the first taste to his tongue. Ruthie palmed her coffee mug with two shaky hands.

"Is something wrong?" he asked. *Gods,* how he longed to crowd next to her on her side of the booth and wrap his arm around her shoulders, but he couldn't imagine she'd find the gesture the least bit comforting.

She focused her gaze on Cupid. "It's just, it's a small town, you know? People like to talk."

So, Ruthie knew the gossip about Zach. Did she believe it? Did she know Cupid had pumped Gail for information? This was all so tricky. Ruth was as skittish as a new filly, and the next wrong move might get Cupid bucked for good.

"Aren't two people allowed to share a piece of pie?"

Her eyes narrowed at his challenge. Cupid bit back his

smile as Ruthie reached for her fork and brought the tiniest morsel of pie to her tongue.

"Oh god, that is really good." She giggled with pleasure, and Cupid vowed right then and there to do everything in his power to bring forth that sound again.

"Have some more."

She set down her fork. "It'll look better on you." She froze as the blush covered her cheeks. Time to change the subject.

"Tell me more about this project."

Visibly relieved, she answered. "I'm converting a spare room into a study where I can read and write."

"You're a writer?"

"Oh gosh, no," she said with a dismissive wave that sloshed her hot coffee perilously to one side. She righted the mug with both hands and brought it to rest on the table. "I *write*. Nothing published."

"Gail didn't mention your writing to me."

"She doesn't know." Judging by the anguish in Ruthie's eyes, she already seemed to regret telling him. "Nobody in my real life knows, besides my husband, I mean."

"Real life?"

"I don't share my writing with anyone I actually know, just the strangers who come across my words on the internet."

"Your secret is safe with me." Cupid sealed his promise with a solemn nod. "What kind of things do you write?" Serious, important articles, Cupid guessed.

"Oh." Ruthie's gaze dropped to the pie between them. "Fiction," she said.

Cupid searched his memory for the last fiction book he'd read. Not for the first time since his fall to Earth, he regretted not taking his schooling more seriously. And he definitely regretted not doing anything to improve his mind since leaving the academy.

Cupid couldn't hope to make up for his deficit all at once, but perhaps he could fill in some of the key gaps. Look how quickly he'd picked up driving and carpentry. Meanwhile, he'd just have to fake his way through. "Fiction, huh? That's great. What do you like to write about?" Cupid braced himself for the worst—science fiction had always confused him.

Ruthie huffed and shook her head. "Nothing you'd be interested in." Her ears turned bright pink at the tips.

Cupid longed to see the lovely blush reflected in her cheeks if only she'd look up for a second. Whatever this was, Cupid was most definitely interested.

He ventured one hand across their table, boldly breaching the midway line marked by the pie. Before she could pull away, Cupid brushed the delicate fingers curled around the handle of her mug and smiled when she looked up with a startled gasp. "Try me," he said, nailing his gaze to hers.

"Romance." She released the word as if someone had dared her to say it, then snapped up her coffee and watched from a safe distance while Cupid's finger trailed back to its own side of the table.

"*Romance?*" Cupid could scarcely believe his luck.

"See? I told you."

"That's amazing. I love romance."

"You do?"

"Of course. Who doesn't? It's universal. I mean, who hasn't known the thrill of falling in love?" Though Cupid was a newcomer to the experience, his feelings could not have been more vivid.

"I guess." So modest, this goddess of his.

"I'd love to read something you've written." He needed to read every word she'd ever written.

"Oh god, no." She narrowed her eyes. "I'd be mortified."

"But you post your stories on the internet for the world to see. Why would you be mortified if someone who"—the dreaded L-word nearly flew out of Cupid's mouth—"if someone who already likes you were to read them?"

Ruthie set down her mug and pulled one of the long scrolls from her bag. "So, basically, I want to add bookshelves along this wall, incorporate a built-in desk here," she said, pointing to an opening below a large window, "and update the colors. Can you do it?" Ruthie lifted her gaze from the page to Cupid's open-mouthed gawp. There she was again, drawing a hard line he'd be a fool to ignore.

Sharing time was over for now but not forever. An ordinary man might have missed the speck of desperation—*See me!*—nearly choked out by Ruthie's tight grip, but Cupid was no ordinary man. He'd spent his whole immortal lifetime finding the weak link in the palace patrol, and he would absolutely find his way inside Ruthie Miller. For now, he'd toe the line and pretend to be a patient man.

"Sure, I can do that for you."

"Are you a builder?"

"Not exactly."

"Exactly what *do* you do?"

"I'm versatile."

She gave him a hard stare, but he took it as a good sign that she hadn't left yet.

"Ruthie."

"Yes?" Her eyes softened. Sitting here, under the influence of his otherworldly charm, Ruthie wanted to choose him, Cupid could tell. The problem would come later. She'd need something solid to justify her decision. He thought of the bookcase drying in Pan's garage, one sad, little project to his name. How could she understand it was all the experience Cupid needed?

"I promise, if I didn't think I could do the job, I would tell you."

Ruthie's mouth turned down at the edges. "That's what my irrigation guy said right before he flooded my basement."

"Ouch." Damn these Earth men for breaking promises and making Cupid's job so much harder. "But I'm not him."

"No, you are definitely not." She folded her hands together, and the plans snapped closed with a jarring finality. "I'm guessing you don't have any references."

He didn't suppose Pan's word would provide much credibility. "If I could just sit down with you and your husband . . ." *and listen for your echo beats.*

"I don't need his permission, Quentin." The sudden shift threw Cupid. "It's my room. My project. I write the checks."

There went that chance, but Cupid had his foot in the door, and he needed to keep it there. "Sure, you're the boss. All I need is one chance to prove myself."

The moment she sighed, Cupid knew he had her. "I must be crazy." Mia had said the same, he remembered.

"You're not."

"Could you stop by one day next week?"

No, he couldn't give her that much time to reconsider and use his inexperience as her latest excuse to talk herself out of this.

"Why don't I come by first thing tomorrow morning, ready to go?"

"Oh."

"Look, Ruthie, if you decide you don't want me to do the job, I promise I'll leave and not give you a hard time, but there's no reason to waste time, right?"

"No," she had to agree, as he'd effectively called her bluff. "I guess not."

14

ON THE JOB

The door chimes jolted Ruth's heart like the blare of an alarm intruding on a deep sleep. Pookie shot out from under the table, tore through the kitchen, and skittered across the marble foyer, where she slammed face-first into the heavy mahogany door, then yipped and scrambled to get her paws underneath her. Pookie's hysteria was like a triple espresso poured over Ruth's already frazzled nerves.

Eight o'clock on the dot. Of course Quentin would be punctual, on top of every other perfect thing about him. This was really happening.

"Hush, Pookie. Sit!" The poor dog was panting like she'd just run a marathon. Even for Pookie, this level of agitation was exceptional. "Calm down, girl." When all her verbal commands failed, Ruth leaned down and scooped up Pookie into the crook of her elbow before reaching for the doorknob. "It's okay, Pooks. Look, he's harmless."

Yeah, right.

The romance writer in her immediately screamed "strapping young man," but the tired cliché didn't begin to do him justice. Yes, obviously Quentin was a fine physical specimen, but his true magic lived below the skin, bursting outward from his flawless form in barely tolerable doses: the deep blue eyes, shimmering with every secret from his past; the childlike smile stretched wide at the mere act of seeing her again; the warmth-oozing voice as he melted her with a simple, "Good morning."

"Morning." Ruth forgot her grip on Pookie for a split second, long enough for Pookie to lunge at Quentin and take a full-tongued slurp across his cheek. "Pookie, behave. I'm so sorry."

"It's okay," Quentin said with a chuckle. "Pookie, is it?" He reached out and swept his fingers through the wavy hair at the crown of her head. The dog calmed instantly, but Quentin's petting—those long, beautiful fingers fluttering so close to Ruth's chest—produced quite the opposite response in Ruth. What the hell was she thinking, bringing this temptation into her home—especially now, when things with Zach were so, er, shaky.

She was giving a worthy man an honest day's work, and in the process, getting herself that writer's study she'd been putting off for years, *that's* what. Would she not be a sexist pig if she were to deny Quentin the job because he was hot? For goodness' sake, she was a grown-ass woman, not some damn lapdog who couldn't control her impulses.

Anyway, Quentin had made his pass at her that first night, and she'd rebuffed him. Case closed. If he were still trying to seduce her, would he have shown up in those baggy, bile-colored coveralls? Quentin looked like a man who was serious about carpentry, not inspiring an affair. Though if Pookie had anything to say about it, Quentin would stand right here and scratch her ears for the rest of eternity.

"Okay, girl, I think we better give Quentin his hands back, huh?" Ruth stepped aside and pressed her back against the open door. "Come on in."

Quentin accepted her invitation with a modest dip of his chin, then breached the threshold Ruth had been guarding with her body and her ferocious cockapoo. She held her breath, ever so careful not to brush the bare skin of Quentin's arm as he passed through the doorway and came to an abrupt halt just inside. Ruth followed Quentin's horrified gaze to the floor, his heavy work boots reversing as quickly as humanly possible off the Turkish rug.

"I'm sorry. I should take my boots off."

Quentin bent forward, and Ruth shot her hand out to grasp his wrist. He blinked up at her with surprise. She imagined he was met by the same expression.

"It's fine, Quentin. It's a rug. It's made to be stepped on." She remembered to release him.

"Okay." He straightened slowly but didn't step onto the rug again. He swiveled around the spacious foyer with his jaw hinged open as he took in the recessed paneling, the hand-dyed silk wallcovering, the intricate crown molding.

Ruth's cheeks heated. Whatever Quentin knew or did not know about custom finishes, there was no disguising the opulence. *Ugh*, why hadn't she brought him in through the back door where both of them would have felt more comfortable?

Why? It simply hadn't occurred to Ruth that she could still feel embarrassed. The Millers lived in a well-to-do neighborhood, attended events hosted by peers with comparable bank accounts, enjoyed extravagant vacations with their friends, shared interior designers and personal trainers and caterers. Ruth's "normal" needle had moved in sync with those around her, gradually enough that eyebrows rarely lifted anymore. They were fortunate people surrounded by other fortunate people. The Millers had nothing to be ashamed of. They were genuinely grateful and disproportionately charitable. Unlike a few of their third-generation wealthy friends, they'd worked hard for every penny. Zach had, anyway.

Ruth hadn't worked in ten years; even then, her annual salary wouldn't have paid for the window treatments in their dining room, let alone the intricate mosaic Quentin was studying with great wonder. She flinched, prepared for the inevitable platitude. The plumber had hit her with, "Do you need a live-in fix-it man? I'm housebroken" last year, and Ruth hadn't been able to call him since. Zach couldn't understand why they were still jiggling the toilet handle in the powder room after months had gone by; Ruth was too embarrassed to tell him the reason.

"This compass rose is just like Poseidon's."

Well, that was unexpected on so many levels. "You're a fan of the Greek gods?"

Quentin's nose crinkled. "Not lately. Poseidon's okay, but—" He looked up suddenly from the floor. "Wait. Are *you*?"

"Of course. They're fascinating."

Something flashed behind Quentin's eyes, excitement at their common interest in mythology? Every time Ruth tried to write him off as just another pretty face, Quentin revealed a new dimension, and the lasso tightened around her heart, drawing her closer to something she could never have. Not that it stopped her fantasies. She pictured the two of them, sprawled lazily on a picnic blanket in the backyard, enjoying a pitcher of fresh lemonade and a plate of homemade cookies while Quentin read *The Iliad* aloud to her. Or wait, no, he'd convince her to read to him while he worked, a wide, contented grin on his face while he painted as slowly as possible to draw out their time together until they'd finished *The Odyssey* too.

Quentin's gaze swept up the wrought iron rail of the curved stairwell, his eyes opening wide at the faux-sky mural overhead. Ruth would never forget the look on Zach's face when she broke it to him how much the decorative painter was charging for "a few puffy clouds."

"Who the hell does he think he is, Michelangelo, for chrissakes?" Zach's outrage faded quickly into a long-running private joke. From that point on, anytime Zach deemed one of Ruth's design choices extravagant, he would tease, "Well, I don't know, Ruthie. Are you sure this knob/carpeting/faucet is grand enough for the Miller Chapel?"

Quentin gawped at the ceiling, his Adam's apple bobbing hard. "Reminds me of home," he said quietly. His eyes filled with a sorrowful longing that seemed out of place on Quentin's easygoing features. Before she could question him further, Quentin changed the subject. "Should we take a look at your project?"

"Yes." That would surely be safer than standing here, sorting out all the longing.

Ruth crouched to set Pookie on the floor. About a foot from the ground, the silly girl wriggled free and scurried to Quentin's ankles, her rump wagging the rest of her body. Who was Ruth kidding? If not for the conventions of common decency, she absolutely would have done the same.

"The room is this way. Just ignore Pookie's shameless flirting if you can. She'll calm down after a bit." Or not.

"She's fine." Quentin chuckled as he tiptoed alongside Ruth to avoid stepping on Pookie's tiny paws with his boots. "How long have you had her?"

"Eight years. Zach thought I might heal quicker if I had a baby to take care of."

"Heal?" he asked.

"Oh. Yeah, after my third miscarriage." Nothing like ripping off the Band-Aid.

Quentin's pace faltered, but he recovered quickly. "The fates can be cruel. I'm sorry, Ruthie."

The fates? Quirky vernacular aside, Ruth found herself unexpectedly comforted by his genuine sorrow. Odd how this near stranger could soothe Ruth's soul. "Thank you."

"Did it help, having Pookie around?"

"I guess, a bit." Ruth glanced down at the playful fluffball running laps around Quentin's feet as they walked. "I love my little pooch to pieces, but she's not exactly the child I wanted." Ruth's steps grew heavy as the nursery door came into view. "I suppose that's why I've left this room as is for all these years."

"If you don't mind my asking"—Quentin reached for the Noah's ark mezuzah she and Zach had bought when they learned she was pregnant that first time—"what is this? I noticed something similar on your front door."

"That's a mezuzah. There's a scroll inside that's meant to remind us of our commitment to creating a Jewish home. Some people believe it offers protection."

"Like an amulet?"

"I guess. This one never really had a chance to protect anything."

"I'm sorry. I didn't mean to make you sad."

She forced the best smile she could, which Ruth imagined was basically a flat line with two hooks for corners. "You didn't. Anyway . . ." She took a deep breath and steeled herself before reaching for the doorknob.

Quentin stepped in front of the door and covered her hand with his. *Ahh*, no wonder those fingers had so thoroughly tamed Pookie. "Ruthie, wait." Quentin's voice, barely above a whisper, pulled her anxious gaze to those mesmerizing eyes of his. "Are you sure you're ready?" He, who had more to lose than anyone if they abandoned the project now, offered a smile so kind and sincere, Ruth felt tears pooling behind her eyes.

A rocky sigh left her. "I guess we'll find out."

He nodded once and dropped his hand away as Ruth opened the door. Pookie took off at a dead run into the forbidden room, flew to the opposite wall and back again, yipping at Ruth, then Quentin, unable to decide who to tell first about all her exciting discoveries. Look! Soft, fuzzy carpeting. Look! A crib. A changing table. A little basket filled with books for chubby toddler fingers. A glider, perfect for breastfeeding in the wee morning hours, draped with the crib blanket Ruth had knitted using gender-neutral yellows and greens because they hadn't found out she'd been carrying a boy until it was already a moot point.

Everything was exactly as Ruth had left it after her last visit on Baby One's miscarriage date thirty-four days ago. Six dates every year—three due dates and three miscarriages—Ruth allowed herself unbridled grief within the walls of the nursery. Aside from Cassie's bimonthly vacuum and dusting, Ruth was the only person to set foot in this room in four years, when Zach had stopped commemorating the events with her. She didn't blame him for deciding it wasn't healthy anymore, but she didn't share his desire or ability to move on.

And now, inexplicably, here she stood with Quentin. Perhaps Ruthie should have warned him what he was getting himself into. What must he think of her foolishness, preserving the nursery as if it were a museum, holding on to baby furniture and hope for eight ridiculously long years? He gave nothing away, standing stock-still beside Ruthie, and as she couldn't bring herself to look him in the eye, the only movement in the room was Pookie's frantic lap running.

This was an epically bad idea.

She'd taken a real chance, bringing Quentin here. A dangerously attractive, attentive young man who'd already hit on her once, then unrepentantly screwed her best friend, he clearly wasn't shy or averse to intimacy with older women. He and Ruth would be alone, together, in her home, for many hours a day, for several weeks.

Would Zach even care? He trusted Ruth, but would he trust this stranger she'd basically picked up in a bar, with minimal experience and zero references? Ruth had nearly worked up the nerve to pull the plug when Quentin crouched down and lifted Pookie into his arms.

"Hey there, girl. It's okay." He murmured sweet nothings in tones as smooth as warm butter until Pookie quieted against his chest. Without another word, Quentin walked toward the big picture window and stared outside, gently stroking his fingers along Pookie's back.

"This would be your view while you're sitting here, at your desk." Quentin seemed not to even see the changing table right in front of him.

"Yes," Ruth answered, surprising herself once again with how easily she committed to moving forward.

Quentin turned slowly, as if he fully realized he might spook her with one false move. "I can see why you're excited about this space." Ruth couldn't respond, and he didn't seem to mind.

He scritched his fingers through Pookie's hair as he paced the width of the room. Once again, Ruth got the impression he wasn't seeing the room as it was but rather, somehow inhabiting the finished space. Pausing in front of the blank wall, Quentin stared thoughtfully from floor to ceiling. "The bookshelves will be perfect here," he said to himself or maybe to Pookie. Quentin had seen the plans only for a minute or two at the diner, but he seemed to have memorized every detail.

If Quentin's interest were purely a desperation for work, he certainly had Ruth fooled. All she could see was a man who respected her demons along with her passions and accepted the full package without judgment. Without swinging a hammer, Quentin had already created the space for her sanctuary simply by stepping inside it with her. The room filled with a profound peace Ruth had never experienced during any of her previous visits.

Ruth closed her eyes and pulled in a deep breath. For the first time, she actually believed she could move forward. Even better, when she opened her eyes, Quentin was grinning at her with that contagious confidence that had a way of ungluing her.

"Let me make this happen for you, Ruthie. Say yes."

A chill blew across her skin, leaving a trail of goose bumps. "Yes."

"I'm hired?" Quentin exclaimed, his excitement startling Pookie out of her sleepy trance. "Oops, sorry, girl."

Pookie barked out an indignant, "Ruh, ruh, rufff!"

Quentin cracked up first, his pleasure so thorough that Ruth found herself giggling right along with him. Pookie's complaints only made them both laugh even harder.

Laughter. In the nursery. Well, that was certainly a first.

15

MODEL BUILDER

Now that he was here, standing at Ruthie's front door, Cupid had to admit his scale model of the project might have been, well, a little too much. *Overkill* was the word Pan had used this morning, watching Cupid glue the final pieces of trim into place. "But really adorable overkill," Pan had added with a gentle nudge that did little to soothe Cupid's nerves.

He half considered hiding the thing in his trunk, but wasn't the whole point for Ruthie to see he could take this job seriously, that he was a professional? Besides, he'd stayed up half the night, lovingly carving each shelf and tiny piece of crown molding with the X-Acto knife he'd picked up at Home Warehouse on his way home yesterday. He sure as shivers wasn't going to send Pan back to that store—and *Rayne*.

Lifting the wood base of the structure practically to his shoulders, Cupid stepped forward and pressed the doorbell, setting off loud chimes and barking and Ruthie's sharp, "Hush, Pookie! Honestly." Cupid smiled to himself, picturing the wild scramble on the other side of the door, and his heart filled, knowing he'd soon be a part of it.

The door opened, and there Ruthie stood, clutching the squirming pooch to her chest with both arms. "Sorry about her," Ruthie said at the same time Cupid said, "Good morning."

"What have you got there?" She peered over the foam core walls, craning her neck until her head nearly touched his chest.

Cupid drew in the scent of whatever she'd washed her hair with that morning—something floral, he couldn't be sure what. Still mostly wet, it was twisted into a loose knot and clipped at the back of her head at an angle that would not have aligned with his T-square but pleased him just the same. A bit too much, in fact. The rest of her outfit wasn't helping any: a crisp, white T-shirt with a pocket stretched this way and that by Pookie's frantic struggling, dark blue jeans, and a pair of tan slippers with a roll of fur hugging her ankles. Cupid swallowed hard. Gods, she was beautiful.

"Ohmygosh, this is amazing, Quentin," she said, drawing Cupid's gaze to the model he nearly forgot he was holding. "You made this for me?"

"Yes. I wanted to show you how I interpreted our conversation and make sure it's what you want."

"Wow, that was . . . *really* . . ." Her voice trailed off with a sniffle and a soft shake of her head, the hair clip losing its grip ever so slightly. She lifted her face. Their eyes met; a tear broke free from hers. "It's *exactly* what I want."

Cupid ached to brush the moisture from her cheek, and if his hands weren't fully occupied, he would have done just that. Instead, he swiped his tongue across his lips, not that it was any use at all, not for moistening them and certainly not for forming words. Ruthie wasn't doing much better, pulling the corner of her mouth between her teeth and sniffling before she finally got any words out.

"That must be heavy."

"It's a bit awkward," he answered, very much wanting the use of his hands back.

"Why don't you come set it down in the kitchen?"

Ruthie knelt to free Pookie, setting her little paws into a furious air gallop before gaining traction on the marble floor and charging at Cupid. He tracked the furry blur until she disappeared beneath the wood platform in his hands and, fortunately, braced for impact just before Pookie slammed into his ankles. Ruthie clucked and fussed—"Ugh, Pookie. So sorry, Quentin"—and Cupid dragged his boots the rest of the way so tiny paws couldn't get trapped underneath.

Cupid settled the model on the granite counter and obliged a very happy Pookie with a belly rub. She flipped onto her back, legs splayed wide, her front paw twitching as if tied to Cupid's wrist. He tried to imagine Cerberus or any one of Actaeon's vicious hounds doing the same, but it was impossible to believe they were even part of the same animal family.

"I can't get over all the detail." Ruthie's awed whisper drew Cupid to her side, causing Pookie to scramble to her feet and yip in protest.

"You can move things around, see?" He poked his finger over the foam core wall and pushed the miniature desk from one side to the other.

"Oh!" A tiny giggle escaped her. "That's handy."

Cupid grinned. Every painstaking measurement was worth it, every minute of sleep he'd sacrificed to do the job just right. "If you need more shelves, we can add some here . . . or over here."

Her head dipped lower, closer. "Hmm." Cupid held his breath while Ruthie studied the model from every possible angle. "I'm not really sure how much storage space I need."

She walked toward her current desk, a built-in wood countertop with cabinets and open shelving above. A quick touch of her fingertip to the corner of the monitor blackened the screen before Cupid could catch a glimpse. Whatever Ruthie had just hidden brought a soft blush to her cheeks.

Cupid unclipped the measuring tape from his belt—*finally, the blasted restraint made itself useful*—and stepped into Ruthie's makeshift office. "Why don't we measure your current storage—" A framed picture caught his eye, and he reached for it without thinking.

A young couple on their wedding day. Bride and groom sitting so close, it would have been hard to say where one ended and the other began. A wide, easy smile on the bride's face, her face angled slightly toward the groom as if he'd surprised her with a joke just before the picture was snapped. *No, not a joke*, Cupid decided. Zach had told Ruthie he was the luckiest man on Earth, and for the briefest of moments on her wedding day, she'd believed him.

"Twenty-three years tomorrow," Ruthie said with a wistful lilt.

"Oh. Congratulations!" Cupid pulled the frame closer. "Wow, this picture was taken twenty-three years ago?" Aside from Gail's comments about the husband, Cupid had no basis to judge his deterioration, but Ruthie had hardly changed a bit unless you counted the way her smile didn't quite seem at home on her face anymore or the lack of twinkle in her once starry-eyed gaze.

"I know what you're thinking. I wasn't always old."

"What?" Cupid's focus snapped back to Ruthie. "I wasn't thinking that at all." Truth be told, Cupid was thinking he wished he were the one putting that glow on her face.

She let out a harsh sigh. "Anyway. The shelves?"

Cupid didn't like it, but he saw the familiar detour sign as sure as if it were a bright orange arrow flashing on Ruthie's forehead, and the last thing he wanted was to give her a reason to push him away now that he'd finally found his way in. He replaced the photo and set about taking measurements.

"How about all this covered storage, the cabinets and drawers? Did you want to recreate the same setup?" Drawers were tricky, but Cupid could practice.

Ruthie opened the cabinets one by one, rattling off lists of what she'd keep and what she'd ditch. She opened the wide desk drawer last, groaning as she lifted a stack of clipped papers. "This should probably go in the garbage, but I don't have the guts to do that either."

"What is that?"

"It's silly." She riffled through the pages at the bottom corner, a loud sigh filling the air around her. "Just something I wrote."

"You wrote a book?"

"*Noooo.* A book has a shiny cover and a life outside of my kitchen drawer. This . . . is a manuscript, a story with no future." With that, she set the stack of pages back inside the dark drawer and slid it silently shut, an act that shook free Cupid's memory of Mia tucking her boys into bed, minus the kiss on the forehead. "My *actual* books are in the mother-in-law suite, overflowing the bookcases. I probably have enough to fill another six shelves this size."

Cupid jotted down the information. "Got it. Okay, this has been really helpful. I'd like to leave the model with you so you can think about the space some more."

"Sure, uh, would you mind very much setting this up for me in the nurs—the room?"

"That's a great idea. You'll get a much better feel for the scale that way."

The more time they spent in the nursery-sanctuary, the better, as far as Cupid was concerned. Ruthie seemed less hesitant this time as she led him down the hallway. He still couldn't help feeling like an intruder. "Where would you like me to put this?"

"Hmm." Ruthie surveyed the room, her gaze pausing longest on the changing table. "I think maybe the floor would be best."

"Sure." Cupid knelt down, using his body as a shield from Pookie as she jumped and sniffed at the delicate walls.

Ruthie swept the dog into her arms. "Don't worry. I'll keep her out of here."

Cupid gave Pookie a playful scratch behind her ears so she'd know there were no hard feelings. "In the meantime, if you're committed to moving forward, we can start thinking about next steps."

"Next steps?" The anxious look Ruthie shot him made Cupid feel like an even bigger jerk, but someone had to get her unstuck.

"Have you thought about what you want to do with the furniture?"

"Not really."

And now they were in extremely uncomfortable territory. "Are you fairly certain you won't be needing it in the future?"

Her hollow laugh sent a shiver down Cupid's spine. "Despite the pregnancy weight I'm still carrying from baby number three, I can assure you, my body is quite out of service." *Gods be damned.* Ruthie would have made the most wonderful mother. "And the adoption window closed a long time ago. By the time I was ready to accept defeat, Zach and I decided we'd waited too long to start considering other options." Pookie seemed to sense her need for affection, choosing that moment to wriggle higher and flick her little tongue all over Ruthie's cheek.

No use rubbing salt in her wound. "If you're sure, then . . ." Cupid waited for her nod before continuing. "I can take care of removing the furniture. You remember my friend Pan, from the club? He has a truck and a connection to some teen moms who could put this furniture to good use. It would be—"

"—a mitzvah." Ruthie finished his thought with a smile.

Cupid didn't recognize the word, but he was pleased his appeal to Ruthie's kind heart had clinched the deal. He'd have to remember that next time she needed convincing.

"Okay if we come by tomorrow with the truck?"

"Tomorrow is perfect. That'll give me the weekend with the empty room."

"I hope you have something else to look forward to," Cupid answered, slightly anxious about the idea of Ruthie spending three whole days in that empty room.

"We're going out for our anniversary on Saturday, so there's that."

"That'll be nice."

She shrugged. "I hear you'll be busy, too."

"I will?"

"Aren't you taking Gail out again?"

"Oh. Right." He'd quite forgotten the plans they'd made before all this construction education began. "Yes."

"Well, it sounds like you're in for a good time, too."

Ruthie's false cheer fell flat, and Cupid couldn't decide which part seemed more forced—the part about him having a good time with Gail or the "too" she'd tacked on at the last second. Either way, it seemed best to pretend not to notice.

16

HAPPY ANNIVERSARY

Zach's troubles began with the doorbell gong, sending Pookie into a yippy tailspin he kiboshed with a stern, "Quiet!"

Ruthie shot Zach a sly glance as she dabbed away the bacon crumbs at the corner of her mouth. Was it his imagination, or was she hiding the beginnings of a smile behind that napkin? She stood, cinching the thick terry cloth robe around her waist.

"Zach? What did you do?"

"Nothing," he answered honestly. Here, he'd been so damn pleased with himself all morning. He'd abided by their long-standing rules: no gifts, flowers, or—God forbid—chocolates. Just the painstakingly selected, cheesy drugstore card he'd set at her place at the kitchen table, a cursive "R" scrawled with a loving hand on the cheery yellow envelope.

Morbid curiosity drew Zach to the front door a few steps behind Ruthie. Who was going to make him look like a schmuck this time? Both sets of parents leaned more toward practical than romantic—where else would Ruthie and Zach both have inherited the tendency?—but his sisters had been known to express themselves florally on occasion.

Well, whoever it was had gone overboard this time. *Two* dozen red roses? *Jesus.* Ruthie could barely manage the vase while hip checking the door closed. "Oh, Zach, you really shouldn't have."

He wanted to take her dismissal at face value, but the flush in her cheeks made Zach wonder if perhaps he really *should* have—not that it mattered now. "I really didn't."

She studied his serious expression for the several seconds it took to be convinced. "No?"

Zach shook his head. He considered reminding his dear wife how she'd bitten his head off the last time he'd broken their pact and spent two hours of his day picking out the exact right tennis bracelet (the tasteful midpoint between scrawny and ostentatious) and how quickly said bracelet had found its way back to Robinsons'. But no good would come of that. After twenty-three years, a husband knows when to keep his mouth shut.

"Huh." The hint of a smile persisted as Ruthie passed the arrangement to Zach and plucked the miniature envelope from its plastic pitchfork. All traces of joy evaporated as she read the card aloud: "Twenty-three roses, one per year of wedded bliss. Thank you for sharing Zachary with us. Happy Anniversary. *Fondly*"—Ruthie fluttered her eyelids at Zach before delivering the final blow with a frightening snigger—"Joan."

Uh-oh.

With surgical precision, Ruthie returned the card to its envelope and tucked the package between the prongs as if undoing the whole unsavory event. She pivoted on her slippers and marched toward the kitchen.

"Wait, where do you want me to put these?"

Her pace barely slowed. "Wherever you'll enjoy them, dear. I'm pretty sure they were meant for you."

Zach could have debated the point; after all, the card was clearly directed at Ruthie, a barb about as subtle as the thorns pricking through his T-shirt. Zach was no fool. He sensed the growing animosity between the two women though both sides of their rivalry struck him as silly.

Joan operated as if she believed that only the pesky wife stood in the way of her complete possession of Zach's leisure time, his passions, and all those wrong places on his body where he felt her eyes lingering too long—places Ruthie barely lingered anymore. But what frustrated Zach even more was Ruthie letting Joan make her feel like the third wheel in her own marriage. Ruthie still made Zach weak in the knees—how corny was that, after all this time?—but what good was his attraction if Ruthie didn't believe him? Instead, she avoided the whole issue and burrowed ever deeper into the online world of her own making.

Bit by bit, Zach had stopped sharing details with both women. It was easier for everyone that way. Ruthie didn't have to pretend to be enthralled by the minutiae of running a nonprofit, Joan didn't have to acknowledge that Zach was still very much in love with his wife, and Zach didn't have to referee. His lifeboat rocked gently this way and that, but as long as the water didn't rise too high on either side, Zach could weather the turbulence until life settled down again.

With a sigh, he retreated to his study and plunked the vase down next to his monitor, where the Trojan horse would not cause further damage. Ruthie rarely breached the man-cave other than by intercom.

The faint clatter of kitchen cleanup filtered down the hallway. Zach had planned to do the dishes today, but housework was Ruthie's therapy. The more troubling the issue, the bigger the muscle groups engaged. Six months earlier, during a serious argument, Ruthie had torn through her closet, thrown every single piece of clothing onto their bed, and reorganized her entire wardrobe. Zach dropped off four fully stuffed garbage bags at Goodwill the next day. Right now, he guessed, Ruthie was more annoyed at herself than anyone else for letting Joan get to her. She'd be fine once she finished off the breakfast dishes.

Zach poked his nose out of the gopher hole and crept toward the kitchen. Ruthie's fingers clacked away at her keyboard, Pookie snoozing at her feet. On the kitchen table behind her sat Zach's half-eaten pancakes, the only evidence of their breakfast in an otherwise spotless kitchen. A spiteful woman might have left the plate as a "Fuck you! Do your own damn dishes," but that wasn't Ruthie's way.

He passed quietly behind her chair, respectful of the invisible boundary of her not-so-private office. Ruthie's fingers paused over the keys. "Hi," she said without turning.

Zach stopped, gave her shoulder a squeeze, and echoed a gentle "Hi." The moment held long enough for the silent acknowledgment to pass between them that neither was going to let Joan ruin their day. The steel band around Zach's heart loosened.

The rest of the morning passed very much like any typical Saturday, a study in parallel play: Ruthie typed away in the kitchen while Zach worked his way through the DVR queue—hours of testosterone-loaded, made-for-cable shows Ruthie wanted no part of. Zach handled lunch, a panini assembly line that would have impressed Henry Ford. Ruthie awarded his effort by watching an episode of *Strike Back* with him before returning to her writing.

Ruthie showered first so she'd have time to blow-dry her hair. Getting dressed had become an increasingly complex (more so for Ruthie) choreography of obligatory checkpoints in the separate silos of their shared dressing room. Punctuality was Zach's deal, whereas Ruthie would usually gallop downstairs a few minutes late, just enough to cast a shadow on Zach's mood but not enough to mention without making himself out to be a jerk. So, when Ruthie appeared at the garage door with four minutes to spare, Zach gave her a grateful smile.

"You're early."

"I believe that's what you asked for last year as your anniversary gift."

Zach nodded and held his tongue. Listing her numerous transgressions in the past twelve months wouldn't win him any points. "I'd like to officially renew my subscription."

"Sure, if you'll renew mine."

"Perfect." Zach beat her to the passenger door and opened it for her. Was it sad his wife had to ask for this morsel of chivalry as her gift?

"Thank you, dear." Ruthie's kittenish smirk awakened his inner Neanderthal man. *Big, strong caveman open door for woman.* If Zach was sometimes bewildered by how little it took to upset their delicate peace, he was all the more amazed by how little it took to set things right again.

He started up the car, grabbed the gearshift, and glanced over at his bride. She'd chosen his favorite cream-colored top and the suede boots she wore when she was feeling good about herself.

"You look beautiful."

"You don't look so bad yourself."

Zach chuckled. Jeans and a button-down. *Woohoo.* At least Ruthie hadn't deflected his compliment. Their ride to dinner was quiet but not uncomfortably so. They'd moved beyond the need to fill every moment with conversation at least eighteen years ago. Besides, their date stretched out luxuriously ahead of them, two hours alone together at a restaurant with happy history, lubricated by alcohol and absent of technology. Zach was starting to like his chances.

The hostess at Ambrosia, a young woman who must have been a toddler on Zach and Ruthie's wedding day, led them to their table. "Happy anniversary, Mr. and Mrs. Miller. Enjoy your dinner."

Ruthie shook her head as she fluffed out her linen napkin, but her smile didn't fade. "Oh, Zach. Now they're going to sing."

"God, I hope not."

A tall, good-looking kid with a cocky glint in his eye came by to introduce himself and take their drink order. Ruthie could barely look at the boy as she ordered her cosmo, and Zach had a good idea why.

With the waiter out of earshot, Zach leaned forward. "Actor wannabe, Brandon Cullinane the third, scrapes together a living waiting tables until one fateful night when a ravishing casting agent sits down in his section."

Ruthie huffed. "Ravishing, huh? I think you have a best seller there. You should totally write that."

"I'm not really feeling the man bun. It reminds me of those hairnets the cafeteria ladies used to wear in high school."

"Way to kill the fantasy."

He continued to tease her, drawing out the awful plot until neither of them could take any more. This was good. They were having actual fun.

He caught the approaching waiter out of the corner of his eye. "Don't look now, but here comes your fantasy."

Zach continued to waggle his eyebrows at Ruthie while Brandon delivered the cosmo with a theatrical pour into her chilled martini glass. Maybe Zach hadn't been so far off with the actor bit after all. Zach's boilermaker was placed in front of him with a cheerful, "Happy anniversary," that sent a pleasant buzz through his body.

It struck him suddenly that their anniversaries were always something Zach had taken for granted. Sure, the pageantry of the actual wedding day made sense: the chuppah topped with Ruthie's zayde's bar mitzvah tallis, the breaking of the glass, the semi-choreographed chaos of the hora, the seven circles his bride had walked around him. Zach fully supported celebrating the milestone of marriage in front of God and witnesses in the time-honored traditions of their ancestors, but did they deserve a medal for maintaining the status quo every year? Before this moment, Zach had never considered *staying* married to be an accomplishment—or a challenge. The realization scared the shit out of him.

Now who's being dramatic, hmm?

Zach shook off the melancholy and lifted his drink to offer his traditional anniversary toast. "To my beautiful wife, the best partner I ever picked."

Their story was relationship lore, told and retold so many times her version had fused with his, and now neither could remember anything different. September 9, 1989, Freshman Econ, day one. Professor Windbag-with-his-name-on-the-textbook ended his lecture with the most useful wisdom imparted that entire semester or, for that matter, Zach's entire life: pair up with a study buddy. Zach scanned the room for the prettiest girl in the packed hall. He made a beeline for Ruthie, "cutting off at least five other guys with the same idea." (Here, Ruthie would always roll her eyes, but Zach knew it was true.) That Ruthie turned out to be a great student was icing on his happy cake. By midterms, they were hot and heavy. At Christmas break, she went home without her virginity.

Ruthie's eyes glistened as she tipped her martini glass to her lips. *Shit.* Those weren't moved-to-happy-tears. "Partner" had become a loaded term, and now he'd gone and plopped Joan in the middle of their table. A swift change of subject was in order.

Zach reached across the table for Ruthie's hand and threaded his fingers with hers. "So, what's going on in your world?"

Ruthie blinked at him, swallowed a hefty swig of cosmo, and set down her drink. She rolled the delicate stem between her fingers. "Well," she began, piquing his curiosity with a ghost of a smile, "I've started a new project."

"Oh yeah?" These days, Zach had no idea whether she was about to tell him about some new story she'd started writing or the latest rabbit hole she'd slipped down or some fundraising effort to lift up one of her internet friends. Zach certainly wasn't expecting the answer she gave.

"Or rather, it's an old project, but I'm really going to do it this time."

The study. Zach knew better than to exhibit eagerness. The cycle was all too familiar—enthusiasm, a creative burst, determination, hope—but when it came time to pull the trigger, Ruthie's crippling guilt inevitably led to a change of heart, followed sharply by paralyzing regret. Pregnancy, loss, and grief, over and over again. What was Zach supposed to say?

"Huh."

Undeterred, she pressed on. "No, really. The whole room is designed. All that's left is choosing the paint color."

"Wow, Ruthie. That's great." At the risk of ruining their evening, he probed to see how committed she was this time. "Sounds like you're ready to put out feelers for estimates."

"Actually," she paused, licked her lips, and glanced up to meet his gaze, "I've already hired someone."

Zach bolted upright in his chair, snapping his hand away from Ruthie's. "You *what*? When did all this happen?"

"We made it more or less official on Wednesday." Wow, she was serious.

"You're not using George again . . . I thought you had some reservations about his workmanship."

Ruthie was looking awfully sheepish all of a sudden. "Um, no, not exactly."

"So, exactly who *did* you hire?" Zach's confidence in Ruthie's choice faded as quickly as her smile. "I assume you've checked references?"

"What's with the twenty questions? You've been after me to do this for months. I finally take some action, and you criticize every decision."

How the hell had this become a fight? "I am not criticizing. Just asking a few questions, same as I would for any project I was managing at work."

Something terrible flashed behind Ruthie's eyes. Zach had just fallen overboard into shit creek.

"This isn't *work*," she said through clenched teeth, "and I am not asking you to manage the project, *dear*."

He held up his hands in surrender. "Sorry, I didn't mean it that way." They both let out a deep breath, sipped at their drinks, and eyed each other like two boxers waiting for the other to throw a punch. The waiter approached; Zach waved him off.

He needed to turn this around right now and switch Ruthie out of defensive mode. Zach dug deep for the most unthreatening tone he could manage. "Ruthie, is there some reason you're not telling me where you found this guy?"

Ruthie met his gaze, then looked away. *What the hell?* "I met him the other night at Versailles, if you want to know the truth."

"So, he's gay?" Did she really think that would matter to Zach?

"Not according to Gail." A hollow laugh left her. "They're seeing each other."

"Wonderful. A random stranger Gail picked up at a gay bar is going to be working in my house?"

"Not exactly. I fixed them up."

This was all spinning out of reach. "How?"

"He asked me for my number, and I gave him Gail's."

Neanderthal man reared his big, fat head again. *Easy, now.*

Zach folded his hands and slid them forward along the white cloth. "A strange man at a club hit on you?"

"Is that so shocking?" Oh, she was pissed now.

"It's not shocking that someone would be interested in you, but did he not see your wedding ring?"

Ruthie glanced down at the 3.15-carat diamond Zach had placed on her finger. On bent knee. With sweaty palms and his heart straining against his chest and the sweetest rush of elation when she'd said yes.

"He definitely saw my ring."

"And asked for your number anyway."

"Yes, but I didn't give it to him."

"No, instead, you invited him to be alone with you in our home for hours at a time, a man who's already blatantly disregarded your marital status once."

"He's apologized, and we're past all that."

Zach wasn't past any of it. "We must know a dozen other contractors already vetted by people we trust. Any one of them would be more appropriate than this, this—" Ruthie raised her chin ever so slightly, preparing to absorb the blow. Whoever this guy was, Ruthie seemed to feel he was worth defending. "This wild card," Zach finished calmly.

"Yes, I'm sure you're right, but Quentin really needs the work, and he's already built a scale model of the whole project, with moving parts and tiny little details that must have taken him hours to put together."

Quentin? "You already have a contractor *and* a model, and you didn't think to say boo to me until now?" And what if Zach hadn't asked? How long would Ruthie have kept this secret?

She slouched in her chair like a discarded jacket. "This all happened so quickly. I didn't want to say anything until I knew I was ready to follow through. I was afraid your doubts might cripple me if I wasn't one hundred percent sure."

Hello, irony.

What Ruthie couldn't know—because Zach had not shared *his* plans for the exact reason she'd just articulated—was how close he was to bringing their days in Tarra, Indiana to an end. Ruthie's timing for executing the home improvement project could not have been worse, but Zach couldn't bear to burst her bubble now. So much for sharing his news about the Glover grant tonight.

"I'm happy for you, Ruthie." Zach lifted his half-emptied glass. "To your sanctuary."

She accepted his peace offering with a soft clink. "Thank you."

"So, when do I get to meet this Quentin?"

17

ECHO BEAT

The right turn onto Third Street provoked a nasty tug inside Cupid's chest. *Cursed gods, not now!* Ignoring his heart pull would cost him dearly, but not meeting Gail at the restaurant she'd picked—"blowing her off," as Pan would say—would make Cupid the kind of unreliable asshole he'd been cleaning up after since he fell. Of the two unappetizing options, Cupid chose to bear the heartache himself.

Staying the course to the restaurant brought first a burn, then a throbbing choke-release, choke-release, then a relentless, mighty squeeze. Beads of sweat rolled down the edges of Cupid's cheeks. Pain tossed his body left and right against the driver's seat like a hydra batting a sheep from one head to another. The gods did not like being ignored.

The seat belt bit into Cupid's shoulder as he thrashed about, but freeing himself from the restraint offered little relief and triggered an irritating warning bell that took turns with Cupid's anguished moans echoing against the walls of the Prius. He wondered if his chest would explode like the eggs he'd blown up in the microwave; he pictured Pan scraping off bits of his innards after they'd splattered all over the car's interior.

After a harrowing twenty minutes with the singular goal of reaching Gail in one piece, Cupid and his wrecked heart arrived at Saffron. The pulsating agony continued even after he exited the car on shaky legs. He mopped his face with the hem of his shirt, but sweat was pouring off him in buckets.

"Hey, you made it." Gail's delight quickly turned to worry. "Holy shit, are you okay?" She rushed over to the entrance and grasped Cupid's arms.

"I'm sorry about this, Gail, but I—*gah!*" A sharp, stabbing pain stole Cupid's breath away. "Can we step outside?"

"Are you having a heart attack? Should I call 911?"

"No, no, I'll be okay." He let out a cautious breath. "Would you mind terribly if we don't eat dinner here tonight?"

"Of course not. Why didn't you just tell me you don't like Indian food?"

"Oh. Yeah, I think—*ouch*—the spices . . ." Gods, he was a terrible liar.

"Jeez, let's go somewhere else. Did you have another place in mind?"

If only he knew. "Can I surprise you?"

Gail's face lit up. "Sure. Are you okay to drive?"

"Yes," he answered, pleasantly surprised to find it was true. He was quite okay the moment he'd decided to follow his heart signal. "Why don't you follow me in your car?" Whatever Cupid needed to handle tonight, he wasn't sure he'd be able to manage Gail too.

Cupid's heart led them both, in separate cars, back to the fateful Third Street crossing where he'd earlier ignored the pull of his heart. This time, he followed the course set by the gods. The occasional twinge tugged at him when the streets didn't quite align with his destiny, but this pain Cupid could bear. In fact, he found a surprising comfort in the external guidance once he got past the idea of being bridled like one of Helios's stallions. Cupid's fate eluded him, but at least he knew which way to turn.

He checked his rearview for Gail every few blocks. Right on his tail, bless her heart. He'd have to remember to tell her she looked pretty when they got wherever they were going.

The zigzag route took Cupid—and, consequently, Gail—to a part of town Cupid had not yet seen. They were definitely not headed toward Ruthie's house, but Cupid fully expected to find her at the end of the journey. He drove under a string of lights stretched across the road, illuminating a grayed wood sign that read Welcome to the Boardwalk. The blacktop street ended with a row of barriers directing cars toward a parking lot. Beyond the barriers, tightly set wooden planks laid on the diagonal invited foot traffic, and there was plenty of it. Carnival games lined the left-hand side of the street; on the other, a series of walk-up food stands boasted gyros and french fries, taffy and ice cream. Whatever this place was, Cupid's heart-motor had reached its destination.

Remembering his date as they both emerged from their cars, Cupid turned just as Gail slammed her car door with a force that surprised him. "We're eating at Pier Ten? Really?"

Cupid didn't have to strain to see the bold neon sign rising from the roof of the sprawling restaurant sitting at the end of the street like Poseidon on his throne, a far cry from the cozy Indian restaurant Gail had chosen for their date. Also, strangely named, Cupid thought, with no water in sight.

"I'm sorry, Gail. I know this wasn't your first choice, but it seems like the kind of place with a big selection."

Her eyes narrowed. Despite Cupid's noblest efforts, he'd

angered her. "Come on, Quentin. You mean to tell me you didn't know the Millers were coming here tonight?"

Aha! His heart had driven him to Ruthie after all. "No, I didn't. I would never have brought you here if I'd known it would upset you so." That was the truth, though how would Cupid have explained showing up here by himself? "Also, you look really pretty tonight. Sorry I didn't mention it earlier."

Gail studied Cupid's face, no doubt seeing only earnestness where experience had led her to expect lies. The hard lines of her irritation softened, and Cupid took advantage of his opportunity.

Grasping her hand, he said, "Gail, I promise I didn't know they were coming here, but what difference does it make? *You're* my date. We're here, and I'm starved. Can we go inside, please?"

Once through the door, Cupid's compulsion returned with a vengeance. Ruthie was nearby.

While Cupid was busy sorting out his signals, Gail slipped in front of him to plead for a table. "I know you're packed, and we don't have a reservation. Whatever you can do . . ."

Little did Gail know, the hostess's pulse had quickened with one look at Cupid. A table miraculously became available.

Heads turned as they walked past. Cupid tried to hold Gail in focus, but there was no ignoring the sideways tug of his heart. Once he caught sight of Ruthie, all pretense fell apart. Even from the back, she was stunning. Cupid dropped out of line, a soldier following the commands of his heart.

Cupid rationed his steps with as much discipline as possible, but the sliver of exposed neck peeking out just above the collar of Ruthie's blouse unraveled him. He'd worked out a greeting during the strange odyssey here—something appropriate, or at least socially acceptable—but before his lips could form words, his fingertips met the soft skin at the back of her neck.

Ruthie batted away the hand and turned with a gasp. "*Quentin?*"

Ruthie's husband stood suddenly, the fork en route to his mouth clattering to the plate, his napkin sliding to the floor. Behind dark, rectangular frames, his eyes blinked slowly as if he were not the least bit surprised to see Cupid standing there and somehow knew every wrong feeling Cupid held for his wife. "Speak of the devil."

"I'm sorry, Ruthie. I didn't mean to startle you."

Ruthie twisted all the way around in her chair. "Gail? What are you *doing* here?"

Gail's hand closed around Cupid's arm. Her answer dripped with tension. "Happy anniversary, guys."

Ruthie's gaze settled on the fingers staking their claim on Cupid. "Really, Gail? You had to bring him *here? Tonight?*"

The two women eyed each other like cobras. "He brought *me*, actually," Gail said. "It was a surprise."

Zach chimed in with a hollow laugh. "I'll say." Stepping to Ruthie's side, Zach clasped his hand onto her shoulder, subtle but effective. Hadn't Hephaestus pulled the same possessive move on Aphrodite countless times? "Ruthie was just telling me about you."

"She was?" Cupid's gaze shifted to Ruthie's. The color returned to her cheeks, casting a warm glow from her forehead to the deep valley of her cleavage.

Zach's head tipped ever so slightly toward his wife. "Yes. You're going to be doing some work in our home?"

"Oh," Cupid said. "Yes, I'm very excited." Zach's eyebrows arched. Ruthie's hand flew to her throat. Gail tightened her grip around Cupid's arm. "Should be an interesting project, I mean."

"Seems so," Zach answered, squeezing his wife's shoulder once more before extending his hand to Cupid. "Zach Miller. Pleased to meet you, Quentin."

Cupid slipped out of Gail's grasp to lean into the handshake. "Please, call me 'Q.'"

"Q," Zach repeated with a grin. "Well, you two have a lovely evening, and send my regards to double-oh-seven." Cupid had no idea who double-oh-seven was, but Zach's dismissal left no room for misinterpretation.

"You, too," Gail sing-songed, shooting Ruthie a smirk.

They were supposed to leave for their own table now, but Cupid couldn't quite tear his gaze away from the sorrow behind Ruthie's eyes. He hated to think their unwelcome interruption had ruined her evening, but wouldn't that be better than the alternative—that Ruthie was already miserable at her own anniversary celebration?

The story of Ruthie and Zach's evening stretched across their table in the steady glow of the mechanical candle. Ruthie's wine glass stood nearly full while her husband's held a mere sliver of dark liquid at the bottom. A single dessert plate sat abandoned at the center of the table, Ruthie's side of the cake untouched. Two people going through the motions that might have worked in the past but seemed to be failing them now.

Cupid's heart sank for Ruthie. No, that wasn't sinking; it was *beating*. And—*did his godly powers deceive him?*—a beat back from Ruthie that met his ears with a resounding *thump-thump-thump*. Ruthie was beating for him! He knew it!

It all made sense now. This was why Cupid's heart had dragged him here tonight. The gods had righted their error. Ruthie was meant to be with Cupid after all. Oh, how happy he would make her!

Cupid closed his eyes to concentrate on their delicious duet. His frenzied *ba-boom, ba-boom* chased after her steady *thump-thump* . . .

Wait, something was wrong. Cupid's beat didn't line up with Ruthie's, and yet, there was an echo. He was sure of it . . .

The truth sucked the air out of Cupid's lungs. He forced his eyes open.

Backlit by the unwavering votive, Ruthie and her Right Love stared back at Cupid.

18

ABOUT MARRIAGE

"This is good," Pan said. "Now you know for sure."

"Wonderful. Watch out for the doorframe!" Sometimes, Cupid doubted whether Pan knew where his body ended and the world began.

"I got it. Keep your panties on."

"You should have let *me* walk backward," Cupid said. "It took me three hours to get the stain finish just right."

Pan kept quiet until the entertainment center was safely lowered into its new space. "You did a great job on this, Q. First table I built, you'd set your beer down on one end, next thing you know, it's sliding off the other side." Pan acted this out with great theatrical flair for Cupid's benefit.

"Your cheering-up routine's not working, but thanks for trying."

Pan's smile drooped. "You knew Ruth wasn't beating for you. Why do you torture yourself?" He slapped his arm around Cupid's shoulders and jostled him as if he could shake Ruthie right out of his system.

"It just doesn't seem possible the two of them are meant to be. They didn't even look like they wanted to share a meal, let alone a life."

"Ah, well, that's marriage, isn't it? How many years did you say they've been together now?"

"Twenty-three."

"Damn, I will never understand monogamy. You want to help me with this cable box?"

Cupid followed Pan's lead, half watching the complicated unscrewing of wires in case he ever needed to manage this himself. "Have you never had a mate you'd want to keep for eternity?"

Pan's huff floated up from the lower shelf. "I guess there were a few I wouldn't have minded as long as I could have banged whoever else I wanted, too."

"Good thing you never married a mortal, then."

"You can say that again."

"What if Echo would've had you? Or Syrinx?"

"Thanks for bringing up those shit shows. I'm not saying this excuses my behavior, but I was half goat back then. And Mount O is not Earth."

"No, but spurned love is spurned love. I'm beginning to appreciate how one might be moved to violence."

Pan popped his head up from behind the electronics. "Do I need to worry about you?"

"Of course not."

The expression of alarm faded from Pan's face, but he kept one eye on Cupid as he set back to work. "Good, because I've got a situation brewing with Euphrosyne, and I can only put out so many fires at once."

"That's fine. I've been thinking I probably need some kind of outside help with this one, anyway."

Pan shot up again, bumping his head on the wall. "Ow.

Fuck!" He scrubbed his knuckles over his scalp. "What do you mean, 'outside help'?"

"Advice from someone who has actually been married. *Earth* married."

"Yeah, that makes sense. What about Gail? She'd know Ruthie better than anyone, right?"

"She's too close to the situation, and frankly, I'm not entirely sure of her motives."

"Beyond relieving you of your pants?" Pan beamed at his own little joke.

"Gail is complicated." While Cupid believed Gail was rooting for Ruthie's happiness, he found it unlikely that Gail would encourage Ruthie to work out her issues with a cheating husband, given her own sordid marital history.

The twinkle of mirth in Pan's eyes mellowed into something resembling admiration—or maybe a surge of pride at his own mentoring skills. "You're learning."

"I was thinking . . ." Cupid took a sudden, keen interest in a loose cable lying near his foot. "I might ask Mia's advice."

Pan stopped working again and shifted his full focus onto Cupid. So much for slipping the idea past Pan's notice. "Mia," Pan repeated.

"She was married."

"Very badly."

"Maybe it takes a person who's been in a bad marriage to recognize how to fix one." At least, this reasoning had convinced Cupid—mostly.

Pan's bushy red eyebrows drew together. "So, this is all about your mission, and not about trying to rekindle something with Mia."

"Absolutely."

"You do realize this has 'fucking terrible idea' written all over it?"

"I can handle it, Pan."

"Dammit, Q, I can't watch you get fucked up over Mia again. You barely survived it the first time."

"Yes, I remember." Cupid's confidence, shaky at best, faltered at Pan's doubts. "I do miss Mia and the boys *so* much, but it doesn't ache like before."

"You also haven't been anywhere near Mia since the day she clicked with her lieutenant."

"True, but look what a mess I was afterward, and I was nowhere near her then. It isn't about physical distance. Once my signal locked onto Ruthie, my heartbreak over Mia faded into the background."

"The gods can be somewhat merciful." Pan stopped there, and Cupid wasn't inclined to probe. "If you honestly believe talking with Mia might help, at least do it over the phone."

"Yeah, that's probably a good idea."

Pan jutted his chin toward Cupid's room. "Go on. I've got this."

"You sure?"

"I have moved at least thirty times since the invention of electricity. I'm decent at wiring shit. Quit stalling."

19

MIA'S ADVICE

Cupid's great idea grew a scary set of fangs on the way to his room. He flopped onto the bed, the exact site where he'd rotted away for days, paralyzed with heartache over losing Mia. But he did not have the luxury of time to wallow now when there was a clear and urgent job to do. Ruthie and Zach's marriage was teetering at the peak of a steep slope, and Cupid needed to steady the boulder before it rolled down the hill and met Sisyphus at the bottom.

Find your center.

Cupid sat up straight, folded his legs, closed his eyes, and inhaled. Pressing his index fingers to the cartilage in his ears, he hummed out the high pitch of the "bee breath" Mia had taught him. After three minutes of the Bhramari, he felt relaxed enough to pick up the phone and dial her number.

"Q! How are you?" Even after everything, her sunny voice sent a pulse of longing through his system.

"How are *you*? What's new with the boys? How's everything going with Patrick?"

Her laughter floated into his ear. "Whoa. Slow down. *Breathe*."

His body complied automatically with Mia's instructions, drawing in a long, deep breath and releasing it purposefully. "It's nice to hear your voice, Mia."

"Yours, too. We're doing great here. I can't explain it, but being with Patrick just feels easy, like we'd been holding a place for him in our lives. He's here now, sitting on the floor with Joe and Eli, surrounded by trucks and blocks."

"Do you need to go? Sorry, I should've asked if you were busy—"

"It's fine, Q. I'm happy to talk to you. Patrick can handle the boys for a little while."

The image of Patrick and the boys pushing toy trucks through a maze of blocks sent a sharp pang of longing through Cupid. It wasn't so long ago that Cupid was the one building a pillow fort with Jonah and Eli and tossing baby Luke into the air. He could still hear their throaty giggles.

"How are they, Mia?"

"They miss you, especially Jonah. He asks about you all the time."

"Please tell him I miss him, too . . . or whatever you think is best."

"Of course I'll tell him," she said. "What have you been up to, more matchmaking adventures?"

"Actually, yes."

"Oh boy," Mia said with a chuckle. "And how's that going?"

"It's"—*excruciating*—"challenging. Actually, I hoped you might be able to give me some advice."

"Me? I thought you were the expert."

"My area of expertise is love, not marriage."

"Marriage? Oh no. You're not trying to do marriage counseling now?"

"For the moment, it seems."

"Pfft, good luck with that."

"I suspected you might say something like that."

"Considering my marriage went down in a fiery blaze, I wouldn't exactly say I'm the best one to give advice."

"I actually need to understand a marriage that's failing. I want to know how two people who've drifted apart might manage to find their way back together."

"Aw, Q." Cupid recognized the pity in Mia's tone. Pan always softened just like that when he was about to shatter Cupid's hope. *Poor you, having to learn the world doesn't work that way.* "Look, you have to admit that sometimes—*many* times—it's best if the two don't find their way back together."

The weight of Mia's bleak observation would have crushed Cupid if he didn't know how happy Mia was now with Patrick, how happy Zach and Ruthie would be again if Cupid could get them past their Liminal Point.

"But these two are meant for each other," he said.

"The heartbeats again?"

"Yes. They are definitely each other's Right Love." The truth stuck like burrs to his tongue.

"Huh. I have to admit, I used to think you were a bit of a nutjob when you started with all that echo beat mumbo jumbo."

Cupid smiled despite her dig. "Thanks."

"Anyway, you sure made me a believer."

"I appreciate that, Mia. There aren't many mort—*people* who are willing to trust in something beyond their understanding."

"I guess love has a way of making its point."

"Until it doesn't," Cupid mused aloud.

"Right. From my brief but agonizing experience with couples therapy, I can tell you most problems come down to sex or money."

"Can't be money. They have tons."

Mia huffed. "That doesn't mean they don't fight about it. Money is power. Sex can be, too, by the way. Once the balance of the relationship is knocked off-kilter, anything can be used as a weapon to gain the upper hand."

"You make it all sound so violent."

Mia laughed. "Haven't you heard the expression, 'All's fair in love and war'?"

"Sure. I just find it disturbing that two people in love can inflict such wounds on each other."

"Nobody can hurt you as badly as the ones you love."

As if Cupid needed reminding, a blunt stab pushed at his chest. Perhaps he should have heeded Pan's warning. "I guess that's true."

"Oh, Q, I'm sorry." There it was again, the pity.

"Don't be, Mia. None of that was your fault." Nor did poking at old battle scars solve Cupid's dilemma. "Let's say the problem isn't money . . ."

"Sex?"

The last thing he wanted to think about was Ruthie having sex with her husband. Cupid hadn't smelled it on her yet, but all that proved was that Ruthie practiced good hygiene. "It's probably safe to say they're not having sex, but from what I can see, neither seems to want to hurt the other."

"That part usually comes later. Obviously, I don't know these people, but intimacy is usually the first to go. Don't get me wrong—two people can have sex without being intimate. It's just not a very good way to keep a marriage alive."

Intimacy. The word rolled around in Cupid's brain. "I'm not sure I understand."

"That special bond that makes the two of you feel like one. Your shared history, the physical attraction you feel, the ways you crawl inside each other's minds and feel at home. That's intimacy, but it's fragile. There are a million ways to weaken the invisible threads that connect two people: stop communicating, violate a trust, take each other for granted, give up on the relationship."

"Yes. This matches up with what I've seen. More of a slipping away than an intentional destruction."

"But no less poisonous," Mia said. "If you don't nurture that sense of closeness, it will die. The outside world intrudes on all of us, no matter how hard we try to control everything. Jobs are lost. People get sick."

"You lose three babies before they're born." Cupid hadn't realized he'd said the words out loud until Mia responded.

"Oh wow. That's hideous."

"Yeah."

"When you stop seeing your own light in your spouse's eyes, it's an uphill battle to try to get that back, and there's almost nothing the other person can do to fix it. How many times can you prop up your husband when your energy is sapped from constant rejection? Then he decides his wife can't possibly love him anymore because he got fired, and he's a big ol' loser, so he finds another woman who makes him feel like the man he used to be. And then, his wife really *is* too good for him because now, he's a lying, cheating sack of shit."

"We're not being hypothetical anymore, are we?" Funny how that same thing had happened when he'd asked Gail about marriage. Was it possible for anyone to be objective on the subject?

Mia chuckled. "Sorry."

"*I'm* sorry, Mia. I didn't mean to dredge up old pain."

"It's fine. Thanks to you, I've put the past firmly behind me."

"Mind if I ask you something personal?"

This time, Mia's laughter was genuinely cheerful. "I believe that ship has already circled the globe."

"When you found out your husband was cheating on you, did you ever consider being with another man?"

"Whoa. Promise me you're not going there, Q. No matter what's happened, you cannot be that guy."

"What if he cheated first?"

"Is she telling you that? Do you have proof?"

"No, she's not saying anything." *It's her friend, the one I'm having sex with, who told me.* "Ruthie doesn't have any idea I'm trying to fix her marriage."

"Oh boy. Are you doing this whole matchmaker routine again because you're stuck on her? Is this some kind of thing with you?"

"It seems to be, for now anyway."

"Has she fallen for you as well?"

Had she? Did it even matter?

"I don't know. She keeps her feelings tucked away. All I know is she beats for her husband, not me."

"Let me go out on a limb and say this woman at least lusts for you. You're going to have to be the one to take the moral high ground here."

"I understand two wrongs don't make a right . . ."

"Here comes a 'but.'"

"What if Ruthie's husband can't make her see that light right now, but I can? I believe he's grown weary of trying to convince his own wife he's still attracted to her. I'm an objective stranger. Wouldn't it help if she knew I'm a complete mess over her?"

"Sounds dangerous. You're not the easiest man to resist. If you were to show interest in her, it's not a fair fight, especially if she suspects her husband of cheating. You start out with a little flirting, a harmless kiss on the cheek, and next thing you know, the two of you are doing the Flying Warrior. She has to live with her conscience. And what if the husband finds out? He might never forgive her even if she can forgive herself. You do not want to be the home-wrecker."

Basically, what Pan had told him from the start—sleeping with Ruthie was a big, fat no-no. So, where did that leave the God of Love?

"There must be something I can do," he said sadly.

"If it's not too late, maybe you could help her, as a *friend*, remember why she fell in love with her husband and why he fell in love with her. If she feels good about herself, she won't be defensive when he tries to lay a compliment on her. Meanwhile, don't let the husband start exploring other options."

"What if he already has?"

"Then they better start working on forgiveness."

In the silence that followed, the weight of Cupid's burden bore down upon him. Nothing less than Ruthie's happiness was at stake.

"You can do this, Q. You're a good man."

"Thank you, Mia."

"Did I tell you Patrick is taking all of us to dinner at his parents' next weekend?"

A disturbing image popped into Cupid's head, bringing Mia and her boys to Mount Olympus to meet the folks. Just your average family, the Goddess of Love and the God of Fire sitting down for a five-course meal accompanied by lutes and lyres in the Grand Dining Hall, maybe the God of War popping his head in to stir up trouble.

"I'm sure Patrick's parents will love you all."

Mia huffed into the phone. "Well, it's all or nothing. Insta-family, here we come."

The miracle of Mia's family rumbled through Cupid's chest, dragging with it the shadow of his own brief glimpse of life inside the frame, the space he'd only been holding for Patrick.

"Hey," Mia asked gently, "are you gonna be okay?"

"Sure," he said. "I've resisted temptation before."

20

PLAYING SPY

"C'mon, girl, let's get you outside." Ruth's heels clattered into the kitchen, and Pookie trotted behind.

"I let her out already."

Ruth gasped at the sight of her husband, hunched over his iPad at the kitchen table. "What the hell, Zach? You scared the crap outta me." Unless the clock over the sink needed a new battery, it was 7:20. "What are you doing home? I thought you left an hour ago."

"And good morning to you too." Zach chuckled as he looked up from his iPad. "Wow, you look nice."

"Thanks." While Ruth wasn't one to lie around in sweatpants, she also didn't make a habit of blowing out her hair or applying lip gloss before her first cup of coffee, two things she had done this morning.

"Lunching with the ladies today?" he asked.

"No." She couldn't bear Gail's gloating or Wendy's interrogation right now. "Just the usual excitement. My car needs gas, I have to return a book to the library, and I thought I might get really wild and do the grocery shopping."

"You look awfully nice for the grocery store."

"I guess I've lowered the bar so far, a pair of nice jeans is cause for alarm."

"Not alarm . . . it's just, if I knew you looked like this in the morning, I might never leave home."

"Very funny. Why *haven't* you left yet?" Zach was clearly dressed for work, all crisp and creased and suited up for his day. "What's going on?"

"What time does your guy start?"

"My guy?" Were they seriously doing this again right now? "Quentin?"

"Yes, Quentin. *Kyewww*, wasn't it?"

Ruthie held her eyes still in their sockets though it took all her might not to roll them. "He'll be here by eight."

Zach checked his watch. "I think I'll stick around."

"Why?"

"I want to ask him a few questions."

"*Why*?" She hoped he caught the warning in her tone.

"I'm not allowed to ask a man in my employ a few questions?"

"*Your* employ? What is going on with you?"

"Look, all I know about this guy is that he materialized out of thin air, hit on you at some sex club—"

"It's a *dance* club. My God, Zach."

"And he pumps out lust like a plug-in air freshener."

Heat rose to Ruth's cheeks. Yes, she had another of her famous crushes again, and this one wasn't just some hot model half her age to ogle through a screen. This guy was real and sexy as sin and on his way over as she stood here arguing with her husband.

"I get it. You don't think I can refrain from throwing myself at him."

Zach sighed heavily, hitting her with the full measure of his long-suffering-husband-of-a-woman-with-an-overactive-fantasy-life routine. "What if he's dangerous? You'll be alone in the house with a man with power tools. Don't you think I have a right to be concerned for your safety?"

"What are you going to do, ask him if he plans to murder me?"

"Yes!"

His reply was so outrageous, it snapped the tension between them like a brittle twig. They passed a grin back and forth. If there was one thing Ruth loved about her husband, he almost always knew when he was being an ass.

She sat down next to him at the table and put her hand on his arm. "Oh, Zach. Quentin is a pussycat. If you don't believe me, ask Pookie. She loves him."

"Great," he grumbled. "I feel so much better now."

Encouraged by the grin escaping from Mr. Serious, Ruth gently cajoled him. "She happens to be an excellent judge of character."

"Actually, she's not," he said with a grimace aimed at the dog.

"Okay, true."

Zach's expression softened as it met Ruthie's. "But *you* are." A sigh left him, a leak in the pressure valve. Always a good sign. "Look, Ruthie, the guy has no experience and no references. I just don't want him to take advantage of you."

"I hired him to do a job, and he's already doing it beautifully. Not for nothing, he's also insisted that I not pay him one cent until the job is finished to my satisfaction—and yours too, if you'd like. Please don't embarrass all of us by giving him the third degree when he gets here."

Zach held her gaze, the gold flecks of his intense, hazel eyes catching the morning sun behind his glasses while he mulled over his decision. "Okay." He stood and straightened his tie. "You know where I am if you need me."

"Yep. At work." Ruth hadn't meant to sound so harsh, but that's what repression would do.

Zach's head turned sharply toward his wife. He seemed to be calculating whether to accept her invitation to fight or let it slide. They both pretty much knew where this one would go. The conversation wouldn't be productive or even interesting.

Ruth had called Zach's bluff years ago about his long hours. They had enough money, more than ten enoughs. She couldn't have cared less about the huge house in a fancy neighborhood, especially once the school system became a nonissue. All she'd ever wanted in a house, after babies had been ruled out once and for all, was this writing sanctuary. When Zach had decided to make his move into the nonprofit world, Ruth could not have been more proud and supportive. She'd never begrudged Zach his time settling into the new role as CEO or tried to make him feel guilty, despite numerous trips out of town to open new playspaces across the Midwest. It was that bitch, Joan, with her invented reasons for Zach to work late, that got under Ruth's skin.

Judging by the look on her husband's face right now, she'd done a poor job of hiding her frustration. Ruth regretted the low blow. Where was that delete button when she needed it?

Zach took the high road first, leaning in to give her a soft kiss on the cheek, which might have been a kiss on her lips if Ruth hadn't just glossed. If only she'd known he'd be waiting for her in the kitchen this morning.

"Have a good day, darling," he said. "I'll text you later about dinner?"

"Sure."

Ruth blinked after her husband as he descended the stairs to the garage.

21

FENDING OFF JOAN

The unbridled power of his M-5 never failed to bolster Zach's mood, but even the rumbling hooves of 520 horses couldn't outrun the haunting truth: all was not well at home. All marriages had their highs and lows, and Zach wasn't so naïve or arrogant to believe his was immune.

In the beginning, Zach had imagined Ruthie and himself as two ends of the same rope, their individual trajectories inevitably meeting and, in doing so, forming a circle. Both families were overjoyed—*a nice Jewish boy/girl*—and careers skipped along down two separate but perfectly compatible paths. Conflicts were rare and quickly resolved. The knot tightened.

Then came the miscarriages, three sharp blades hacking away at the fibers until the circle opened into a flimsy line with the two of them holding on to opposite ends, floating toward an unanchored, unimagined future with only each other as a tether. With compassionate guidance and time's inevitable march, Zach had buried or at least successfully compartmentalized his dreams of fatherhood: nuzzling his face into warm folds of baby pudge; tossing a son over his head and reveling in the tiny bundle's absolute faith that his father would catch him; chasing a giggling toddler up and down the beach; tucking in his daughter with homegrown fairy tales and lingering at the bedroom door, just to absorb the rhythm of her soft snores; teaching his son to tie his shoes, offering patient encouragement when the loops slipped through clumsy fingers; playing catch in the backyard, hotbox when two kids were coordinated enough to run and throw; cheering them on through dance or piano recitals or swim meets or karate competitions with his heart in his throat; hosting noisy, messy, multigenerational holiday dinners where kids were interspersed with adults, not sequestered at a folding table with separate platters of gefilte fish; straining to understand his children's lively debates about the newest technologies and medical advances; and later, *much* later, opening his and Ruthie's circle to absorb significant others and spouses and grandchildren.

Healing did not happen without effort. Zach would be the first to admit that Ruthie suffered on a whole different plane, but their intimate, shared sorrow created a momentum of its own. The brilliant fire of youthful passion mellowed into a smoldering, enduring tenderness. What conflict could possibly warrant choosing opposite sides after all they'd survived together?

Their tacit strategy not to inflict wounds over "the small stuff" filled Zach with a not-so-secret pride. He and Ruthie became *the* couple to double-date. No embarrassing squabbles in front of their friends, no babysitter to cancel on them at the last minute. Perspective was a double-edged sword, though, as Zach was only now beginning to realize. Had "letting things go" turned into taking each other for granted? How did one distinguish what was "worth the fight"? Three dinners missed for the sake of a new job? Ruthie spending more time inside her computer than with Zach on his days off? Ten days without sex? A month?

Zach roared through the streets of Tarra in his armored cocoon, a machine embarrassingly overqualified to navigate the unchallenging straightaways of his faux city. Well aware of the looks fellow motorists would give his car as he wove in and out of rush hour traffic, Zach didn't seek or relish the attention, but was he not entitled to enjoy the fruits of his labor? Inside his bubble, undistracted from his troubled thoughts even by the morning radio talk shows, Zach wondered if his revelation had come too late. Had their marital knot frayed, one sinew of negligence at a time, to the point where the raggedy ends could no longer hold together?

Zach swung the front end into his parking spot, the Reserved for CEO sign providing a much-needed dose of validation. Whatever his failings as a husband, Zach excelled at CEO-ing. The national headquarters of Brighter Tomorrows sat at the top floor—fifteen—of the tallest building in downtown Tarra. The city's architecture reflected "value" property, structures that sprawled thriftlessly over wide concrete swaths of recession-cheapened land and extended upward almost as an afterthought.

Zach's corner office afforded him an unobstructed view in two directions of the ever-unchanging landscape, a perfect place to ponder life's big questions, and today's was a whopper. He sank into his leather throne and spun toward the east. With his focus fixed on the faraway horizon Zach had always assumed would be his and Ruthie's future, he let the question in: *Am I losing my wife?*

"Rough morning?"

Zach startled at Joan's voice in his doorway. There was a lot of that going around today.

He turned away from his marital woes, stowing them in their airtight compartment, at least for the next ten hours. “All good.”

She eyed him skeptically, arms crossed over her no-nonsense suit. Regardless of the season or the lack of contact with the outside world, Joan followed the adage, *Dress for the job you want.* Zach had to admire her ambition, even if she’d chosen his back to prop up her ladder.

“I was looking for you earlier.”

“I just got in,” Zach said without a trace of apology. Then, though he immediately regretted it, Zach added, “Ruthie and I had some things to discuss this morning.”

Joan’s nose twitched as if a garbage truck had just rolled by. She tolerated Zach’s marriage in the abstract, but any reminder of the *actual* wife led to passive-aggressive backlash in the form of wildly inconvenient meetings with potential donors or crises only Zach and Joan *together* could resolve.

“Did you have any comments on the redlined doc I sent you over the weekend?” Ah yes, another of Joan’s favorite tactics to hold Zach’s attention—excruciating revisions.

“Haven’t had a chance to look at it yet.”

“We have to submit our final materials to Langston by Friday so he can send out a pre-read for the board meeting. I don’t think I need to remind you we’re only going to get one chance at the Glover Foundation—”

“No, Joan. You don’t.”

In fact, Glover had been their main thrust since Zach accepted the CEO position. He and Joan had been working toward national presence for almost two years, strengthening their brand, expanding into six states with twenty-eight new sites, a wildly ambitious vision he could never have achieved without Joan. Her demands stretched Zach beyond even his own outsized ambitions, igniting a creative spark he had never accessed before, which was—Zach would be the first to admit—addictive.

So maybe, when Joan intruded on his personal time, Zach didn't object as strenuously as he should have. It was complicated, as they say, especially when his labors bore results even Ruthie couldn't dispute. They'd wooed the crap out of Glover to chase this grant opportunity, and they were so close to finally achieving their dreams, Zach could almost hear the children's laughter in the centers of the future.

Joan plowed forward. "I've reworked the outcomes section, but you're the genius when it comes to articulating vision. I thought we could stay late tonight and push through it."

"Sorry, Joan, I can't tonight."

"What's going on with you, Zach?"

"Nothing. We're in the middle of a home renovation project."

"Smart. Increasing your property value before you put your house on the market."

"Right. So, I need to"—*make sure the contractor isn't banging my wife*—"be there for Ruthie."

Joan huffed. "No offense, but since when are you helpful with anything around the house? Please don't tell me you're attempting a do-it-yourself project."

Now, *that* was funny. "No, Ruthie's hired someone."

"So, what does she need you for?"

She'd hit the nail right on its damn head. *Ugh*, and now Zach couldn't help but picture a larger-than-life, hammer-wielding handyman, flexed muscles on full display, much to his wife's delight. *Who's making the garbage face now?*

Joan lit up with recognition. "*Ohhh.* This 'someone' happens to be hot?"

If only Zach had thought to say he'd never met the handyman, he could have easily thrown Joan off before she realized she'd struck a vein running rich with pure gold. He busied himself with the pile in his inbox, praying she'd take the hint and back off.

No such luck. Joan's tenacity was legendary. It's why the big bucks came flying into their coffers. Zach was screwed.

Joan's no-nonsense pumps clicked across the walnut floorboards to his desk. She perched on the edge of the seat opposite Zach's, raised one elegant, stocking-clad leg across the opposite thigh, and hooked her foot nearly full-circle around the ankle. Zach couldn't look away from those legs, twined together like two strands of strawberry licorice, begging to be peeled apart.

Joan caught him staring, which was, of course, the entire point. The performance resumed. She slid her folded hands along her skirt until they came to rest over her kneecap. Balanced just so, on the ball of that one foot touching the floor, Joan pressed forward and teetered precariously over the edge of the chair.

"Zach, you cannot seriously be worried about your wife looking at another man."

He froze. Who says these things out loud? "Joan—"

"Wow. You *are*." Her disbelief might have been flattering had she not crossed so many lines. "C'mon, Zach. Be real. Do you not have any idea how attractive you are?"

"This conversation is wildly inappropriate." Yet there he sat, having it.

Joan eyed him carefully as she processed the new data. She was nothing if not adaptive.

"You know I'm here for you, Zach. Whatever you need."

Zach had no clue what he needed, but he was certain whatever that was should not be supplied by Joan.

22

SHOWDOWN

Despite Pan's warnings to "slow down and try to behave like a human," Cupid made remarkable progress his first week. By day, he worked harder than any servant at his mother's palace, ripping up old carpet, stripping wallpaper, repairing trim, and priming the walls for their first coat of paint. Each night, Cupid returned home, inhaled his dinner, and headed straight to the garage-workshop, where he spent the next four hours measuring, cutting, and assembling bookcases.

More importantly, Ruthie was moving forward. She'd wandered in and out of the former nursery over the course of the week, sighing less and less and smiling more and more.

Bright and early Friday morning, with two cans of freshly mixed Cornsilk Yellow paint hanging from one hand, Cupid knocked on the back door of the Millers'. Through the windowpane, Cupid watched Pookie tumble down the stairs first. Seconds later, a pair of low-heeled ladies' shoes appeared, then gray dress slacks flapping around Ruthie's ankles, and finally, a pretty lavender sweater that bounced up and down in time with her footfalls. Ruthie was dressed for something other than watching Cupid work.

"Morning, Quentin," she said as she opened the door. After sixteen hours apart, it was both wonderful and terrible to be so close again.

"Good morning. You look nice."

Her blush made Cupid blush, too. "Thank you." She stepped aside to let him pass. "I'm just heading out, and I won't be back till at least two. Would you mind letting Pookie out around noon?"

"Sure. Does she need anything else? Food? Water?"

"Nope, she'll probably drive you nuts, wanting to play every second, but other than that, she's low maintenance," Ruthie said with a chuckle. "Thanks again."

"No problem. Have a nice day."

Cupid peered through the second-story window as Ruthie's car snaked down the driveway. On the one hand, Cupid was pleased Ruthie trusted him enough to leave him alone in the house for six hours. He'd make the most of this opportunity to earn her faith by taking the best possible care of Pookie and being super productive today. Maybe he'd even surprise Ruthie with the first coat of paint when she returned home.

On the other hand, he already missed her.

Having viewed hours of paint instruction on YouTube, Cupid was more than eager to try his hand. He made three trips out to his car for rollers and drop cloths and brushes and paint and his ladder, each time carefully navigating the two flights of stairs with overfilled arms and a dog running circles around his feet. With the last of his supplies organized on the floor, Cupid crouched down for a heart-to-heart with Pookie.

"Okay, girl," Cupid said, giving her a good scratch behind the ears, "I'm going to open the paint now. Can I trust you to sit right there for me?" She plopped onto her bottom, and Cupid interpreted her cheery *yip-yip* as a yes.

Keeping one eye on the dog, Cupid popped the lid off the first can. Pookie panted and shook but stayed put.

"Good girl," Cupid crooned. "Now, *stay* . . ." He lifted the can and poured it into the tray. So far, so good. Cupid reached for the roller. In the split second he turned away, Pookie jumped into the tray and hopped around like a child playing in a rain puddle.

"No! Bad girl!" Cupid tossed the roller away and scooped up the messy dog before she could track paint all over the house. "I thought we had an agreement."

Clutching Pookie tight against his coveralls, he sped to the nearest bathroom. She yelped and squirmed, but Cupid wasn't about to be outmaneuvered by the little monster again. He stuffed her paws into the sink, turned on the cold water, and washed off the paint. Grumbling at the naughty girl as he dried her paws with the hand towel, Cupid caught their reflection in the mirror. How silly was he to be angry at a dog for playing?

"*Hmph.* Some responsible pet-sitter you are."

He carried Pookie back to the nursery and set her down just outside the door. "Give me a minute, girl." She whined when he shut the door.

Working quickly, Cupid cleared the floor of all dangerous and potentially messy obstacles. When he was sure the room was Pookie-proof, Cupid opened the door. The dog bounded inside and sprinted from one end of the room to the other, looking for trouble and not finding any. Pan would tease him mercilessly if he ever found out, but Cupid had to admit he enjoyed the little critter's company, especially once she finally settled down for a snooze inside a beam of sunlight.

Setting his mind to the paint job, Cupid grabbed the roller and started in. Straight stripe up, zigzag down. He made efficient strokes, quickly mastering the pattern he'd studied. Occasionally, Cupid would hear the soft tinkling of Pookie's tags and turn to see her head lifted as if to supervise. "What do you think, girl?" he'd ask. "Am I doing a good job?" She'd blink at him until her eyelids grew heavy, then flop down and fall back asleep.

The soft swish of the roller soothed Cupid's nerves. In fact, he'd thoroughly enjoyed all aspects of the construction project: drawing plans, fashioning the pile of wood planks into cabinetry and trim, and now this, adding a splash of color to the walls. If not for his punishment, Cupid might have completely missed out on this pleasure of creating with his hands. Perhaps he would redecorate his bedroom at the palace when this was all over and he ascended home. The thought of returning to his old life filled him with melancholy.

Pookie let out a low *woof*, scurried onto her paws, and trotted to Cupid's side.

"Easy, girl," Cupid said absently, climbing the ladder with a brush in hand so he could tidy the ceiling line.

He worked the end of the bristles into the corner and drew a steady line of paint along the molding. Pookie's chirps turned into urgent, full-body barks directed up the ladder.

"Hey, Pookie, what's got you all riled up?"

"That would be me."

Cupid whipped his head around toward the doorway of the nursery, where Zach leaned against the doorjamb. A cold shiver ran down Cupid's back where his wings once hinged. What was Zach doing home in the middle of the workday?

"Sorry," Zach said. "I didn't mean to sneak up on you."

"No problem," Cupid answered, though Zach definitely had

snuck up on him, and Cupid couldn't believe he'd accomplished such a feat by accident.

Cupid scurried down the ladder and lifted Pookie into the cradle of his arm. "Shh, it's okay." Cupid petted her head and murmured comforting noises, unclear if he meant to calm Pookie or himself.

The two men regarded each other warily, Cupid waiting for Zach to state his purpose and Zach watching with awed fascination as Pookie calmed against Cupid's chest. "Wow, Ruthie was right." Whatever Ruthie was right about caused Zach's expression to sour. "You seem to have all the females in this house wrapped around your little finger."

Not good. Cupid braced for a punch, though honestly, he had no clue how to defend himself. On the Mount, nobody would have considered physically harming the son of Aphrodite. Cupid made a mental note to ask Pan for some lessons.

"If you're looking for Ruthie, she's not here."

"Yes, I'm aware of my wife's schedule. She volunteers at the playspace from nine to noon, followed by a manicure."

So, Zach had come for him, then. "Is there something I can do for you?"

"Yes, actually. My wife seems intent on keeping you to herself. I wanted to stop by and get a sense directly from you of how the project is going."

"Sure. Give me one second?" Cupid gingerly set Pookie onto the floor, replaced the lid on the paint can, and set the brush on top. "Everything is moving along. We're right on schedule. Ruthie seems happy."

Zach nailed Cupid with a sneer. "Yes, isn't she though?"

"Is that bad?" Mortals could be so confusing.

Zach shook his head and stepped all the way into the room. Cupid's gaze chased Zach's around the walls. Every raggedy edge and errant paint streak jumped out at Cupid. "I've only applied the first coat. I'll even it all—"

Zach pivoted to face him. "How did you talk Ruthie into getting rid of the baby furniture?"

How on Earth did Ruthie keep up with this man? Zach changed direction faster than Mercury running from a winged boar.

"She said she was ready."

"Huh." Zach's focus drifted to the walls again. "Why yellow?"

"Ruthie and I researched colors that inspire creativity." Cupid also happened to know Erato's favorite color was yellow. It never hurt to appease the Muses.

"When will you be finished?"

"Three more weeks ought to do it."

Zach nodded, and Cupid allowed himself to believe he might just escape unscathed after all. "*My wife* is"—Zach turned to glare at Cupid—"very trusting."

"I'm keeping track of my hours, and I can assure you, I'm not taking any liberties." Cupid wouldn't have considered charging Ruthie for the hours he spent honing his skills late into the night.

"I wasn't referring to the work. My *wife*," Zach said, then paused in case Cupid had missed the unmissable the first time, "likes to help people. Sometimes they draw incorrect conclusions from her kindness."

"Incorrect conclusions?"

"I don't think Ruthie realizes she sometimes comes off as flirty. She's basically a lover of people."

"Yes, I've noticed that. I mean the lover part, not the flirting. Not that she loves me . . ." A sick feeling came over Cupid. This conversation was getting away from him. Confident it would bolster his case, Cupid added, "She's very shy around me."

"Despite your advances."

She'd told him. Cupid raised his hands in surrender. "I asked her for her phone number *once*, and she shot me down right away. I can take a hint."

"And yet, here you are in our home."

"She needed this room built."

"Needed . . ." Zach muttered under his breath. "You're telling me you don't have designs on my wife?"

"Absolutely not. She gave me work, and I am appreciative. I am not a"—*what was the expression Mia had used? Oh, yes*—"a home-wrecker."

Zach weighed Cupid's explanation for what felt like days before delivering his verdict. "You do seem to know what you're doing with the carpentry."

"Thank you."

"And you don't look like a psycho killer."

"Definitely not." It wouldn't help to explain he was the consummate lover, not a fighter.

"I haven't quite figured out how, but you seem to have sparked something in Ruthie. She's . . . *different* since she met you. I wish to hell I'd been the one to help her move forward—God knows I tried—but I certainly won't let my ego stand in her way. You have my seal of approval." Zach extended his hand, and Cupid grabbed it before Zach changed his mind.

"Thank you."

Maybe Aphrodite was right about making Zach a Worthy after all. It felt strange to root for Zach while Cupid was still trying to swallow his own profound loss.

They both released a long breath before Cupid spoke again. "Does Ruthie know you're here right now?"

"No," Zach answered, somewhat sheepish for the first time.

"Are you planning to tell her?"

"I have no secrets from my wife," Zach said, his tone shifting swiftly from defense to offense, "and I fail to see how that is your affair."

Cupid's cheeks flared with heat, an unfortunate response to Zach's unfortunate choice of words, which, also unfortunately, Zach did not fail to notice. A slew of inappropriate replies popped into Cupid's head. Unpracticed as he still was at lying, Cupid had at least learned when to keep his mouth shut. Sometimes, though, saying nothing said everything.

Zach threw his head back and rolled his eyes toward the ceiling. "Unbelievable. Fucking Gail!" Pookie scrambled onto her paws and let out a startled *woof*. "She's filled your head with a load of crap about me, hasn't she?"

Cupid didn't trust himself even to shake his head.

With an audible sigh, Zach pushed his fingers through his hair. "*Christ*." Clearly, he was frustrated, but Cupid couldn't discern whether it was because Zach felt wrongly accused or rightfully exposed. "I am not having this conversation with you."

Not a confession, not a denial.

Nothing good would come of challenging Zach, and Cupid certainly did not want to be the cause of a marital spat. If Cupid had reached an impasse on his primary mission, at least he could make progress on the construction project.

"I should probably get back to work."

"Yeah, me too," Zach said with a huff. "You missed a spot under the windowsill," he added as he strode out the door.

Pookie's rear end wagged the rest of her body as she faithfully stood guard by Cupid's feet, her tiny ears perked until Zach's footfalls faded out of range. She lifted her face to Cupid's, then cocked her head as if to ask, "What was that about?"

Cupid chuckled, crouching to scratch Pookie's chin. "Looks like I've got my work cut out for me, eh, girl?"

Pookie's lips parted into a grin, revealing two tiny rows of teeth and a soft, pink tongue that quivered as she panted.

"Are you laughing at me, you little stinker?"

Pookie leaned into Cupid's attentive fingers, indifferent to the Cornsilk paint clotting on the paint brush, Cupid's work schedule, and Ruthie and Zach's marriage. Her jaws opened with a high squeak, and she yawned so hard her whole body quaked. She ambled over to her sunbeam like the last guest to leave the Bacchanalia, circled the warm spot on the new carpeting, then flopped to the floor, closed her eyes, and began to snore.

23

FANNING FLAMES

There was only so much wife-wandering a god, especially one with self-esteem issues, could take. In recent weeks, Aphrodite's level of hero worship for Ares had progressed from the occasional, manageable swoon to a constant gnawing at Hephaestus's manhood.

Hephaestus would have been lying if he denied a grudging respect for the God of War—ingenuity, good looks, *and* brass balls. Sadly, Heph could no longer miss the obvious manifestations of his wife's dangerous fascination: stolen glances below the belt of Ares's chiton, a quickened flutter of her treacherous lashes, the rosy flush in her cheeks, a breathy lilt whenever she spoke to him.

And what of the "private strategy sessions" called on a moment's notice at Ares's whim? Hephaestus could only imagine—and he often did, in torturous detail—exactly what Aphrodite and Ares were up to behind closed doors at the compound. Hephaestus took little reassurance from his own occasional conjugal couplings with Aphrodite, who returned his romantic attentions with legs barely open and eyes tightly closed.

The longer Cupid sojourned on Earth, the more perilous grew Hephaestus's marital situation. The first trial had taken Cupid less than two weeks to sort out; this new punishment was already into week five. Frankly, Hephaestus hadn't seen much progress, hence his fixation on this new Worthy couple.

Hephaestus felt for Ruth. He'd spent centuries in her shoes, drying up in the corner like last year's raisins while the juicy new grapes plumped on the vine. It was neither here nor there whether Zach had cheated on his wife. Her insecurity alone would be enough to ruin their marriage.

Enter Cupid, a charming admirer, slavishly devoted to Ruth's happiness. Even with the best intentions, the boy could not necessarily be relied upon to discern short-term comfort from everlasting happiness. Hadn't Cupid proven that by diddling Mia in that parking lot?

Hephaestus had been quick to judge Cupid's indiscretion, even convinced Aphrodite to impose a second labor. It was the right move, but oh, he was kicking himself now. The Divine Council surely would have overruled Cupid's ascension, but at least they would have taken over his case and supplanted the unholy alliance of Aphrodite and Ares.

With those two manufacturing excuses to draw out Cupid's punishment, Hephaestus could no longer stand idly by. The time was upon him to set his plan into motion. Aphrodite would be angry at first, but the nobler part of her, the part Hephaestus had fallen in love with over and over again, would eventually win out. Above all else, she was a mother who loved her son. Once Hephaestus got Cupid home, Aphrodite would appreciate the enormity of what he'd done for her. She would forgive, and somewhere down the road of eternity, she would respect her husband not only for rescuing Cupid but also for restoring Aphrodite to her finest self. Her attraction to Ares would wither and die without a purpose to nourish its existence.

If his plan worked.

Generally speaking, Hephaestus lacked the discipline of his nemesis. Today would have to be different. He suspected his first chance might be his only chance, and he'd damned well better get to it before Aphrodite caught wind of his scheme.

It was helpful that Cupid had settled into a routine: report to the Millers' by eight, put in an impressive day's work, and close up shop at four; debrief and dinner with Pan, though lately, Pan tended to be out more often than home; another three to four hours devoted to study and practice of his new craft before Cupid would fall into bed and surrender to Hypnos.

It was just after four now in Indiana. Hephaestus fixed his stare through the gaiascope and located Cupid in the nursery. The boy was talking to himself as he sealed paint containers, packed up brushes, and tidied his workspace. Cupid had taught himself well.

A pang of paternal regret agitated Hephaestus's heart. If only the boy had shown a morsel of interest, Hephaestus would happily have taught Cupid the finer points of construction. He allowed himself the brief fantasy of crafting side by side with the boy in true father-son fashion upon Cupid's return to the palace. *But no*, this Earth-Cupid would not be the one returning to Mount O, if he returned at all. It was one thing for a winged preteen to manage the bow he was born to; wielding a hammer was an entirely different story.

Movement drew Hephaestus's attention back to the glass. Cupid skipped down the stairs and out the door, the little furball hot on his heels. Heph's pulse quickened. *Am I really about to do this?* If his plan backfired, he might well find himself on the other end of the gaiascope at the mercy of Ares, if such a quality existed.

He could see the whole sordid ordeal, playing out in his mind as clear as that humiliating day he cast his golden net over the two adulterers, his wife with his own brother. There they would be, wife and lover, naked in each other's arms, frolicking in Hephaestus's marital bed, the two of them laughing at the fool suffering his punishment on Earth below until their mutual passions fizzled out, and they allowed his ascension . . . right around *never*.

Happy are those who dare courageously to defend what they love, or so said Ovid.

Setting aside paralyzing thoughts, Hephaestus jumped off the bed, gaiascope shaking between his hands. "Let's go! Let's go!" he yelled at Cupid, even as the boy's footsteps turned away from the driveway. "Get in the car! What are you doing down there?"

Oblivious to Hephaestus's meltdown, Cupid jogged across the grass behind the house, picked up a colorful disc, and tossed it to the opposite end of the yard. The dog bounded after it, rushed back to Cupid's feet with the toy in its mouth, and stood there panting until Cupid wrestled the toy from its jaws. Hephaestus groaned in frustration as the disc crossed the grass again and again until the pup finally trotted over to the bushes, sniffed around, and squatted. Her tiny body quivered for several seconds, then she pranced over to Cupid as if she'd just sculpted the *Jockey of Artemision*. "What a good girl you are," Cupid cooed at her.

"Alleluia!" shouted Hephaestus. "A pile of turds. Now get in your car . . ."

Cupid batted playfully at the little rat, spilling her onto her back in the grass and knocking her off-balance again each time she regained her footing and scampered back for more. Hephaestus paced and muttered curses into the glass until Cupid finally led the little mutt inside and emerged from the house alone. All that waiting time had strengthened Hephaestus's resolve. He was as ready as he'd ever be.

Cupid started up the Prius, and Hephaestus commandeered the controls. Aphrodite controlled her son's heart, but the God of Fire could still handle a hunk of metal.

Cupid gripped the steering wheel tighter at first, surprise turning to panic as he fought the force of Hephaestus's will. To the boy's credit, Cupid quickly figured out that stabbing at pedals and spinning the wheel had no impact on the speed or direction of his vehicle. With a resigned sigh toward the clouds, Cupid slumped back against the driver's seat and left the driving to the god above.

What a good boy you are.

"What are you grinning about?"

Aphrodite had breezed into their boudoir earlier than Hephaestus had expected. All the better to impress her with his cleverness in real time.

"Just turning up the flame under Cupid's bottom."

"What?" Aphrodite snatched the gaiascope out of his grasp. "What did you do?"

"I figured out how to get *our son* home."

Aphrodite snapped her head up from the Earth scene. Oh, how her pretty mouth twitched with the effort of not correcting him. But there were bigger issues at stake than parentage, and Aphrodite was not easily sidetracked. "Do tell, husband."

"The way I see it, we need to motivate the boy to leave Earth and keep him out of trouble in the meantime. I've engineered a solution that accomplishes both." Taking Aphrodite's awed expression as encouragement, Hephaestus puffed out his chest. "Cupid fornicates with Pan's girl, thereby mucking up his friendship with Pan for good—part one—while giving him a safe place to relieve his appetite—part two."

"Why?"

"Did I not explain my reasoning?"

"What you did not explain is why you decided to stick your nose into the situation and take action without consulting me."

Not exactly gratitude, but that would come later. "The opportunity arose, and you were not here to consult."

"*Ares* and I have *our* son's situation under control." And there it was.

"I see. And how is your little scheme to get the boy home working so far?"

She answered her husband as if speaking to a small child. "You seem to forget there's more to this than simply bringing Cupid home. He needs to be taught a lesson."

"And which lesson is that?"

Aphrodite sighed. "Have we not been over this a hundred times?"

"Indulge me, *wife*."

"Love is not a game? People's hearts are not to be trifled with for the entertainment value? Sound familiar?"

Did she not see the irony?

"Hmm," Hephaestus began, "to clarify, then, the idea would be to teach Cupid the lesson with minimal suffering to the boy and the least amount of collateral damage. Is that correct?"

Aphrodite tossed the gaiascope onto the bed and paced to the window, robes swishing along the floor behind her. "Not necessarily. We want the lesson to really sink in. So naturally, some pain is . . . constructive."

Ares had worked his hooks into Aphrodite even deeper than Hephaestus had allowed himself to imagine. He could no longer hold his tongue. "*Constructive?*"

"Pain lingers in the memory long after other emotions dissipate."

"No need to remind me of that, my love," Hephaestus shot back.

She half turned toward him but changed her mind. "As for collateral damage, humans do a fine job muddling their own affairs."

"Interesting choice of words."

"Fie!" She wheeled around, moral indignation renewed. "The situation was well in hand, I assure you. Yes, the measures we imposed were strict but doable. Now, what you have gone and done?"

"I simply moved Cupid's car in the direction that would be most fruitful."

"You moved a car?"

"Yes, dear. Have you forgotten I command the power to manipulate metal?"

Her lips curled into a hideous sneer. "I did not forget your powers, oh big, mighty god. I just cannot believe you took such a liberty."

Hephaestus could feel the pressure hammering in his ears. "So, it's okay for my brother to cause a multi-car collision and . . . *kill . . . a human . . . being*"—Hephaestus's tirade broke into separate, clipped words, as if their meaning would be too evil to withstand if strung together—"but not for *me* to safely deliver Cupid into a lover's arms?"

Aphrodite leveled a hard glare at Hephaestus. "I was none too pleased with Ares about that maneuver of his, if you'll recall."

"I recall that you accepted his judgment as I would expect my wife to respect her husband's." *I dare you,* his glare said.

"Oh, Heph." Not exactly the affirmation he was hoping for. "What makes you think Pan even cares about that girl? He hasn't seen her in weeks."

"He'll care when Cupid sleeps with her."

Aphrodite rolled her eyes. "Men."

Great, now the conversation had devolved into pity and disdain. He needed to jolt them back on track.

"Tell me, Aph, why were Ruth and Zach chosen? What makes them Worthies?"

Aphrodite's shoulders fell, all the fight seeping out of her. She glided over to her favorite chaise and sank onto the cushions. "They were a beautiful match, one of my very best," she said without a trace of boastfulness. "One's dreams found nourishment and light in the other."

In all the centuries piled upon centuries of marriage, had Hephaestus ever heard the Goddess of Love express her ideal? Now that she'd laid out the definition of Right Love like the answer to a test, could he ever again delude himself that he was Aphrodite's? *Best not to think about it.*

He shifted uncomfortably and stole a glance at Aphrodite. She seemed fully absorbed in the mortal union. Her tone held a faraway quality. "You know I rarely intercede in the work of the Fates—"

"A quality I've always admired in you, sweetheart." If only the Olympians would leave each deity to his realm, how much less drama there would be on the Mount and on Earth.

"It wasn't easy, but I held my tongue when Atropos took the first baby from Ruth's womb. After the strain of the second miscarriage, I could no longer remain silent." *There's my fierce tiger*, Hephaestus mused with an unexpected gush of warmth. "I pleaded with Clotho to intercede on the unborn baby's behalf, but you know how intractable the sisters can be." Aphrodite's lovely forehead pinched in anguish.

Hephaestus regarded the physical form draped along the frame of the chaise. Goddess. Wife. *Woman*. So powerful, so tender.

"Yes," Hephaestus answered gently, shuffling toward his wife's side.

"There was no changing Atropos's mind once she'd decided to take the third child." Aphrodite sighed wistfully. "Ruth would've made a wonderful mother. They didn't deserve this."

"Would a strong marriage not survive even such misery?"

Aphrodite blinked up at him. Were her lashes moist? "That remains to be seen, doesn't it? They both believe themselves diminished in the other's esteem. Ruth is not the wide-eyed, confident girl who caught Zach's eye, and he's not the all-powerful protector he might once have thought himself. Instead of seeking answers together, they've drifted down separate paths. They've lost their way as a couple."

Hephaestus set his hand on Aphrodite's shoulder, pleased when she didn't flinch at his touch. "Then help me bring them back together, my goddess."

"What do you think I'm doing? I put my best soldier on the ground, right on top of the situation."

"A soldier who's charming the pants off the wife."

One of Aphrodite's perfectly sculpted eyebrows rose in challenge. "Once in a great while, temptation can be resisted, I hear."

"Maybe so," he said, noting the triumphant gleam in Aphrodite's eye, "but do you honestly believe it wise to subject Ruth to Cupid's charms while her husband's loyalty hangs by a thread?"

Hephaestus could have sworn he caught a devious grin flicker across Aphrodite's face. "I believe the Council will look favorably on the added challenge when evaluating Cupid's progress."

"Which will be a moot point if Cupid fails to get them past their Liminal Point."

"Aren't you the one who keeps telling me to have faith in Cupid? Have you lost yours?"

Generally speaking, no, he hadn't, but there was that immediate gratification factor Hephaestus just couldn't be sure Cupid had mastered. "It's the mortals who have me worried, my love.

If either of them strays, they may never recover. You'd be condemning your son to a life on Earth away from you. Is that what you want?"

"People heal from unfaithfulness. Look at us." Aphrodite craned her neck and smiled cruelly.

How would it serve Hephaestus to admit their marriage was a sham? So instead, he railed. "That's your solution? Just let them follow their carnal desires and hope they'll find their way back?"

"I'm done coddling the boy," Aphrodite said, with an inflection that sounded all too much like the God of War's, "and I strongly suggest you do the same."

Her barely veiled threat blew an icy breeze across Hephaestus's heart. He walked soundlessly to their bed, a feat for the big man, picked up the gaiascope, and retired to his workshop to watch his scheme unfold.

24

BRO CODE

Pan pounded the heavy bag, his fists throwing off clouds of chalk and dust into the still gym air. The abuse felt good, his need for physical release so intense it almost scared him, but what else could he do? There were only so many boys he could fuck in a day.

Jagger was always game, but charming as he was, the stripper lacked Cupid's bright-eyed view of love, and his eyes were the wrong shade of blue, and he didn't get half of Pan's jokes. Pan tried to backfill the missing pieces—one from Boy A and another from Boy B—as if he could assemble the perfect mate like some Lego project. But no matter how many parts Pan collected, the picture just wouldn't add up.

He needed to be mindful at the gym, especially when his system kicked into overdrive. You don't pile twice your body weight on the bar and expect to go unnoticed. The uber-jacked regulars knew exactly what a body that lifted 400 looked like, and Pan didn't have one. Suspicions would be aroused. If this compulsion to punish his muscles persisted, Pan would have to reconsider installing a home gym—*ah,* but then, he'd miss out on the locker room. Nothing quite compared to the communal, naked lounging in sauna and steam rooms, especially when Pan was cruising for a hookup.

As spent as he was, the walk back to the locker room triggered a predictable response, an urge Pan had recently stopped resisting though these bathroom tumbles only offered temporary relief. His all-you-can-eat buffet was starving him for what he really craved. At least there didn't seem to be any backlash beyond Pan's growing weariness. In a cosmos stirred by capricious deities, "no harm done" worked for Pan.

Dripping with sweat and body odor and exhaustion, he pushed through the locker room entrance, sniffing out his options like a lion hunting for dinner. Pan's eye caught on a lean, dark-haired twenty-something who'd bent over to untie his shoes. He had a runner's body, slim and toned. He would do.

The boy lifted his head, smiled at Pan, and pumped out an intoxicating bouquet of want. Pan smiled right back and jutted his chin toward the toilet stalls. A warm curl of desire snaked through him as the boy peeled off his shirt and fell into step behind him.

As they passed the last row of lockers, Pan heard the muffled ring of his phone. No mistaking the "Stupid Cupid" ring tone. Pan darted off course toward locker 134, and the boy, not comprehending, followed him.

Pan turned and addressed him as if they'd known each other for years. "Sorry, I've got to take this call."

"Oh." Still dazzled, the boy asked, "Should I wait?"

Pan chuckled. "Sure, if you're not in a hurry." To sweeten the deal, Pan pulled the sodden tank over his head and drew his hands, at the ends of artfully flexed arms, through his sweaty ginger locks.

The boy grinned. "I'll wait."

Pan nodded and even tossed in a wink. "I'll meet you in the shower."

"All right," the boy said, drinking in one last look at Pan's midsection before turning away.

Pan grasped the key dangling from his wrist and pushed it into the keyhole. The metal door fell open, and the ringtone blared louder. *Shit.* How long had Cupid been calling? The workouts were Pan's one cell-free refuge. Had he overplayed his freedom?

Pan unzipped his leather gym bag and dug through the clothes until his fingers met metal. He tapped "answer" and slapped the phone against his ear. "Everything okay?"

"Yeah, I think so."

Dodged a bullet. "What's up?"

"Cheri's asking about you."

"Cheri? She called you?" Here, Pan had thought Cheri *got* him, was cool with what they had.

"No, not exactly. I'm at her house."

Dread crept up Pan's spine. "Why would you go there?"

"I didn't exactly go anywhere, more like I was driven. Think about it, Pan. I didn't even know where Cheri lived until she answered the door."

"Wait, are you saying your heart-thing took you to Cheri? She's your next . . ." Bad thoughts came easily to a god who'd witnessed so much evil. "Q, for fuck's sake, tell me you're not fucking *in love* with Cheri!"

"No. Just Ruthie." A humorless laugh followed. "It wasn't my heart this time. It was my car. I swear, Pan, it literally drove itself here."

Pan leaned inside his locker in case any mortals were within earshot. "Your car steered itself?"

"Yes. I didn't even have a change of clothes with me. I peeled off my coveralls in the driveway, but there's paint splattered all over my boots, in my hair . . . I'm a mess." As if a little evidence of a rough-and-tumble workday wouldn't make Cupid even more desirable.

A string of curse words fluttered through Pan's mind, but none met his lips. Q was telling the truth, Pan was sure of it, but that didn't unfuck the situation.

"And now you've reasoned you're meant to screw Cheri, so you're calling me for permission?"

"I don't know. I'm confused."

"Damn straight, you're confused. Cheri is mine."

Wow, where the hell did that come from? Okay, calm the fuck down.

Pan pulled in a deep breath, then immediately wished he hadn't. Locker room air, a thousand times more potent to Pan's sensitive snout. Dirty socks and smelly pits and sweaty jocks and that ever-present pre-mildew of damp towels.

Despite Pan's growing agitation, Cupid pressed boldly on. "I know you and Cheri were together for a while, but the gods must have delivered me here for a reason, right?"

"It's a test, Q. They love to test us, remember?"

"But Cheri's not my Worthy, and she's not married."

Pan pinched the bridge of his nose, a nervous tic that did little to relieve his stress but helped—marginally—with the stench. "Okay, look, I know you're unacquainted with the Bro Code, so let me fill you in. A guy doesn't go sniffing around his best friend's territory."

"Oh." Cupid's end of the conversation went silent, and Pan assumed he was working out the rules. "I think she asked me to call you before we . . . because she wants to know if you still care about her, Pan."

"That is between Cheri and me. You need to stay out of it."

"Why?"

"Because keep your dick away from Cheri, that's why. I am warning you, Q."

"I'm not blind, Pan. Ever since that night at Versailles, it's been a nonstop parade of men in and out of your bedroom. And your truck," he added. And Cupid didn't even know about the locker room.

"All of that is none of your business and totally beside the point."

"How?"

"*Why? How?* What are you, a child?" Wasn't Cupid supposed to take Pan at his word? "Whatever happened to your fuck buddy . . . Gail, was it?"

"That's disgusting, Pan."

"Oh, gimme a break. What would *you* call it?"

"Over." A few beats went by before Cupid spoke again, his voice calm, as if he'd assumed the advisor role. "I can't see Gail anymore. It's causing problems. But that's not important right now. What should I tell Cheri?"

"Hmm, how about, 'Been nice catching up. Goodbye'?"

"Fine," Cupid said quietly.

"*Fine?* That's it?"

"Yes, Pan. That's it. You know I'd never do anything to hurt you, not on purpose, anyway."

Huh. "Thanks, Q. I appreciate that, and obviously"—an unexpected lump welled up in Pan's throat—"I feel the same."

"I know," Cupid answered in his trusting, gentle tone. "See you at home?"

Home with Cupid. That would be a nice change of pace from Pan's frenetic night-crawling. "Yeah, be there in a bit."

Pan kicked off his socks and shoes and tossed them into the locker, quickly followed by his shorts and jock. Strutting like the demigod he was, Pan made his way to the showers and located his bonbon. The boy had a pretty face: interesting, almond-shaped eyes, a nose that blended in without calling attention to itself, and a pair of cherry-pink lips that opened into a wide smile at Pan's approach.

A mild wave of guilt hit Pan as he pressed the boy's back to the tile wall and closed in for a kiss. He'd spoiled Cupid and Cheri's fun, and here he was, taking all this for himself. But he needed to shower, and *someone* had to soap all his nooks and crannies.

That was the right thing to do, Pan convinced his reflection as he gargled and spat. A sated Pan was less vulnerable to Cupid's allure. By the time Pan opened his locker again, he'd erased his conscience of any residual crumbs of guilt.

He hummed to himself as he pulled out his bag and set it on the bench. Out of habit, he checked his phone: two text messages. He'd learned his lesson earlier—Pan rarely made the same mistake twice—and before reaching for his boxers, he tapped in his password and opened the messages, both from Cupid.

Said our goodbyes, went to leave, car wouldn't budge.

So much for Pan's good mood. With a sinking feeling, he opened the second message, sent roughly ten minutes later.

Cheri's OK having us both. Guess I'll be home when the gods allow.

Oh, hell no. Fuck Q. Fuck Cheri.

Pan tapped the screen so hard, he felt the aftershocks in his fingertips long after the message was sent:

DO NOT BOTHER COMING HOME!!

25

KICKED OUT

Cupid woke before his 6:30 alarm, slipped quietly out of Cheri's bed, and showered without waking her. He was much relieved not to have to make conversation with her this morning after a fitful night spent dreaming of fire-breathing, redheaded monsters and herds of angry, wild goats. Cupid's thoughts were gnarled, and his words could not be trusted. If last night was, indeed, a test, Cheri would have awarded him the highest marks. Cupid could be proud of that much.

The hot shower was a much-needed gift. Dried paint blobs came back to life under the stream. Thick, yellow snakes slid from Cupid's hair, shimmied down his body, and slithered into the drain. At least his body was clean. He hastily dressed in yesterday's underwear, T-shirt, and coveralls. Lucky for Ruthie, her nose would pick up only a mortal's fraction of his stench; still, Cupid would have to keep his distance today.

If the gods were displeased, they had left no discernible evidence. (Out of habit born of recent necessity, Cupid had carefully examined his genitals before, during, and after sex with

Cheri and noted no anomalies.) That Cupid could drive himself to work without outside influence over heart or steel seemed like a good omen as well. Painting occupied Cupid's hands but freed his mind to grind over his problems.

Pan's text was a worry. He didn't understand this bro-code concept any better now than when Gail had accused him of taking Zach's side. When his car wouldn't leave Cheri's, and then she so willingly consented, Cupid had assumed any obstacles had been cleared. All Cupid knew for sure was that he'd turned out to be a shitty friend—and to Pan, of all people.

Pan had never been able to hold a grudge for long. If Cupid could plead his case in person, Pan would see the sincerity written all over his face. After work, Cupid would head home, or what used to be home, and beg forgiveness.

At four o'clock, Cupid sealed the paint cans, folded his drop cloths, and took Pookie outside to do her business. As the inevitable confrontation drew closer, anxiety bloomed like a welt from a physical blow. What could he say to make Pan believe he'd meant no disrespect? Would Pan even listen? Maybe if Cupid could get Pan to consume enough of those nasty beers he loved so much . . .

Of course! Cupid would bring a host offering to Pan. Not just any gift, but one that would also weaken Pan's resolve to stay angry with him. It would have to be something special, an upgrade from Pan's normal swill. A nice bottle of wine on par with the cabernet Cupid had taken to Mia's that first time.

Unlike Pan, Cupid did not have Dionysus's cellar at his disposal, but luckily, the mortals in Ruthie's neighborhood consumed remarkable quantities of fine wine. The local shopkeeper was happy to point Cupid to two "perfectly delightful" choices, and all Cupid had to decide was whether he preferred black cherry or tobacco undertones, which seemed like a trick question.

Something felt off about using Pan's credit card to buy the gift, but until Cupid finished his job at Ruthie's, he had no other source of funds. As he signed the slip, Cupid vowed to pay Pan back with his very first sixty-three dollars earned. He set the bottle gingerly on the passenger seat beside him, vaguely wondering if it would help to spring for tulips.

All of his internal organs seemed to rise into his throat when he turned onto Pan's street. He started up the driveway and pressed the button on the garage door opener. As the door *click-clacked* up its tracks, the full measure of Pan's fury became clear. All traces of Cupid's workshop—the shelves he'd crafted, his tools, his worktable—had been removed. In their place, in the middle of what had been Cupid's side of the garage, sat a single green plastic trash bag tied off in a knot. Taped to the front was a lumpy, white envelope with the letter "Q" scrawled in thick, black marker.

Cupid parked the car in the driveway, stepped out on shaky legs, and plucked the envelope off the bag. Inside was a small key on a plain, metal ring and a folded piece of lined paper ripped from the pad in the kitchen.

> ***I've moved your building supplies to a storage locker at the South Side Apartments. Sleep wherever you want (oh wait, you already do)—anywhere but here. Keep the car. Keep the phone. Use the credit card to buy whatever you need. Do not contact me. I will be in touch.***

Not "good luck" or "I'll miss you, old friend" or even a goodbye. Not a single indication of any personal connection. Pan would have offered more warmth to a stranger on the street.

Cupid stood frozen to his spot in the garage, staring at the door leading into Pan's home, a door he was unlikely to ever walk through again. So much for working it out. Pan's truck was here; he had to be inside. Was he listening to Cupid's movements from the other side of the door, heart beating out of his rib cage too? Or was he settled indifferently on his couch with a beer in one hand and his TV clicker in the other? Gods, how Cupid wished he could jump onto the cushions beside him.

He hadn't thought it possible for his heart to break so completely in this new way. How much more did Cupid have to learn about the throbbing organ in his chest?

Hoisting the giant bag over his shoulder like a thief, Cupid lumbered to his car, swung the bag into the back seat, and closed the door with a thud. He climbed into the driver's seat and scrubbed his hands up and down his face. Tears stung his eyes.

The wine bottle mocked him from the passenger seat, the peace offering that never had a chance. No use keeping it for himself. Cupid grabbed the bottle by the neck and forced his body out of the car a second time. He opened the passenger door—what used to be *his* side—of Pan's truck and placed the bottle gingerly on the seat. Because the wine was expensive, Cupid drew the seat belt across the bottle and locked it into place.

Cupid took one last wretched look around the garage, then trudged back to the Prius and closed the garage door. He stared through the windshield at his Earth-home where he no longer belonged. *Now what?*

His first instinct said "Mia's," but even Cupid could not be that selfish. Mia was the one relationship he'd gotten right (in the end). If the gods were keeping tally—and they always were—Cupid needed to keep that point on the scoreboard.

He considered contacting Gail, but her home had never been an option before, and it certainly wasn't one now. Cheri was tempting, but Cupid knew better than to rub fresh salt into that open wound if he hoped to have any chance of repairing his rift with Pan. The logical choice was the hotel where he and Gail had rendezvoused, or any number of other hotels in the downtown area, but the idea of a cold, lonely, anonymous room left Cupid with an ache his heart would not survive.

There were other fallen deities living across town where Pan had stored Cupid's supplies. Pan could have set him up in an apartment there. *Why didn't he?*

A bright spark of hope flared inside him. Perhaps Pan knew their rift would be short-lived. *"I will be in touch,"* he'd written. Either that or—

Cupid rubbed his chest as the more likely explanation occurred to him: Cupid wasn't worth relocating because he'd be gone soon enough. Little did Pan know, Ruthie's marriage had deteriorated, if anything. Yes, Cupid had figured out the two Worthies he was supposed to bring together, and yes, they were already married to each other, but did Cupid have any clue how to bring them to their Liminal Point? Not a one.

But say, by some miracle of luck and love, Cupid did sort them out. Say the gods were pleased with Cupid, and they returned him to Mount Olympus. How could he and Pan ever repair their friendship from the distance of two different worlds when their hearts were so far apart now? How could Cupid put his whole heart into fulfilling his mission when success would bring him so much more pain? What would happen to all of them if he failed Ruthie and Zach as friendship and love seemed to have failed Cupid?

A howl of despair escaped him and bounced off the walls of his car. Time to go.

Cupid started the engine. Utterly lost and alone, he waited for his heart or his car to guide him. *Nothing.*

"Tell me where you would have me go," he wailed to anyone who might be listening.

Craning his neck toward the upper edge of the windshield, Cupid cast his eyes to the sky and watched, transfixed, as the veil of evening turned to night, and milky blurs of light sharpened before his eyes. The constellations were so much clearer on Mount O, but there was no mistaking the familiar head of Taurus, the symbol of fertility and power.

Much could be said about Zeus—the more outrageous, the more likely the story was true—but the Ruler of the gods wasn't afraid to go after what He wanted. If that meant turning Himself into a bull and mingling with the herds of Europa's father to attract the girl's attention, He barely gave a second thought. Of course, Zeus almost always won the girl, and here was proof of His undying love—His gift to Europa, a constellation to live eternally in the night sky.

A motivated god was a force. How hard would it have been for Aphrodite to send Mercury down with a simple message? An "I miss you" or "I love you" would have gone a long way in those first days after the fall. Cupid told himself it didn't matter; at the ripe old age of three thousand, give or take a few years, he'd surely outgrown his need for Mother's affection. And yet, he couldn't help but feel like an abandoned child.

Without realizing it, Cupid had set his car on course for Ruthie's. How was it fair that Aphrodite could discard a child without a care, when Ruthie, a woman who'd wanted to be a mother so very desperately, had been tragically denied three times? How fickle were the Fates, how merciless the Divine Council.

With a full head of righteous steam, Cupid parked his car in the Millers' driveway, same as he'd done every morning for the last two and a half weeks, heaved the trash bag of belongings over his shoulder, and approached their back door.

26

INTRUSION

The motion-sensitive floodlight came on, reminding Cupid of the first time he'd dropped by Ruthie's home uninvited. Would tonight's arrival be any more welcome?

He announced himself with a firm knock on the glass—enough to set Pookie off, which, in turn, triggered Zach's sharp, "Hush, Pookie!"

A pitter-patter crossed the room and skipped down the back staircase. Pookie tumbled down the stairs first, eager to have a catch with her new playmate. Zach's slippers came into view, then gray sweatpants, a college T-shirt, and Zach's wary expression as he squinted at Cupid through the door.

Cupid gave Zach a friendly wave. It didn't help. Zach looked confused, then *pissed*, as Pan would say. Zach opened the door but blocked the entrance with his whole body.

A terrible storm churned up from the bottom of Cupid's stomach. "I'm so sorry, I—don't know what I'm doing here."

"What *are* you doing here? Construction emergency? Did Ruthie *call* you here?" Zach grew agitated, checking over his own shoulder for Ruthie and over Cupid's shoulder, for an army, perhaps.

"No!" Cupid threw his hands up to try to slow Zach's momentum. The bag slid to the ground. Zach eyed it and Cupid with great misgiving.

"Little early for Santa Claus, isn't it?"

"I guess." Cupid had no energy for humor. "I'm truly sorry to disturb your evening. Do you think I might speak with Ruthie? *Please?*"

Zach scowled at him for several eternal seconds while Cupid valiantly attempted to appear less like a bedraggled off-duty carpenter lugging around all his belongings in a garbage bag. "I know all about you," Zach announced finally.

Cupid's mouth went dry. "Excuse me?"

"There aren't many Quentins in Tarra." A self-satisfied smile settled on Zach's face. "You are quite the hero, Mr. Arrows."

"Oh. *That.*"

Zach's eyebrows arched high into his forehead. "You're hiding something else?"

"No. Of course not," Cupid spluttered. "I wasn't hiding that either. I just don't like to draw attention to myself."

"Right." Zach frowned as if disappointed not to have a reason to turn Cupid away. He stepped out of Cupid's path and waved him inside with all the hospitality of the Minotaur receiving his next tribute into the labyrinth. "Wait here."

Pookie yipped at Zach's retreating slippers but made no move to leave Cupid's side. Inordinately grateful for the affection, Cupid crouched to scratch her ears. Their love fest was disturbed by a rising argument upstairs.

"How do you know he's not some bum living out of his car?"

"So what if he is, Zach? He's doing a great job. You've seen for yourself, *remember?*"

"Then tell me what he's doing here now, showing up like a beggar in the night."

"I don't know. Here's an idea. Why don't I ask him?" Ruthie's voice, short and clipped, was barely recognizable.

What was Cupid thinking, coming here like this? This fight was entirely his fault. How would he even begin to explain to Ruthie what he was doing here?

"*Jesus,* Ruthie. Can't you see? He's using you . . . *and* Gail."

"Using us for what, exactly?"

"Come on, Ruthie. Set aside your wild fantasies for one goddamn second and ask yourself what a young, good-looking guy like that would want with a couple of middle-aged women."

Cupid listened into the terrible silence. Ruthie was either too sad or too angry to respond. Cupid strained his ears for a whisper, a sob, any clue of Ruthie's emotional state. His heart pounded for her with so much love and pain, he could hardly distinguish one from the other, but Cupid's wasn't the only heart beating.

Louder than their words and their awful silence, Ruthie and Zach's heartbeats echoed as powerfully and unmistakably each other's as ever. At least Cupid hadn't managed to mess that up—yet. If he snuck away now . . .

No, that would be the coward's way out. Besides, the damage was done. He couldn't leave Ruthie like this.

The floor creaked with hasty footsteps. Ruthie's slippers appeared. Cupid rose on wobbly legs, unsure how much of the overheard argument to acknowledge. His heart twisted when her tear-streaked face came into view.

"I am so sorry, Ruthie. I didn't mean to create problems for you."

"Never mind him," Ruthie said with a dismissive wave. Her gaze ran up and down his body. "Are you okay? Come in."

She didn't wait for Cupid to answer before leading him inside. Cupid slogged up the stairs behind her, dragging the sack of clothes he wished he'd left in the car.

"Here. Sit."

Cupid had walked past this room every day, coming and going, but this was the first time he'd entered the space. The room radiated Ruthie's brand of warmth—soothing natural tones, soft fabrics, inviting seats that faced other seats—not like Pan's, where everything faced the TV. Like the rest of their home, this room was neat to the point of looking uninhabited, except for the electronic device and half-full drink on the table in front of the couch, where Zach must have been sitting, watching TV, before Cupid's untimely arrival. Cupid made sure to choose a different chair.

"What can I get you to drink?"

"Nothing, I'm—" He was thirsty. And hungry. He'd been so focused on the fighting and the heartbeats, Cupid had failed to notice the mouthwatering smells coming from the kitchen. Had he eaten anything today? "I'd love a glass of water, actually. If you don't mind."

"Be right back." She looked at him through sad eyes as she left him there. They both could use a hug, he thought.

His gaze followed her to the kitchen, where Zach stood with his arms crossed, watching Cupid as if he were a common thief. He wished he had the right words to assure Zach he hadn't come to steal from them, but Earthlings were mistrustful, and it seemed to Cupid that those who had the most were often the ones who trusted the least.

"Here you go," Ruthie said gently, handing him a tall glass of ice water as she sat down in the chair beside his. She waited for Cupid to take a long drink, not asking any questions, not demanding any answers.

"Thank you," he said, for both the water and the time to gather his thoughts. "I'm sorry for interrupting your dinner," Cupid said again.

"Please stop apologizing. Have you eaten yet?"

"No." There was no way he could have pulled off a lie, especially when his belly gave a loud rumble. Ruthie's lips curled into a gentle smile.

"You'll join us for dinner, then."

It wasn't a question, and Cupid was in no position to refuse. He softly thanked Ruthie, avoiding Zach's glare as if meeting it might turn Cupid to stone.

She leaned in, closing Zach out of their discussion. "What happened to you, Quentin? Why did you come here?"

"I made a mistake. A bad one." Cupid swallowed the lump in his throat. Ruthie would surely think less of him once she learned what he'd done. "With a woman."

"*Gail?*"

"No, I'm not seeing Gail anymore."

"Oh." Ruthie looked visibly relieved. At least Cupid had made one good decision.

"You remember my friend Pan? From the club?"

"The burly redhead?"

"That's the one. Well, I, uh, went to see Pan's . . ." Cupid refused to repeat the disgusting term Pan had used, but he didn't know what else to call it. "They had sex a few times, but I guess I wasn't supposed to—"

"I thought Pan was gay."

"Pan's a bit of everything."

A faint blush edged up Ruthie's cheeks. "Oh."

"Anyway, we had a horrible fight over it. He's kicked me out, and I'm not sure he's going to forgive me. Ever." Saying it out loud lent an air of finality that broke Cupid's heart all over again.

"Oh no. I'm sorry to hear it." Ruthie wrung her hands together in her lap. Cupid could tell she wanted to reach out and comfort him, and he wanted that, too, but not with Zach standing in the next room shooting daggers at the two of them. "You two have been friends a long time, right?"

"Yes."

"Well, I'm sure you'll work it out. Until then, you'll stay here," she added without hesitation. "We have a whole wing that goes unused fifty weeks out of the year."

Zach cleared his throat. Ruthie shot him a look Cupid had seen Aphrodite use countless times on Hephaestus: *I will not be intimidated.*

Zach rolled his eyes and blew out an exasperated breath. "By all means," he said, sweeping his arms open with huge drama, "stay as long as you want, *Henry*."

Ruthie's mouth dropped open. She stood suddenly and clapped her hands together. "Why don't I show you to your room, and you can settle in?"

Cupid had rather liked her suggestion of eating dinner, but a change of clothes first was probably a wise plan. Ruthie rose and walked past Zach without looking at him, and Cupid picked up his bag once again and followed, head down, until they reached the front stairs.

"I shouldn't have come here," he said. "The last thing I wanted to do was put you in a rough spot."

Ruthie climbed the stairs, face forward, shoulders squared. "That wasn't really about you."

"Would it help if I talk to your husband?"

Ruthie shook her head and tried to chuckle, but what came out held no mirth. "Thanks, but no."

"I'll find somewhere else to stay tomorrow." How bad could a hotel be? "I promise."

"Don't be silly. We have the space." Ruthie continued down a hallway Cupid had not explored before, set away from the rest of the living quarters. She opened a door, and an entire world revealed itself: a huge bedroom with its own bathroom and kitchen area and a separate sitting area with a sofa and TV, and shelves overstuffed with unruly stacks of paperbacks and hardcover books.

"Wow. These are all the books for your new study."

"I'll probably leave the nonfiction behind." Ruthie crossed her elbows over her chest and rubbed her upper arms. "It's a little chilly in here. You can adjust the temperature however you like."

Cupid dropped the bag next to the bed as he looked around in wonder. Paintings as beautiful as anywhere else in the house covered the walls. Elegant draperies adorned floor-to-ceiling windows. Plush carpet gave way under his heavy boots. "This place is a palace."

Ruthie laughed for real this time. "I don't know about that, but it works. We wouldn't want to make Zach's parents too comfortable. They might never leave."

I might never leave.

Ruthie seemed to read his thoughts. "Feel free to make yourself at home. Put your clothes in the drawers. There are towels and soap and shampoo in the bathroom."

Her kindness was almost unbearable. They were standing too close to each other, too close to the bed, awkwardly restraining themselves from the physical contact Cupid craved and sensed Ruthie did as well.

"Thank you, Ruthie. I can't tell you how much I appreciate this."

Their eyes met for a brief, charged moment before Ruthie waved away his thank-you and started for the door. "You can come down for dinner whenever you want. I'll fix you a plate. You don't have to sit with my grumpy husband."

"Hey, that reminds me," Cupid said. "Who's Henry?"

"Oh." She halted just outside the door as if her feet had suddenly grown roots. "Nobody. Just one of my characters."

Hmm, this was getting interesting. Cupid had been dying to learn more about Ruthie's writing ever since she'd changed the topic in the diner. "What kind of character?"

"Oh, uh, he-might-be-a-handyman."

"A *romantic* handyman?" Cupid grinned. Ruthie blushed. "I'd really love to read that story."

"I don't think so."

"Okay, fine. I'll read anything you've written. It doesn't have to be about me." He gave her a wink.

"You probably weren't even alive when I wrote that."

It was working. Ruthie was loosening up.

"I'm older than I look, Ruthie."

"Whatever."

Cupid took a chance and ambled ever so slowly toward Ruthie. He leaned against the doorjamb, careful not to brush his shoulder against the silver box mounted at an angle. Cupid couldn't afford to anger any more gods.

"So, what do I have to do to get you to share that story with me?"

Ruthie shook her head, but a slow grin stretched across her face. He had her now.

"Okay, fine, you can read it. After I edit out the juicy parts."

Great Zeus! The handyman's tale had juicy parts? Had Ruthie been thinking about that story while she watched Cupid work?

"*No!* You can't!"

"Goodbye, Quentin."

She wouldn't have believed him, but Cupid could have sworn Ruthie looked ten years younger than she had before this conversation started. Cupid wondered if Zach would notice. And then he wondered if that would be a good thing.

27

FIXER UPPER

Ruth paused outside the room that was no longer a nursery but not quite her study, admiring the meticulous stroke of Quentin's brush along the edge of the windowsill. The man was a perfectionist. A perfect perfectionist.

She knocked lightly. "Good morning."

Quentin smiled at Ruth and waved her into the room. "I'm glad you're here. What do you think about the Linen White trim?" He took a few steps back to examine his work alongside her.

"I think it looks great, especially with the morning sun streaming in." She might actually be able to keep a plant or two alive in here.

"I agree. Glad you're happy, Ruthie."

This room made her happy, anyway. "I just popped in to invite you to come down for a cup of coffee and some breakfast."

"Oh." Quentin rubbed his belly as if he hadn't considered eating until she'd mentioned food. "That's sweet, but I'm fine. I can get something when I'm through for the day."

"Through? That's three meals from now."

Quentin chuckled. "I don't really get hungry while I'm working."

At times like these, Ruth wondered about the boy's mother. "Good thing I reminded you to eat, then. Zach's not here. It's just me and the ferocious watchdog." Ruth jerked her chin toward the dozing dog curled up by the window. In another life, Ruth would gladly curl up and snooze at Quentin's feet all day. All night.

"She's good company."

"Let me feed you something, please. I'm Jewish. It goes against my DNA to let anyone go hungry under my roof."

"Actually, a quick bowl of cereal might be nice." Quentin set the brush across the top of the paint can and followed Ruth downstairs. Pookie trotted after them.

"Coffee's made." Ruth filled the waiting mug on the counter while Quentin checked his phone, then stuffed it into his pocket. "No word from Pan?"

"Not yet." Quentin wrapped his hands around the mug and brought it to his lips. "*Mmm.*"

"Cream or sugar?"

"No, thank you. You don't have to wait on me."

She pulled out the least fibrous cereal choices from the cabinet, placed a bowl and spoon down next to them, and reached into the refrigerator for the milk. "I'll stop if you promise to help yourself."

Quentin took the hint. He chose a box and poured some cereal into the bowl. "So . . . how was everything this morning?"

"You mean is Zach still being an ass?"

Quentin grabbed the milk and turned away so she couldn't see the smile he was doing a poor job of hiding.

"He left before my alarm went off, but that's not unusual. I'm hoping the three of us can sit down to a civilized meal tonight."

"I think it might be better for everyone if I just stay out of his way."

"I want you to feel at home here. That reminds me, what kind of snack foods should I pick up for you? Do you like a cold beer at the end of the workday?" Zach never had, but Ruth was game to provide whatever Quentin needed—*foodwise.*

"I am not a fan of beer," he said, tucking into his cereal as if to banish the taste of the imagined beer. "Please don't worry about feeding me. I have a credit card and a car, and that microwave and refrigerator upstairs will be more than enough for me."

"*Ohhhh*, I get it. You don't like my cooking."

His huff made Ruth smile. "What? No. I loved your barbecue chicken last night. I just don't want to make any more trouble for you. I should get back to work. Thank you again for breakfast."

He wolfed down another couple of spoonfuls, tipped back the rest of his coffee, and placed his dishes in the dishwasher. Even performing the most mundane human activities, Quentin moved through the kitchen with an elegant ease and subdued strength that sent Ruth's head reeling to that other space she'd been fighting so hard to ignore: *What's going on under those bulky coveralls?*

Shame on you, Ruthie. Objectifying is so, so wrong.

—True, but I admire so much more than his body.

As if that makes it better. This man is a guest in your home.

—Yes, a ridiculously hot guest, showering just down the hall . . .

Quentin tapped her computer monitor on his way out, popping her internal dialogue like soap bubbles. "Don't forget, Ruthie, I'm waiting for our love story."

"I was kind of hoping you'd forgotten about that." In fact, Ruth hadn't hoped that at all.

Quentin turned back and shot Ruth a panty-poofing grin.

"I never lie, and I never forget." And just because her heart was still beating, though barely, Quentin zapped her with a killer wink.

She debated—*should I or shouldn't I?*—for all of ten seconds before her decision was made. It had been almost two years since Ruth had written *Fixer Upper*, before she'd learned the perils of dialogue tags and nuances of narrative voice, but she still genuinely liked this story—probably because she loved the Henry she'd created so much.

Fixer Upper weighed in at fifteen thousand words, one of her heftier stories. Ruth knew exactly where to find the racier passages—both inside her characters' imaginations and after, when all erotic hell broke loose around the three-quarters mark—and she searched and destroyed without mercy. Where the chunks removed were too large to easily substitute with something tame, Ruth simply dropped in an ellipsis and left Quentin to fill in the blanks.

After the most egregious scenes were sanitized, Ruth searched for incriminating mentions of body parts, any and all conjugations of "fuck," and overly dramatic gazes, kisses, or touches. She couldn't help tinkering a bit with the phrasing, but she didn't allow herself to go overboard with nitpicks. Once she'd finished all her edits and saved the file under a new name, "FU4Q," she reread the whole story from the beginning.

It was . . . awful. And it barely resembled her story. The exercise had proven what Ruth had always hoped: the sex scenes were not gratuitous but integral to the story. Take away the graphic bits, and you lost Henry's sheer joy in expressing himself physically, the unhurried tenderness in every touch, and the way his sense of humor bridged the awkwardness of their first time. Without that, he was a watered-down, one-dimensional cliché. Is that how she wanted Quentin to experience her writing?

Screw it. Before her better judgment could overrule her brash decision, Ruth printed out the original, unabridged story, punched holes, and snapped the pages inside a bright red binder. She floated upstairs with all the wild anticipation of hitting the "Post" button—for an audience of one this time.

At the doorway of the former nursery, Ruth's hands extended the binder toward Quentin as if she no longer controlled her own limbs. "I can't really believe I'm doing this, but . . ."

Quentin's attention shifted to Ruth, his eyes lit with glee. He dropped the paintbrush into the open can and jogged toward her as if he, too, recognized Ruth's reckless offering might be retracted at any moment. Holding Ruth in his gaze, he gently pried the plastic binder from her grip. A rush of giddy pleasure washed over her as Quentin flipped open the cover.

A smile spread across his cheeks as he read aloud: "Thea should have turned tail and run from the dilapidated house, but there was something about the ramshackle exterior that drew her in. 'Needs a little TLC,' the real estate agent said. Maybe Thea did, too."

"Whoa there, pal. You're gonna have to read this to yourself . . . after I get far, far away."

He chuckled but respected her wishes. "How do you expect me to get any work done when I know Thea and Henry are waiting for me?"

"Should I hold on to this for you until 4:01?" Ruth made to grab it from him, but Quentin tucked the binder tight against his side.

"*Ohhh* no. There is zero chance I'm letting this story out of my sight." With the utmost reverence, he cleared a space on his worktable and set it down. "It'll stay right there until I'm done with my work for the day"—he turned to waggle his eyebrows at Ruth—"and then Henry, Thea, and I are gonna get busy."

Ruth moaned into her hands. "You have to promise me we will never, *ever*, discuss this." The die was cast; Ruth turned to leave.

"Ruthie."

"Hmm?"

"Thank you for trusting me. It means a lot to me."

28

HONEY-DO

The moment the garlic reached Cupid's nose, he knew he'd made a grave mistake. There was no chance his slab of meatloaf from the prepared foods case could possibly compete with whatever Ruthie had simmering on the stove. Nevertheless, he'd made a promise to stay out of Zach's way, and Cupid was a god of his word—but, *curses*, did Ruthie have to cook spaghetti tonight? It made his mouth water.

He buried his sigh in the brown paper grocery bag and bounded up the garage stairs into the kitchen. There stood Ruthie with her back to him, angled over a pair of thick loaves splayed open on the counter like a girl with her skirt pushed up too high. Ruthie's shoulders dipped and swayed with the rhythm of the brush, slathering the surface of the bread with the pungent spread. Above the music pouring through the ceiling speakers, a sweet sound arose—a singing voice so carefree and uninhibited, Cupid was shocked to realize it was coming from Ruthie.

She had never let down her guard like this in front of Cupid, and she would surely be mortified to know he'd caught her unawares. *Let me just witness this beautiful abandon a few more seconds,* he gambled, but the risk of discovery quickly overtook his selfish inclinations.

As if just cresting over the top step, Cupid trod forward heavily, adding extra ruckus by crinkling the paper bag cradled in his arm. "Something sure smells good in here," he called out over the music.

Ruthie spun around. "You're back. That was quick."

Cupid plunged his hand into the bag and presented Ruthie with a bunch of orange tulips wrapped in cellophane. "These are for you. A small token of my appreciation for letting me stay here."

Back to her carefully composed self, Ruthie busied her fingers with the cheery yellow ribbon tied around the stems. "You didn't have to do that."

"It doesn't feel like nearly enough, to be honest. If you can think of other ways I might repay you and Zach for your hospitality—finish up any other projects around the house, put a fresh coat of paint somewhere, build shelves—I'd really like to do that. Obviously, your study is my top priority. Anything else would take place after my workday is finished."

Ruthie pulled the bouquet to her chest. "Oh, Quentin, you don't have to sing for your supper." His singing voice was nowhere near as lovely as Ruthie's, but he couldn't tell her how he knew that. "You're our guest."

A guest. *Right.* No doubt, Ruthie had intended to make Cupid feel welcome, but her choice of words reminded him in no uncertain terms this wasn't his home. Ruthie was neither his wife nor his mother. Cupid was a visitor in this house—on this planet, in fact—and he had a vital job to do.

"If you'll excuse me, I'm going to head upstairs. I'll see you in the morning, Ruthie." Her wistful gaze followed him out of the kitchen.

Tucked away in his spacious suite, Cupid closed the door, as if the potent swirl of home and hearth could somehow be barred from entry. He filed away his groceries, setting aside one of the red apples. He checked his phone one last time before giving up on hearing from Pan for another day.

Cupid's self-inflicted solitude did provide one consolation: he could now freely dive into Ruthie's story without fear of interruption. He rubbed the apple on his sleeve until it gleamed, took the binder from his nightstand, and sank into the deep armchair.

"Needs a little TLC," the real estate agent said. Maybe Thea did, too.

There it was, right there on page one, impossible to miss: Ruthie's cry for help. Could he bear to read the rest?

Cupid sighed, lifting his eyes from the words. If he could see through the ceiling and roof, would he find answers in the clouds? Who better than the God of Love himself could solve the puzzle of how to put this couple back together?

He bit into the apple and slurped up the sweet juices. The apple tried its best to curb Cupid's hunger, but a mere piece of fruit could no more be expected to satisfy the craving inspired by the aroma of Ruthie's homemade Bolognese than the occasional, brief conversation with Ruthie could satisfy Cupid's cravings of the heart. He sank his teeth into the soft apple flesh again and again until there was no more to consume, and still, he was famished. Putting his hope in the meatloaf, Cupid rose from the recliner and crossed the room toward the kitchenette.

Downstairs, a door opened and closed. A pair of voices rose and fell beneath the din of Ruthie's playlist. Zach was home early, and Cupid had a feeling he might be the reason.

Eavesdropping lived on that thin line between honesty and deceit. For the sake of his mission, Cupid forced his attention to the conversation downstairs.

"Everything is fine. Can't a guy leave work at five?"

"Of course. It's a lovely surprise."

"Flowers? Do I even need to ask?" *Was that irritation in Zach's voice?*

"He's just expressing his gratitude, Zach. He feels terrible for causing a fight."

"We're not fighting." *Squeak, squeak, squeak, pop!* "Can I pour you a glass?"

"Thanks."

"It smells amazing in here, by the way."

"I can have dinner on the table in fifteen minutes."

"Should I set the table for three?" Zach's tone was unreadable.

"No. He's keeping to himself."

Drawers opening and closing. The clink of plates and silverware. "At least when I'm home."

Ice cubes falling into a tumbler. The whir of the water dispenser.

"He asked me for a list of odd jobs he could do around the house. He feels guilty for imposing, wants to pay us back the only way he knows how."

"You should do it, Ruthie. Make him a list. A man needs his pride." *An accusation lobbed at his wife?*

Table-setting noises were replaced by the clang of pots and pans, *tap-tap-tap* of a knife on the chopping board, the buzz of the timer.

"Dinner's ready."

Dinner—as if Cupid's belly needed the reminder. He spooned the mashed potatoes onto a plastic plate, slid the cold, gray slab of molded meat on top, and slipped the plate inside the little oven. The rattle and hum of the microwave muted the voices downstairs to where Cupid could barely make out their conversation without straining, and that suited him fine. He'd heard enough civil discourse between husband and wife to eat his dinner without worrying about the imminent collapse of their marriage.

He set the binder open on the small dining table and tucked into both story and meal. *Oh, Ruthie.* It was no wonder she'd spent so much time blushing in Cupid's presence. By the end of chapter three, Thea had inspired a burning physical desire that was overpowered only by Cupid's need to learn Ruthie's mind. He finished off his meal, pushed the dishes aside, and dragged the words closer.

Henry's perspective was no less tame, Cupid was delighted to learn. The fictional fix-it man had a thing for *cougars*, the term Gail had used to describe herself.

A soft knock at the door pulled Cupid out of the story. "Quentin?"

He closed his finger inside the binder to mark his spot, stood, and opened the door. Despite a vivid description of Thea quite distinct from the woman standing in front of him, Cupid realized he'd read every word of the story with Ruthie in mind—her gentle smile, her melancholy eyes, her fiercely restrained passion. He stared for a beat longer than usual while, right before his eyes, Thea merged with the Ruthie familiar to him.

"Hello, Ruthie."

Ruthie gave him a puzzled look, then seeing the binder in Cupid's hand, blushed madly. "Oh boy."

He had a hundred questions, but remembering their pact, Cupid eyed the slice of pie Ruthie was holding and asked simply, "Is that for me?"

"Oh. Yes. Here."

"Thank you. It looks delicious," he said, setting the pie down on the table. "Would you like to come in?"

"Just for a second. Zach and I discussed your offer, and we decided to give you this. Only because you asked." She pulled a sheet of paper from her pocket and unfolded it. "I can go over these with you tomorrow if you'd like."

Kitchen faucet leaks.
Laundry rm door sticks.
Light bulbs – basement . . .

"Thank you, Ruthie."

"Also, this." She handed Cupid a slip of paper with his name and $4,000.

"Oh. No, I couldn't possibly take your money for fixing these things. That's the whole point. It's a gift to repay your hospitality."

"I'm sorry I wasn't clear. This check is for the study."

"But you've already paid for my supplies."

"It's a progress payment. You're nearly finished. It's the least we can do."

"Ruthie, I don't want—"

"Hush. It's either take the money or start eating my cooking."

"Oh, gods, no." He swooped away the check and folded it into his pocket. Teasing aside, Cupid had earned a paycheck for the first time in his life, and it felt good. Besides, he owed Pan for that wine.

Ruthie glanced once more at the binder before turning away. "Have a relaxing evening, now."

Fixer Upper was more agitating than relaxing, but hearing Cupid say so would only embarrass Ruthie further. "See you in the morning, Ruthie."

When Saturday morning rolled around, Cupid found himself

in a quandary about what to wear. His weekday coveralls seemed a bit extreme for changing a lightbulb. Luckily, since his clothes were mostly brand new, even his T-shirts and jeans were respectable enough for hanging around the Millers'.

Thanks to Jagger's casual morning-after strutting, Cupid knew to keep his face out of Zach's first cup of coffee. The laundry room project would do, well out of the way and not loud enough to disturb anyone downstairs. Cupid spread a clean drop cloth and set to work on the hinges. He should have known Pookie would find him, yapping and jumping at Cupid's ankles as he grabbed the door with both hands and lifted.

"Hey, girl. Watch out, now. Don't wanna clomp you on the head." He set the door down, carefully avoiding tiny paws. Pookie took Cupid's empty hands as an invitation to play. She made him laugh, nuzzling her nose right up into his crotch and running back for more each time he tossed her away. Best not to get too attached, Cupid reminded himself with a sigh.

Pookie watched with great interest as the plane swept across the bottom edge of the door, sending thin curls of wood onto the cloth. When Cupid was certain he'd worked off enough, he set the door back into its hinges, tested the swing, and tightened up the screws.

Pookie sniffed at the edges of the cloth, prancing in circles—dead giveaway. "Need to go out, girl? C'mon!" He jogged down the stairs and into the kitchen with Pookie tumbling along beside him.

Zach looked up from the device resting on the counter and attempted a smile. "Morning."

Cupid wanted to ask where Ruthie was but didn't want to risk upsetting the peace. "Morning. Okay if I take Pookie out?"

"Sure. Thank you."

"No problem."

Pookie quickly located an acceptable patch of grass, did her business, and dragged the Frisbee over to Cupid. She was an excellent diversion, this little furball. Cupid could have tossed that Frisbee all morning, and she would have happily obliged. It was easier staying out here than indoors where Zach was, but Cupid had work to do.

By the time Cupid wandered back through the kitchen, Zach was gone, replaced by Ruthie, typing away at her desk. "Morning."

She spun around, hand on her heart. "Oh! You scared me."

"Sorry, I'll make more noise next time." He glanced at the computer screen. "Working on our sequel?" Before she could answer with more than a blush, Cupid winked and jogged up the stairs.

Cupid's least favorite of all the odd jobs was changing the basement bulbs. Not that he had a problem with a six-foot ladder or the mechanics of screwing in a bulb, but the fixtures didn't want to hold still in the flimsy ceiling. Every time Cupid knocked one of the tiles askew, a shower of dust and dead insects rained down on his head. At the sound of Ruthie's footsteps, he tried to shake the dirt out of his hair, but there was no way to avoid looking as if he'd spent the afternoon toiling at Hephaestus's furnace.

"Oh, dear. Is everything okay down here?"

"Was there an earthquake recently?"

Ruthie giggled. "Not that I'm aware. Sorry it's such a mess."

"It's fine. I'm almost done, and I plan to have a long, hot shower."

Something wicked flashed behind Ruthie's eyes, and Cupid got a quick glimpse of Thea and that shower scene in chapter four he'd read three times last night—just to make sure he had all his facts straight.

"I hope you don't feel like you have to work all day again tomorrow. Even God took a day off."

Cupid harrumphed. The gods barely worked at all. "I'm going to bring all your shelving and cabinetry over so it's ready to install first thing Monday morning."

"You're getting close," Ruthie said. Did he detect a note of sadness, or had Cupid layered his own emotions onto her words?

"Yeah, I should be done by the end of next week."

"Where will you go next?"

As if he had a clue. Would he ascend? Would Pan take him back? Would he be exiled to the South Side to live alone in one of the anonymous apartments?

"I'm not sure. It's not your problem, Ruthie, but thanks for worrying about me."

"You know, someone is always renovating something around here. Kitchens, bathrooms, basements . . . I can get you more work than you could handle. I can't promise your next customers will provide you a room though."

No, the last place he wanted to be was down the street from Ruthie. "That's kind of you, but I think I should try my luck in a different neighborhood."

"Different neighborhood, same story. Trust me, I've invented enough to know truth really is stranger than fiction."

"Speaking of truth and fiction, do most handymen work without their shirts on? Have I been doing it wrong?"

Ruthie folded her arms across her chest and swiftly changed the subject. "Zach and I are about to head out for dinner and a movie."

"Have a nice time." He wanted her to. He needed her to. And yet, *ouch.*

"There's leftover spaghetti in the fridge, and I made you a fresh salad."

"You didn't have to do that."

She shrugged. "Can't really help it. You know, you don't have to stay locked in your tower. Feel free to watch TV in the family room if you like."

Cupid chuckled. "Oh no, you don't. I have my evening's entertainment all lined up. Chapter eight: Power Tools, if I'm not mistaken?" He winked a very Henry wink, which she answered with a very Ruthie blush.

"Good night, Quentin," Ruthie said.

29

THE FUTURE

"You look like shit."

"Happy Monday to you too, Joan." Today was going to be a long damn day to start a long damn week.

"You, sir, require coffee." *Click, click, click.* Off she went on her serious shoes.

Zach spun his chair to face the windows. The sky was clear as a bell, but Zach couldn't see much beyond his immediate surroundings lately.

He walked to the east-facing window and pressed his forehead to the cool glass. Bigger *was* better; more money meant more centers, not for personal glory but for the families they served. To repair the world. Wasn't *Tikkun Olam* the whole damn point, or had the bright light of Zach's ambition blinded him to what was real and right in front of his nose?

They'd talked about this all along, he and Ruthie, taking the playspace concept to the biggest possible market, synergies, leverage. Eventually, their shared vision would move them to that bright, shiny life glittering in the distance—culture, diversity, opportunity. Ruthie had cheerfully and faithfully supported the cause and her husband though she'd never fully embraced the concept of moving. As the vision materialized into bricks and mortar, more bricks and more mortar, Ruthie seemed less and less excited to have that conversation. So yes, it had been a while since the topic had intruded on their day-to-day, and if Ruthie had maybe started to believe the expansions were going to continue without impacting their life in Tarra Heights, Zach hadn't felt particularly inclined to upset her apple cart—and hence, his own.

Click, click, click.

Joan crossed straight to the windows with his coffee. Boundaries never much concerned her.

"Splash of cream, one Splenda." Observant, that one.

"Thank you," Zach said, turning back to the present.

"More trouble with Bob the builder?" All *too* observant.

"Ah, you mean *Henry* the handyman."

"Henry?"

Zach had spilled more than he'd meant to; he wasn't about to out his wife to Joan. "Did I mention he is now our boarder? Well, not exactly a boarder—that would imply he's paying rent. He's more like a really hot exchange student." Zach also hadn't meant to explode in sarcasm, but damn, a little edge of cruelty felt good, if he were being honest.

"What? Why would you let him move in with you?"

"That is a long story."

"Give me the Twitter version."

Zach smirked, sipped his coffee, and attempted to gain some control over his runaway mouth. "Hashtag: my wife is a softie." Which made Zach the hard-ass.

In fact, he was starting to feel like the warden in his own home. Quentin stayed holed up in his room. When he occasionally popped his head out for air or to take Pookie out or to work off an item on Zach's neglected honey-do list, Quentin and Ruthie would talk in that same careless way she and Zach used to, as if the two of them were continuing a conversation with no beginning and no end. Eventually, one or the other of them would sneak a guilty glance at Zach, and Quentin's prison yard time would come to an abrupt end.

They were all trapped. Only leaving the house offered any measure of relief, but now all Zach could think about was what the two of them were doing in his absence.

"Anyway, bottom line, I haven't been sleeping very well."

"How much longer till the home improvement project is done?"

"He's finishing up the trim and installing the shelves. He'll hook up the computer, move the books and files, and then hopefully, he is out by Friday."

"Hopefully?"

Shit. How had Zach gotten caught in this twisted replay of Saturday night's argument with his wife? He'd finally coaxed Ruthie out of the house, and how had he used their alone time? To pick a fight with her about how Quentin seemed to be vying for a permanent position as their houseboy. Her answers had been vague and unsatisfying, to say the least, but they were also none of Joan's goddamn business.

"Let's move on, shall we?"

Joan, every bit the intuitive woman Zach admired, wisely changed course. "By Thursday at noon, we'll have DC locked up, and we'll *all* be moving out. I've been googling homes in Potomac. We should stay an extra day and have a broker show us around the area on Friday."

Zach's gut twisted. "Don't you think you should wait to count your chickens?"

"By failing to prepare, you are preparing to fail." Zach rolled his eyes as hard as he could, to which Joan responded with a tilt of her head, "Benjamin Franklin."

"Isn't there a quote about planning for success but preparing for failure?"

"You know, you're really depressing lately. This"—she waved as if she might be able to make this unappetizing version of Zach disappear—"isn't the man we need to put in front of the board. How are we going to fix you before Thursday?"

"Hmph. Maybe I should sleep here tonight." Zach started to laugh, then worried he might not be able to stop. "Hell, they'd probably like that."

"You don't really think there's something going on between them, do you?"

"Something physical? No, of course not. Ruthie would never be disloyal, even if the guy is a constant source of temptation." A flicker of intrigue passed behind Joan's eyes, arousing in Zach an inexplicable spike of jealousy. Was he losing his damn mind?

"So, what are you worried about?" she asked. "Doesn't matter where she gets her appetite as long as she eats at home, right?" Joan tossed in a wink she probably meant to lighten the mood, and perhaps it would have worked if Ruthie's last "meal with Zach" had been more than a compulsory anniversary screw, and not a particularly inspired one at that.

"You're a walking *Bartlett's Quotations* today."

"Sorry, motivation isn't exactly my area of expertise. I'm trying here."

"I know you are. I appreciate it. I'm sorry I've been so morose." Zach exhaled heavily and dropped his face into his hands.

"*Zach?*" The tremor in Joan's voice shook him.

"What?"

"You *do* want the Glover grant, right?"

"Of course I do. It's absolutely the next logical step for Brighter Tomorrows."

"And for you as well, no?"

"Sure." Not that Zach was entirely sure that mattered anymore. Langston had climbed out on a limb, agreeing to let this unknown regional fledgling company make their case to the board. As he'd made clear early on to Zach, they weren't about to throw money at Brighter Tomorrows without securing the hotshot CEO and his dynamo of a fundraiser.

Maybe Zach had fooled himself as much as he'd fooled Ruthie, believing that once they reached this point, momentum would carry them both right across the finish line. Ruthie would see there was nothing holding her here, not really. No family, no kids in school, no job to tie her down. Frankly, it was a wonder they'd stayed here this long. Tarra-*fucking*-Indiana.

Uprooting a life was never easy, but he could see them moving forward together as a couple in ways they couldn't here. An exciting new start in a world of possibilities, devoid of ghosts. Ruthie could make new friends in a new place, plus now she had all those online fans who'd find her just as easily in Washington. In his most optimistic scenarios, Zach had Ruthie taking a significant role in opening the new playspaces, the two of them working side by side.

If only Zach had known a wild card named Quentin would drop into their lives, he could have told Ruthie the conditions of his deal with Glover before she committed to repurposing the nursery. Whether they'd recover their investment in this nursery conversion depended on what the new owners had in mind for the room. Ironically, they'd most likely sell to a young couple looking to fill the rooms with children. The money didn't matter, but he could have saved Ruthie from getting so invested in that writing sanctuary he was about to rip her from.

How could Zach break the news to her now? How could he *not?* Every day was another lie.

"We are going to knock 'em dead at the board meeting, and then you can tell your wife the great news. It's all gonna work out."

"Of course it will."

Zach gazed at the blank wall just beyond Joan's tense figure. The blur of his future sharpened into a chillingly clear picture: he and Ruthie on opposite sides of a deep, yawing chasm.

30

CONVINCING

The loud whir of a drill overhead answered Ruth's question: Quentin was up and hard at work, er, working hard. Screwing, drilling, nailing . . . *Damn you, Henry!* Rereading her naughty story until three a.m. might not have been the smartest idea, but with Zach out of town and nothing on her calendar for Thursday, there was no guilt in staying up into the single-digit hours.

Ruth didn't love that Joan had accompanied Zach for the Glover presentation, but what could she do? *It's just one night.* Zach would surely win them over and secure that grant, and Ruth would have her husband back.

Now, if only she could grab a battery-operated tool of her own to relieve this delicious ache. Even with Quentin's power tools buzzing, she couldn't risk it. That man was always seeing and hearing things Ruth would not have thought humanly possible. No, there would be no diddling with her toys while Quentin was underfoot, and no more late-night erotica sessions until he moved out—*which might be tomorrow,* she realized with a heavy heart.

Of course, the silver lining to losing Quentin's company was a finished writing sanctuary. Ruth couldn't resist a peek before heading downstairs.

"My desk!"

Quentin craned his neck toward Ruth's voice and shot her a brilliant smile. "You like?"

"It's gorgeous." Ruth crossed the room quickly, nearly tripping when Pookie ran between her legs. "Wow, this came out great." She ran her palm over the mahogany top and tested each drawer, admiring the smooth glide and perfectly squared lines. Ruth Miller knew quality work when she saw it.

"Can you picture writing your best seller here?"

"Best seller might be a stretch, but plugging away at my keyboard? Definitely."

Quentin shook his head and added one of his I-give-up grins. "Whatever you say, Ruthie."

"I say, 'Carry on.'" Ruth set her hands on her hips and regarded her dog. "I don't suppose you want to come downstairs with me, Pooks?"

Pookie panted, wagged her tail a couple times, and plopped back down in her sunny spot. *Poor Pookie. You are going to miss Quentin even more than I am, aren't ya, girl?*

"Nah, didn't think so. You two have fun, now."

The drill hummed again before Ruth reached the doorway, and the comforting reminder of Quentin's presence followed her all the way into the kitchen. She sat down in her well-worn leather chair, leaned onto the cool, black granite desktop, set her fingers atop the old, familiar keyboard with the rubbed-off *n*, and angled her body unergonomically toward the off-kilter screen.

8:40 AM, read the clock at the edge of her taskbar. A sympathetic chill ran down Ruth's spine. Zach would be called into the board meeting any second now. If public speaking didn't come so easily to him, Ruth might have worried for him. But that husband of hers was cool as a cucumber. Still, it couldn't hurt to send some good karma Zach's way:

I'm sure you're wowing the board.
Can't wait to hear. Love you. xoxo

Love you. Easier written than said. Why the hell was that, after twenty-three years of marriage? Probably something else Ruth should avoid thinking too hard about. What better escape from thinking than ShouldKnowBetter's Facebook page? Ruth held her coffee mug in one hand and the mouse in the other. *Rabbit hole, here I come.*

Truth be told, Ruth had basically been living her fantasy—minus the mind-blowing sex—since Quentin slammed into her at Versailles. Ironically, Ruth hadn't written a word since.

Too close? Too soon? Too real?

It's not that she'd ever intended to write a sequel to *Fixer Upper*, but when characters jumped around in Ruth's head, she tended to let them out to play. Good old Henry had plenty to say these days, no matter how hard Ruth shushed him and that damn dimple of his. Fiction and truth were a confusing blur lately, but with Quentin's imminent departure, all would soon be sorted out. The line between reality and fantasy redrawn with a fat, black Sharpie. Until then? Repression, avoidance, and coffee.

To post or not to post . . . and about what? Those were the questions.

Ruth was sitting on a gold mine: the gorgeous young man with a disposition to match, talented with his hands, generous with his time, flirty and eager to please. A single stealth photo of Quentin would earn her over a hundred likes, more if he showed that dimple or bared—Ruth fanned herself—what were sure to be amazing abs. She pictured the romance book covers that graced her newsfeed every day; how about that oh-so-natural pose where the model just happens to have the edge of his slightly grimy undershirt pulled way up over his shoulder for reasons that could only be understood by buying said book? Hell, Quentin would pose for the photo in a heartbeat if Ruth asked him to.

She let that fantasy swirl around in her head for a few happy minutes but kiboshed it again before the idea could gain any traction. They'd never understand Ruth's undefinable relationship with this stranger, and she didn't want to explain it. Screw the social media currency to be gained if the cost was giving away pieces of Quentin.

Scroll, scroll, like this post, angry-face-in-solidarity that one. Scroll, scroll, leave a heart-hug-wink. Scroll, scroll, click. Take the Buzzfeed quiz to find out which cartoon princess I am.

A toasted English muffin later, Ruth had caught up on the news of the world as curated by her newsfeed. She watched the tiny clock with one eye and tried not to worry, but shouldn't she have heard from Zach by now?

"Excuse us!" Quentin called as he barreled through the kitchen with Pookie at his ankles. "Somebody's got an emergency."

Yeah, this is your life.

Ruth stood to refill her mug with lukewarm coffee when the email came in from Zach:

We got it! $15MM for 50 new centers over 5 years. Still reeling!

Holy shit! Ruth collapsed into the chair. They'd gone for the full package. Zach had to be over the moon.

Wow! That's amazing! So proud of you.
Can you call? Can you even speak?

Not right now—heading over to office for a tour. Also, sorry for short notice but Langston wants to trot me out on the stage at the annual black-tie shindig tomorrow night to stir up the crowd for the live auction. Obviously, they'd love you to be here. I know getting here's a hassle and it's not your scene (pantyhose, heels, and a bunch of rich white folks pretending we can dance). Please don't feel bad if you can't make it. Joan's gonna stick around so I won't be sitting here all alone looking like a tool in my rented tux. :)

"Ruthie?" Quentin rushed to her side. "Hey, what's wrong? Bad news?"

"Hmm? No. Great news, actually. Zach got the grant." She gestured toward the screen and reread the email while Quentin caught up.

"Wow, that's great. Congratulations! You're going to Washington."

"No, Quentin. Zach doesn't want me there." He already had a date—the perpetually ready, willing, and able Joan.

Quentin squinted and moved closer to the screen to reread the message. "What do you mean? He asked you to come."

"Look at the language. That's not an invitation. It's an *un*-invitation. '*They'd* love me to be there,' not Zach. I don't fit in with his fancy new crowd. I'm not the woman he wants to 'trot out.' He'll take Joan and forget all about me."

"Wow." Quentin pushed away from the desk as if he'd touched hot coals. "You know, you sound an awful lot like Thea."

"Thea?" Ruth moaned into her hands. "What about our agreement?"

Surely, Quentin would respect her feelings and go away now. He'd go upstairs and do his job and leave her alone with this misery, and they wouldn't speak of it again.

But he didn't. Not this time.

Quentin grasped the arms of her chair and spun her around to face him. He waited for her to meet his ridiculously blue eyes. "I finished your story last night. I liked it. A lot."

"Thanks?" *Dear god,* had they been reading the same words at the same time last night, separated only by a few yards of hallway? "And your point is?"

"My point is Thea doesn't see herself clearly."

How did he turn her to mush with that earnest routine every damn time? She had to be the world's biggest sucker. *Occupational hazard of the romance writer, don't you know?*

"I hate to break it to you, Quentin, but Thea's not real. The story is not real. It's just a dumb fantasy."

"Fantasies aren't dumb. They're a window into hidden desires, a way to start a conversation."

"A very embarrassing conversation I definitely should not be having with you." She hated to be so harsh with him, but he'd never been quite so thick or pushy before.

He shook his head, and Ruth breathed a sigh of relief, but it was premature. Quentin dropped into a crouch at her feet. "Ruthie, I'm sorry if I'm embarrassing you, but what if Henry hadn't spoken up? Thea would never have realized how beautiful she was."

"I'm not Thea."

"And I'm not Henry."

"And that's why it's called fiction, folks."

"Yes, but you have to admit you share a few qualities with Thea."

Thea, the sex-crazed, head-in-the-clouds cougar with a heart of gold. "Maybe a couple."

Quentin smiled tenderly. "And please tell me you realize you endowed Henry with the traits you admire most in your husband? He's smart, confident, good, generous, doting . . ."

Please don't mention his enormous penis.

Ruth huffed. "Zach doesn't see himself in Henry at all."

"He's read your stories?"

"Yes. Every word."

"What does he think of your writing?"

"He's sweet, supportive. 'Nice chapter, hon.' He thinks it's a nice hobby, gives me something to do while he's out saving the world, being someone else's hero."

"He's not your hero?"

"It's so much more exciting to impress someone new."

"You think he wants to impress this Joan woman?"

"Oh, she laps up every word. If only I'd paid attention, made more of an effort." She remembered with a fresh pang of guilt how Zach complimented her the other morning, just for putting on lip gloss. "It should be me sitting next to him at that table." *Shit, and now I'm crying.* "Look, I appreciate your concern, but—"

Quentin lifted her out of the chair and pulled her into his arms. "Shh, it's okay, Ruthie."

Damn, it felt good to have a pair of strong arms to hold her up again, a safe person to vent to without worrying everything she said would be thrown back in her face. Someone she could trust with all those fears she'd been clutching with such a tight grip, they were strangling the life out of her. Quentin held her while she purged the venom from her system.

"That barracuda has been trying to get her fangs into Zach since the night they met. I made it so easy for her to steal him away."

"Oh, Ruthie. You don't know that."

"She sent him flowers on our anniversary."

Quentin pulled back suddenly. "*What?*"

"I know. It's crazy, right?"

"Ruthie." His hands slid up her arms, kneaded her shoulders. "That doesn't make sense. Why would she do that?"

"I think . . . they might . . ." She gasped, sucked an air bubble into her lungs, and coughed.

Quentin cupped her cheek. "What?"

"I think they're *sleeping* together."

His eyes filled with pain, *her* pain, as if taking it upon himself could relieve Ruth of her burden. "No," he said. "No, he wouldn't."

Ruth would never know who moved in first or which set of lips crossed the halfway point between them. He was so close she could taste his sweet breath on her tongue. God, how Ruth wanted those lips on hers. It was a miracle she'd resisted as long as she had.

Because you're married.

"Oh god." Ruth turned her head just in time, placing her hand on Quentin's chest to hold the space between them, but also, if she were honest, because she wasn't quite ready to let go. "I'm so sorry. That was completely my fault. I send out signals." How many times had her friends warned her about this?

"No, Ruthie. That was me. One hundred percent." His pretty mouth twisted into a terrible grimace. "I know better. And I promised both of us I would not do that again. Please forgive me."

"It doesn't even matter who did what. That's not the point. My heart strayed, and . . . it's not the first time."

"What do you mean?"

"I've met people—*men*—online." She couldn't tell if Quentin felt confused or betrayed. When the almost-lover you almost-kissed feels cheated on by your imaginary lovers, your life is officially surreal. "It's intoxicating when a total stranger falls for whatever persona I put out there."

"You mean 'you.'"

"Well, some version of me that doesn't have cellulite or stretch marks or a mansion in the suburbs. Just the parts I want someone to fall for, I guess."

"Don't we all share just what we want with the world?"

"You can't exactly hide when you're married, living twenty-four seven in plain sight. Maybe there are some parts of ourselves we just can't handle being exposed."

"To your husband or yourself?"

She let out a harsh sigh while she pondered his question. "Both, I guess. That's why just chucking it and starting over seems so alluring. Picking up the shiny new toy. *Being* the shiny new toy. It's a turn-on. And it's a hell of a lot easier than trying to hold someone's attention for twenty-three years."

"Something tells me you fully have your husband's attention. Did you see him that night I showed up here?"

"Oh yes, what a treat. Angry and possessive and disgusted with his wife, and you got to see all of that."

"Ruthie, that's not what I saw at all."

His gentle tone brought her up short. She wiped her tears and met Quentin's tender gaze. "You know I'm afraid to ask, but what did you see?"

He took her hand from his heart and held it in his own, wove their fingers together to let her know he wasn't running away. As much as Ruth didn't want to admit it, she drew great comfort from Quentin's touch.

"I saw a man desperate to hold on to his wife. He's seen me as a threat from the first time we met."

"It's not you, Quentin. Our problems started long before you showed up." All those nights she pretended to be asleep, gave Zach less attention than her computer world, stopped making plans to go out as couples, complained about Joan, whined about getting dressed for those rubber chicken dinners.

"I guess the important question is, do you want him back?"

"Yes, of course. He's my husband, and I still love him with all my heart."

"Even if he has . . . done something?"

Well, now. There was a question to make a wife suck in her breath and pause. "I've always liked to think I'd be the kind of person who could forgive and move on."

Cupid nodded. "I suppose none of us really knows what we'd do unless the situation arises."

"I guess I found out I wouldn't kiss you if I had the chance." Ruth allowed herself a smug grin, and he gave her a crooked smile back.

"You sure did."

"You probably would have stopped first."

"No, Ruthie. I'm ashamed to say it, but stopping wasn't on my mind. That was all you."

"I'll be kicking myself over this one day."

"No, you won't." He squeezed her hand, and she knew he was right.

"Do you think it's too late for Zach and me?"

"Absolutely not. If you want him, you should go to that event."

"It's tomorrow!"

"I understand airplanes can travel great distances in short periods of time."

"Very funny. I don't have anything to wear."

"What time do the stores close?"

"I don't know, nine?"

"That gives you"—he checked his phone—"eight hours to find something."

"But I can't just . . ."

"Ruthie, *breathe.*"

Sigh. "Okay, but how can I . . . with *her* there?"

"How can you *not?*"

"What about Pookie?"

She woofed, and Quentin picked her up. "Lucky for you, you have a live-in pet sitter."

31

MEMO FROM THE GODS

Hephaestus's crappy Monday just got a whole lot crappier. Thankfully, visits from Ares were rare, but whenever he deigned to drop in on his "favorite goddess and her absurdly fortunate husband," he arrived without warning.

"Did you see?" Ares burst into the solarium where Aphrodite and Hephaestus sat huddled together over the gaiascope.

Aphrodite turned too eagerly from the glass between her husband's hands. "We did." To imagine his wife in Ares's thrall was agonizing; to see the evidence before him, in the flesh—Aphrodite's flushed, supple flesh—was downright intolerable.

Hephaestus rounded on Ares. "How did you get here so fast?"

Ares's smug smirk widened. *Damn him.* If seducing Aphrodite delighted the God of War, then taunting the cuckolded Hephaestus doubled the bastard's joy. "I had my team hitched when the Worthy's husband left town yesterday. Something was bound to happen."

"Oh, fie!" Hephaestus waved his hand over the gaiascope. "What's the big deal?"

Ares arched a confident brow. "Cupid crossed a line. He violated the law of the land."

"But he didn't."

A knowing glance passed between would-be or possibly-already-reunited lovers. "Heph, he was going to kiss her," Aphrodite said. "He would have, if not for the wife's pushing him away. He said so himself."

"So now Cupid is to be punished for his intentions?"

"Intentions are the gateway to virtue," Ares remarked, as if lecturing to the populace.

"Really, *Virgil?* Who among us could live up to those standards?" Hephaestus made a point to stink-eye his wife.

"Fortunately, *we* are not the ones on trial, darling."

"Does saving the mortals' marriage not mitigate Cupid's guilt?"

Aphrodite nodded to Ares, who took his turn answering as if the two had rehearsed. "We're teaching a lesson in ethics, not military tactics."

Hephaestus tensed. "Ironic."

Aphrodite set her palm on Hephaestus's chest though her full body weight would have been as effective as a water reed in the path of a charging bull had Hephaestus decided to lunge.

"Dearest," Aphrodite said through clenched teeth, "we don't know yet if the marriage is saved. The couple has not reached their Liminal Point."

"I'd wager the palace treasury on it," Hephaestus answered.

Ares rushed to Aphrodite's side, shot her a meaningful glance, and tenderly removed her hand from Hephaestus's chest. "Your point is moot, brother. The boy's inappropriate behavior is enough to warrant another punishment. I've already drafted our report to the Council."

"How convenient." Hephaestus huffed, then turned on his wife. "I know what you're doing, Aph. You're not fooling anyone."

"What do you accuse me of, husband?"

"At the very least, wreaking havoc on your own son's life just for the excuse to sniff at Ares's robes. It's beneath you."

Aphrodite's delicate hands balled into fierce little fists. Oh, she was livid. "I require an excuse to move about Olympus? Am I your prisoner now?"

"No, just my wife." Hephaestus heaved a sigh. "Frankly, sweetheart, I thought we were through with all this. Do you plan to cuckold me again? Have you already?"

"No, of course not." That she'd only answered one question did not escape Hephaestus's notice. "This is not about you or me or Ares. This is about my son."

"I see. So, this is about creating new tortures for Cupid at every turn, celebrating his slightest misstep with utter glee, rushing to persuade the Council to rule against his ascension?"

Aphrodite attempted a softer approach. "I miss the boy as I'd miss my right arm, but we all agreed, Cupid must be properly vetted before he can return. You have to admit, he mastered his desires much better this time despite his close quarters with the human."

"Until she gave him that *story* she wrote." Ares nudged Aphrodite and had himself a hearty chuckle.

"Oh, Heph, don't you see? The punishment is working. He's maturing, gaining respect for the idea of love. The kiss was an impulse. He was weak. That only means he has more work to do."

Hephaestus had lost, but he could still twist the knife. "You do realize the longer he stays down there, the less he will want to come home again."

"My son will come home when I tell him to come home."

"Of course he will. What choice does he have? But have you considered what eternity will feel like with a mopey adolescent underfoot?"

"He'll get over it. He'll get his wings and his arrows back. I'll throw in an extra servant to fix his favorite dishes."

"Your big plan is to replace sex with a plate of souvlaki?"

"Oh dear," Ares piped up, "I certainly hope you're giving it to her better than that, old man."

Hephaestus leveled Ares with a dangerous glare. His temper was getting the best of him, and Hephaestus could ill afford to draw first blood on the God of War.

Aphrodite's decision made, she turned to Ares. "Deliver our recommendation to the Council. In the meantime, we should begin strategizing Cupid's next Worthy."

"I cannot wait to begin that conversation with you," Ares said.

Hephaestus could take no more of their nauseating collusion. "I will not have a hand in this. Cupid's misery will not be on my conscience." Gaiascope in hand, Hephaestus turned on his heel as gracefully as he could manage with his shriveled foot and limped out.

32

MAKING UP

Cupid had a dilemma. For five long days, despite the pain of being cut off from his best friend and only liaison with home, Cupid had faithfully obeyed Pan's direct order and refrained from contacting him. But Cupid had made an equally vital promise to Ruthie to care for Pookie while she was away. The trusting little creature balled up in Cupid's lap was counting on him for food and water and trips to the yard, basic needs Cupid could easily manage—unless he suddenly ascended. With Ruthie on her way to Zach with the express purpose of mending her marriage, Cupid had every reason to believe the couple would reach their Liminal Point in the next twelve hours, casting his immediate fate into the hands of the gods who'd punished him.

Though Cupid tried mightily, he could not come up with a solution that didn't involve Pan. And so it was, with heavy heart, Cupid put the welfare of Pookie before his pride and sent a desperate message to Pan: *Please call me. It's an emergency.* If their final exchange of words had to be a fight, so be it.

Pan's call came swiftly. "*What?*" His voice was terse, but a rush of affection swept through Cupid. He knew Pan could never turn his back on him.

"I might need your help."

"What have you done now?"

"I, um, might have messed up. Or I might have fixed them. I don't know."

"Dammit, Q. Just give me the facts."

"I'm afraid I might need you to watch Ruthie's dog for me."

"You called me to dog-sit? This is your emergency?"

"I volunteered to take care of her while Ruthie and Zach are away, working out their problems," Cupid said.

"Have you forgotten how your little foray into babysitting turned out last time?"

"How could I?" Cupid sighed, forcing away memories of squealing tires and metal-on-metal. "Look, I didn't have a choice. Ruthie needed to leave quickly, and I've been living here, so I said I'd—"

"*That's* where you're living? Un-*fucking*-believable."

"Look, Pan, if I'm here, I can watch her, but if I vaporize, it'll be kind of tough. I really don't want Ruthie's dog to die of starvation or pee all over their house."

"I don't understand. Did you fuck up, or did you fix it?"

"I don't know. I tried to kiss her—"

"Fucking hell! What did I tell you about that?"

"I know, I know, but the thing is, she didn't let me."

"Well, good for her, but that's not gonna change a damn thing for you."

"I know. It's okay, though, because I think she and Zach are gonna work it out now. So, even if I get"—Cupid paused to rub his heart—"punished again, I can handle it if Ruthie's okay."

"You are really something else, you know that?" It didn't

sound like a *good* something else, but at least Pan was still on the line.

"Pan, I'm so sorry, for everything."

"Q." A weary groan filled Cupid's ear.

"Did you get the wine I left for you? Not that a bottle of wine fixes everything, but I just didn't want you to not see it in your truck or have someone sit on it by accident."

Pan chuckled, and Cupid pictured him with the beginnings of a grin. "It was very lovingly tucked in under the seat belt, thanks."

"Okay, phew."

"Dammit, Q, I've missed the hell out of you."

"I've missed you too, Pan. So much. I know I probably shouldn't have come to Ruthie's after you and I had our fight." Remembering that awful conversation brought a hollow feeling to the pit of Cupid's belly. "I swear, I never meant to stay here longer than one night, but Ruthie was so kind, and I was so alone."

"I'm sorry I got so angry at you. I usually have better command of my emotions, but you just seem to get under my skin like nobody else."

"I'm trying to follow the rules, truly I am. But it's all so confusing sometimes, and I've only been doing this for a little while."

"Fifty days."

"You're counting?"

"I have a chart for all my fallens."

"Oh."

"I don't count days for any of the others," Pan offered, a life preserver to a drowning man.

"So, I'm still your favorite?"

"Yes, you idiot."

"Thanks, Pan. You'll do me this favor, then? You'll take care of Pookie if I ascend?"

"Of course. What do I have to do?"

"Could you come over and meet her, just so she's not scared? And I can show you where they keep the food and where she likes to pee and everything." *And it would be so great to see you again.*

"Yeah, okay, I can do that."

"They have a lot of really big TVs. We could hang out. You could bring that wine, or I can pick up some beer."

"You hate beer."

"Yes, but *you* don't."

"How long are they gonna be away?"

"Until Sunday if all goes as planned. Hey, maybe you could set up Ruthie's computer."

"Sure, no problem."

"And help me hang the curtains?"

"Any other manual labor I can do for you?" Pan was definitely grinning now.

"Yes, actually. There are about ten boxes filled with books I need to move and load into the bookcases."

"Well, why didn't you say so? Sounds like a blast."

Damn, it felt good to talk to his best friend again. "I thought so too."

Pan chuckled. *Oh, he was kidding.* "Do I have time to make a few calls first? I have some other irons in the fire."

"Sure. Ruthie's about to land in Chicago, and she has to switch planes. The flights are awful."

"Nothing beats having your own set of wings, eh?"

"To be honest, I'm not that eager to have my wings back. Or anything else."

"Q, careful . . ."

"Right. She's going straight to the event tonight. Zach doesn't know she's coming."

"Wow. Brave lady."

Sigh. "Yeah, I'm so proud of her. Anyway, Zach is making some big speech, plus they have a lot of issues to work through, so I don't think it will happen right away."

"Okay. I'll be there in a bit. Have they got anything to eat in that mansion, or should I pick up a pizza?"

33

GLOVER DINNER

There she stood at the precipice of the tallest cliff she'd ever considered diving off, or at least that's how Ruth felt, teetering on skinny, impractical heels and clutching her tiny, impractical handbag at the entrance of the grand atrium of the Hay-Adams Hotel. This was about the bravest thing Ruth had ever done.

Oh, she'd written the grand gestures up and down the page. After all, where would a romance be without them? But to *be* that girl who jumped on a plane, shimmied into the sparkly dress purchased only hours before, and walked into a thousand-person event where the only two people she knew were the husband she was determined to win back and the woman trying to steal him away? That took guts.

"Okay, Zach. Come out, come out, wherever you are," Ruth sing-songed under her breath, lest the good folk of the Glover Foundation think her insane.

It was uncanny how well her Zach-dar worked, the two of them had often remarked, and boy, did it come in handy at these massive events. No sooner would they arrive than Zach would be drawn away to press hands with some donor or investor, or Ruth would wander from his side to check out the silent auction items up for bid. They both rather enjoyed moving independently through the crowds of fellow philanthropists, to regale each other with their separate adventures when reunited. If worse came to worst, they would always find each other at the dinner table, but Ruth much preferred their private game of cat-and-spouse, especially when Zach would light up with, "*There* you are," as if he'd been missing her terribly the whole twenty minutes they'd been apart.

She leaned onto her tiptoes and scanned the room—*nada*—before stepping boldly forward into the abyss. *Chin up, smile on.* The important thing was to look like she had a destination. Thank goodness, there was always a bar.

Once she started moving, she felt less awkward and out of place though she was both. Either she'd find Zach before she reached the bar, or she'd soothe her nerves with a generous pour of chardonnay—a win-win scenario. She wasn't quite prepared for option C: coming upon Zach from behind and discovering Joan's perfectly manicured hand resting possessively on his shoulder.

How dare she put her dirty mitts on my husband? Not that he discouraged her.

Gather your wits, Ruthie. You didn't come all this way to make a fool of yourself.

No, she'd come to stand by her husband's side, and as another woman had apparently claimed one of Zach's sides for herself, Ruth had arrived none too soon. She steeled herself, waited for a lull in the conversation, and stepped into the gap between Zach and the gentleman to his right.

The stranger greeted Ruth first, with a warm handshake and introduction, which Ruth forced herself to return.

"Ruth Miller, eh?" the man said with a grin. "Any relation to this guy?"

The moment of truth.

Zach shifted. The tux jacket that brushed her arm was a rental; he smelled of foreign bath products. If she were honest, Ruth would have to admit she didn't really know this particular Zach in this unfamiliar crowd in this unfamiliar city. Though she wanted to believe she knew his heart as well as she knew her own name, Ruth had no idea if Zach would be happy to see her or bummed that his wife had intruded on a perfect evening with his mistress.

"*Ruthie?*"

Her mouth locked in a tense smile, she spun to face Zach. "Surprise!" A twitchy jazz-hands routine ensued while Ruth attempted to regain control of her extremities and facial features.

Joan's hand slipped off Zach's shoulder. *And good riddance.*

"You came!" Zach's expression contorted from shock to pure delight. He was that boy in the lecture hall again, setting eyes on her for the very first time. She might have been the only other person in the room. Had she been a fool to question her marriage, or had her spontaneous appearance reset their romance?

"I came," she echoed quietly. "I'm so proud of you."

That old pilot light of theirs still burned, after all. A loyal, beleaguered soldier standing at attention through thick and thin, waiting for Ruth's grand gesture to ignite this fire. The evidence was as plain as the glow heating up Ruth's insides and the flames licking behind Zach's eyes. *You done good, Ruthie.*

Zach set his hand on Ruth's waist and leaned in for a kiss. Not one of those corporate air-kiss jobs and not even the welcome-home, Ward Cleaver variety. No, this was a *kiss* the likes of which Ruth and Zach had not shared in months: the kind that tingles your toes and tickles your belly and makes you forget you're standing in the middle of a gigantic corporate event. *Whoops.* Ruth might have felt silly if Zach hadn't looked so damn sheepish.

"I'm excited you're here," he said, "in case you couldn't tell." They both chuckled. "Have I seen this dress before?"

"Nope." Ruth trembled in anticipation as Zach craned his neck to see around back. He'd always been a sucker for a halter top.

"Wow, Ruthie," he whispered. His fingertips skimmed across Ruth's bare back, raising goose bumps all over her skin. "You look gorgeous."

How his words could still make her blush after all these years, Ruth would never comprehend, but moments like this validated every last one of her romantic fantasies.

"I did the best I could, but I had a really early flight. I had to blow-dry my hair at six this morning."

"You know I love your hair down like this." Zach's wandering hand drifted up the back of her neck, disappeared into her hair, swept around the sensitive shell of her ear. If he kept this up, she'd need help standing. "I really can't believe you're here. How did you manage this? What about Pookie?"

"Quentin's watching her."

"Ah, Quentin. Of course." Was that the sound of the coach turning back into a pumpkin?

"Yes, *Quentin*, and as soon as we get back, he's leaving, Zach."

Ruth watched the gears turn in Zach's head. Ruthie was here; the hot handyman was leaving. *Advantage, Miller.*

"Zach?" *Joan*, drawing him back to her world.

"Right. Oh, Ruthie, let me introduce you to—"

"Evan Walters," Ruth said. "Yes, we just met."

Zach rubbed his adorably muddled head. "Of course."

Evan chuckled. "Looks like you two have a lot to catch up

on. Pleasure to meet you, Ruth. Zach, we'll talk soon." He lifted his glass and faded into the crowd.

Joan shot forward with outstretched arms. "We're so glad you could make it, Ruth." *Ugh*, always making herself into the plural of Zach.

"Thanks, and congratulations." Ruth dipped for the air-kiss do-si-do, which Joan delivered with an oppressive dose of *eau-de-I'm-easy*.

"It was all Zach. He was amazing. I wish you could have seen him in action."

The erotica writer in Ruth couldn't let that one go without arching her eyebrows at Zach. "I hope to later."

Zach grinned and slipped his arm around Ruth's waist. "Let's get you a drink."

"You're not drinking?"

"I have to give a speech after dinner." Zach rolled his eyes, but Ruth knew better than to fall for it. While she thrived behind the computer screen, Zach adored the spotlight. He'd have the room eating out of his hand, and he'd love every minute of it.

"I'll stay sober in solidarity."

"Fine. We can get hammered together later."

"And stay up all night?"

"I'm game." Zach shot Ruth a look that melted her heart. There was no question he'd caught her reference to their all-night sex marathons in college. "C'mon, I can't wait to show you off to the rest of the board. Joan, could you make sure they set a place at our table for Ruthie, please?" Without waiting for confirmation, Zach led her away from Joan, which was the exact direction Ruth wanted to travel.

Zach navigated through the crowd like the pro he was, plucking out the bigwigs to introduce to his "better half" as the Glover folks gushed about how lucky they were to be able to back her visionary husband. Ruth had almost forgotten what a turn-on it was to watch Zach in his element—and in a gorgeous tux, to boot—but Ruth wasn't just a bystander. Zach had turned her into the main event. *Say hello to my wife. Look who surprised me!*

That hide-and-seek they liked to play during cocktails? Not happening. Zach wasn't letting go. He wasn't usually one for PDA, but Zach was different tonight. Even as they moved through the tight crowd, his hand warmed her back. He leaned in to share a private tidbit whenever the mood struck. His thumb traced a soft arc across her shoulder. He was sexy and attentive, brilliant and accessible, familiar and brand new. Ruth couldn't wait to get him alone.

Alas, that wouldn't happen for hours.

Even as Ruth wished for the night to speed up, she was dismayed to hear the dinner chimes echoing through the room. Time for the dreaded sit-down dinner: forced conversations with assigned tablemates, endless thank-yous to corporate sponsors, mystery gravies, and rich desserts the skinny girls had no trouble pushing away. The speeches usually weighed down her eyelids, especially after a couple of glasses of wine, but tonight, she couldn't wait to soak in as much information as possible. Ruth was beginning to understand how profoundly out of the loop of her husband's life she'd been.

Zach led her to a table right up front, where Joan sat waiting for him like the teacher's pet. In typical fashion, Zach chose the seat between the two women warring for his attention. He pulled out the chair to his left, and as Ruth scooted into place, Zach's palm grazed her backside.

Took you long enough, she smirked at him. He always loved the feel of her barely-there panties under a fancy dress. If he could have, Zach would have happily left his hand right there all night. But he couldn't, so he shook his head and grinned at her instead. *My naughty girl.*

"Ah, you must be Ruth. I'm Peter Langston, big fan of your husband." Ruth knew precious little about the man taking the seat next to her, but she quickly picked up on the fact that he and Mrs. Langston had made the most of the open bar.

With Joan's claws currently deeply sunk into Zach, Ruth had little choice but to engage the Langstons. Predictably, Peter started the conversation with, "So, what kind of work do you do?"

Usually frustrated by this question, Ruth took advantage of the opening to talk about her volunteer work with Brighter Tomorrows. Langston nodded along, friendly and encouraging. Also predictably, Bunny Langston leaned over her husband's filet mignon and dauphinoise potatoes—the proper potato term known to Ruth only because of the calligraphed menu left at each place—to ask about the Millers' children. Peter choked and coughed and shook his head violently to try to head her off. Fortunately for all involved, Ruth was well prepared with an answer that usually shut down the conversation, and while Peter was recovering from his coughing fit, she simply told Bunny, "We were unable to have children."

Just when Ruth might have pulled rank on Joan and used Zach as an escape, one of the evening's production crew requested Zach's presence backstage. He swiped his napkin across his mouth, turned to Ruth, and said, "Wish me luck."

"You don't need luck. You're a star."

He gave Ruth's knee a squeeze under the table. Before she could recover from the shock, he winked. Winked!

More to herself than anyone else, Ruth shook her head and muttered, "Boy, I need to bottle some of this DC water to take home with us."

Langston chuckled heartily. "Soon it'll be running out of your taps."

Huh? "Sorry?"

"I assume you'll be following Zach here fairly soon? After tying up the sale of the Indiana house?"

"Following Zach?" *The sale of the Indiana house?* Ruth's head seemed to be shaking like a dashboard hula doll, but she couldn't stop it.

Langston's jaw dropped. "Oh, dear."

A cold sweat broke across Ruth's forehead. How long had Zach known? Had she really missed something this huge, or had Zach simply kept this detail from her, knowing how she'd likely respond? Wow.

Her fight-or-flight instinct screamed, "Run for the hills!"—or at least, the ladies' room—but how could Ruth leave with Zach climbing the steps onto the stage, waiting to be introduced? She reached a shaky hand for her water glass and forced herself to sip slowly, drew in and released a deep breath, dabbed her forehead with her napkin, and turned her attention to the stage.

Except directly in Ruth's line of vision sat the evil Joan, whose smug, calculating glare was fixed on Ruth. Whatever Ruth's feelings—and she couldn't decide between profoundly sad and ragey mad—the last person on earth she'd reveal them to was the vulture now scooting into Zach's empty seat beside her. Ruth angled her chair toward the stage, slapped a neutral expression on her face, and lifted her gaze well above Joan's head.

Not one for subtlety, Joan fired her cannonball into Ruth's lap. "He never told you?"

How Ruth would have loved to have told Joan to butt the hell out, but the truth was, none of this had anything to do with Joan, never had. This was Ruth and Zach's marriage, and they were the only two who could fix it. Luckily, Stuart Glover had stepped up to the podium, and all Ruth had to do was point. Joan couldn't be caught talking while her boss's new boss was speaking. She snapped her head around, and Ruth breathed a temporary sigh of relief.

Glover's words were amplified by the microphone, but Ruth's thoughts were louder. Zach's deception stung. And the cruel irony of selling their home now. How could he have let her pour her heart and soul into the writing sanctuary when he knew—or at least, the chances were pretty damn good—they'd be putting their house on the market? Was it possible they'd sprung the move on him yesterday, a new condition of the grant? Still, he'd gone ahead and accepted the terms without consulting or even informing her. What kind of marriage was that?

Her gaze shifted to Zach. *What else are you hiding?* She'd shrugged off her suspicions for months now, not truly able to believe he could cheat on her. But now? This feeling of distrust was so alien to Ruth, she couldn't reconcile it with the kind, familiar face staring out into the bright lights.

". . . with that, I turn the microphone over to the extremely talented Zachary Miller."

Applause rose throughout the room, shaking Ruth's attention back to the moment—this enormous moment for Zach. In her heart of hearts, she understood why he'd waited to tell her. *Of course* she would support him. He knew this. In a way, didn't his omission demonstrate a certain faith in their bond? Or was she acting the fool?

Zach shook Glover's hand. The applause died down. "Thank you very much for that warm welcome. I would first like to thank Peter Langston for reaching out to Brighter Tomorrows and showing the courage to share our vision." Ruth swiveled to applaud Langston, who nodded and waved to the adoring crowd. "And of course, our gratitude to the board of directors for approving this grant for *fifteen million dollars* over five years to increase our reach into *thirty* states!" Applause. "We could not be more thrilled to partner with you, and I promise we are going to make every Glover investor proud to be a part of this work. Maybe I shouldn't confess this, but . . . oh, what the heck? The papers are signed, right, Peter?" Peter nodded gamely, waiting for the punch line with a smile on his face. Zach leaned dramatically into the microphone and covered his mouth as if he were telling a secret. "Our model is embarrassingly simple." Titters of laughter. Zach stood tall again and clicked off the points on his fingers. "Excellent vocational training. Strategic corporate partnerships. One-on-one support and supervision for our clients. And the heart of our program, ladies and gentlemen: outstanding volunteers like my wife, Ruthie, right there at the head table. Yep, I quite literally would not be standing up here right now if not for my amazing, warmhearted wife."

Oh no, he didn't. But yes, he had, and she was fairly certain he was about to share a slice of Miller lore retold nearly as frequently and lovingly as their first encounter. Ruth bunched her napkin in both fists and held on tight.

"Ruthie first volunteered at the Tarra center three years ago. That evening over dinner, she couldn't say enough about the gifted teachers, the impressive facility, and the warmth and sense of community in the classroom. These centers are first-rate day care, and that is not to be taken for granted, but the real magic is this: while the kids are busy finger painting and singing and having tea parties or"—he stole a smile at Ruth, and a furious blush made her grateful for the dim lighting—"sitting in my wife's lap being read to, their parents are either out earning a decent paycheck, or they're down the hall, improving their vocational skills.

"I was intrigued. I sat down with the officers of Brighter Tomorrows, who quickly convinced me of the sustainability and replicability of the model, and let me pause here to tell you, I am not the easiest man to convince. Ask my wife if you don't believe me." Laughter from the crowd, tears from Ruth. "So, I did what any reasonable man would do: I quit my job and joined the team. Best day of my professional life."

Zach's gaze swept the room, then landed dramatically on Ruth like a spotlight over her head. "The moral of the story is marry a good woman."

The crowd gave out a collective, "*Awww*," while Ruth struggled to keep her mouth from twitching. *You're in big trouble, Zach Miller*, she said with a shake of her head.

He nodded. *Worth it.*

Lucky for both of them, Zach didn't wink again.

"Fast-forward to tonight. Thanks to your generosity, we will be able to build ten new Brighter Tomorrows centers per year for the next five years. At an average of eighty families per center per year, *you* will move over 12,000 families to sustainable financial independence in the next five years alone and 4,000 every year thereafter for a fraction of your capital investment."

A roar went up in the crowd, and Zach stepped back from the podium to add his own applause. Ah, the darling of the perennial charity fundraiser: the big, fat slap on the back for writing that check.

"Speaking of your investment," Zach went on, "I hear we have some outrageous vacation packages to auction off, so grab those paddles and don't be shy. Thank you so much."

Zach gripped the podium while the standing ovation gained momentum like the wave at a Colts game. On her feet with the rest of his admirers, Ruth soaked her napkin with tears. Zach lifted his hand to acknowledge the applause, mouthed a few thank-yous, and exited the stage.

Ruth's heart swelled as she watched him make his way back to her, shaking hands thrust at him as if he were walking the red carpet. He locked eyes with Ruth as he approached the table. Zach's steps lightened as a gorgeous smile broke across his face. He was close enough now for Ruth to see the tears behind his glasses. There was nothing that choked her up like her husband's tears.

Neither of them noticed Joan step into Zach's path, her arms spread wide to receive him. Zach nearly plowed right through her. He bounced back as if stung, grabbed her right hand, gave her a couple of quick pumps and a pat on the opposite shoulder, and said, "Thanks, Joan. Excuse me, won't you?" Ruth couldn't be bothered to take her eyes off Zach, but Joan had to be fuming.

Langston peered over Ruth's shoulder. "Well done, Zach. I know better than to keep you from this little lady. We'll talk later."

He disappeared before Zach could thank him. Finally, alone—*ish*.

Zach opened his arms and shrugged. "How much trouble am I in?"

"A lot. Oh, Zach." Ruth fell into his chest and wrapped her arms around his neck. They rocked gently together, holding each other up while the emotions shook their way out. "I'm crying all over your tux," she said.

Zach laughed. "It's a rental."

She pulled back and stared into his moist eyes. "Is that the speech you were going to make before I showed up?"

He shrugged. "I have no idea. I was gonna wing it."

"Only you, Zach."

He ran his palms up and down her arms, settling his hands tenderly on her bare shoulders. "Have I mentioned how"—he leaned in to whisper—"*fucking* happy I am you're here?"

One last sob spilled out with Ruth's laughter. "Me, too. I am so proud of you, Zach. All you've accomplished and all the great work in front of you."

"Look, Ruthie, there's something I should have mentioned sooner—"

"We're moving."

Anguish crinkled his forehead. "Joan told you. I'm so sorry, Ruthie."

"Actually, no, but that doesn't matter. How did we get to the point where we don't talk about these things?"

"I don't know, but I hate it. I feel like we have so much to catch up on."

"Yes." Normally, the "we need to talk" line set off warning bells in Ruth's gut, but right now, it was exactly what she'd needed to hear.

Zach glanced over his shoulder at the stage. "This isn't the most conducive atmosphere."

How had Ruth not noticed the auction barker riling the crowd? And there they were at the epicenter right up front, the seats reserved for the big spenders. "No, it's really not."

"Hey, why don't we stay the weekend? Did you bring any clothes? Oh, who cares? We'll buy you a new wardrobe." He was eighteen again, lit with passion for her, for his work, for life. His enthusiasm was contagious.

Ruth giggled. "I left a small suitcase in the coatroom. I brought you a pair of jeans and a couple of shirts. I was hoping maybe we could make a little vacation out of it, see the sights?"

"I like the way you think." Zach grazed her skin with his thumbs. "Actually, full disclosure here, I, uh, went out with a real estate agent this morning, and there's an adorable pied-à-terre in Georgetown I'd love to show you. I thought we might start out living in the city, just until we get our bearings?"

"That could be a really nice change for us."

"Seriously?"

"Yes, Zach. Are you so surprised?"

"I know you love our house in the suburbs, and you were really looking forward to writing in your new study."

"I love *you,* and I can write anywhere."

"I think you're going to love this place. There's a sunny room with floor-to-ceiling bookshelves on two walls and French doors leading out to a little patio and small yard for Pookie. I've already imagined you sitting at your desk, typing away."

"Sounds like heaven," she said, tipping her head toward the line that had formed behind Zach, "but I think we should discuss this later. Your fans want you."

"I'm sorry, Ruthie."

"Don't be."

He leaned in and kissed her cheek. "I'll find you as soon as I can."

"Go. Be adored. I'll be fine."

"I know you will, but you just got here, and I don't want to let you out of my sight." He sighed. "I've missed you, Ruthie." He wasn't referring to the last thirty-six hours, and they both knew it.

"I'll meet you on the dance floor."

The shocked expression on Zach's face was worth every ounce of pain soon to be inflicted by Ruth's wildly impractical shoes.

34

REUNITED

Pan pulled his truck up tight behind Cupid's Prius in the driveway. He wouldn't be surprised if one of the neighbors had already called the police. *Heh,* the good folks of Tarra Heights would never have believed who was hanging out on their ritzy-titzy street tonight. He grabbed the pizza box and liquor store bag off the passenger seat and headed to the back door Q had directed him to use.

This is not a date, Pan reminded himself, though his loins seemed to have decided otherwise. The time apart had been sheer misery for Pan's soul, but his libido had enjoyed a much-needed rest. Pan had been on full tilt since his friend's arrival. Even for the god of the hunt, that was a whole lot of arousal.

A few days into Cupid's absence, Pan had started feeling much more in control again, and he'd secretly begun to believe he might have built up some kind of immunity. The ride over had blown that theory to bits. Pan was stiff as a board and emotional to boot. What a perfect time for bourbon.

He suspected Cupid had heard his truck roll up but knocked on the glass pane just to be sure. Or maybe he wanted to light a fire under Cupid's ass to even the playing field.

"Be right there," came Cupid's voice.

Pan peered through the window, excited beyond reason when Cupid's sneakers rounded the corner and hit the top step. His old buddy appeared in the frame, one delicious inch at a time. Immunity, my ass.

Hot on Cupid's heels, a blur of white fur tumbled down behind him. In one smooth motion, Cupid bent down, gathered the barking dust bunny under his arm, and opened the door. "Thanks for coming so quickly."

Pan swallowed the raunchy comeback, even as Cupid's scent brought every repressed desire straight to the fore. Damn, he'd missed Cupid more in these last six days than in the two thousand years they'd been separated, and it wasn't just the physical attraction. Pan had nearly convinced himself this earth life wasn't lonely, that leaving everyone and everything he knew on Mount O was an easy trade for the riches of relative autonomy and the animal delights afforded by his human—and rather exceptional, if he did say so himself—form. Then Cupid fell, reopening that gaping hole Pan had learned to ignore while filling it at exactly the same time. The self-imposed separation had only reminded Pan of the farce.

And here they were, together again, even if only for a few hours more. And there stood Q, silently imploring Pan for forgiveness while stroking his fingers rhythmically through the dog's hair. Was Cupid struggling as mightily as Pan to keep his hands to himself? Between the dog nestled in Q's arms and the pizza box and bourbon bottle in Pan's, there would be no satisfying body contact anyway.

"You have got to be shitting me. This little mutt?"

Cupid lifted the dog so his face was level with Pan's. "Pookie, meet my friend Pan. Sometimes, he can be a bit gruff, but his bleat is worse than his bite."

Pan shook his head at the hairy rat. "I have to tell you, I pictured something more dignified and less . . . mophead." If Pan's friends at the muscle gym ever got wind of this, he'd never live it down. Still, he had to be grateful. If not for the little rodent, he and Cupid might not have repaired their friendship in time.

"She's very cuddly, and she loves to play catch."

"You don't have to sell it, Q. I'm doing the job," Pan said, cuffing Cupid on the arm as he pushed past him into the extravagant playground of the Millers' great room. "Wow, no wonder you wanted to live here. This house makes mine look like a dump."

Cupid scurried up the stairs behind him. "No, Pan. I miss your place."

Pan wasn't ready to have that conversation yet. "Hungry?"

"Yes. That pizza smells amazing. Is that sausage?"

"And pepperoni."

"*Mmm.* What's in the bag?"

"Bourbon." Pan chuckled at Cupid's expression. "Yeah, you'll hate the first few sips."

"Let me grab some plates and glasses."

"Plates? What do you think the box is for?"

"I don't think Ruthie would approve." *Ruthie, right.* Their invisible hostess. Cupid bent down to release the dog, who made a beeline to Pan's ankles.

Pan shooed the dog away—"Go see Daddy"—which, of course, only made her want Pan more. Each time she skittered back, he gathered her in his palm like a bowling ball and rolled her away. She'd slide halfway down the hallway, scramble onto her paws, and rush him again. "Hey, you remember how Mia's kid wouldn't leave me alone? What is it with puppies and babies?"

Cupid tossed a grin over his shoulder as he plucked two glasses off the shelf. "Too young to know better?"

"Funny." Pan rounded the counter and gave Cupid a friendly hip check. A low growl trilled in Pookie's throat.

"Better watch it, Pan. She's very protective."

"I'll take my chances," Pan said with a confident grin. He pulled the Knob Creek out of the brown paper bag, peeled off the wax, and worked the cork out.

Cupid watched warily as Pan poured a generous shot into each glass. He considered offering a splash of water or a couple of rocks, but why dilute good alcohol?

Pan raised both glasses and handed one to Cupid. "To old friends in new places," Pan started, taking stock of the massive kitchen.

"And forgiveness?" Cupid offered his toast with a hopeful gleam.

"Absolutely." They clinked. "Hang on. Don't drink yet. First, you want to take a good whiff. If you were human, I'd tell you to stick your nose in the glass but—don't."

Cupid lifted his face well above the rim, took the lightest sniff possible, and screwed up his nose. "Wow, that's strong."

"It needs to rest a few minutes. Oh, *I* know. We can put the pizza on our plates while we're waiting. Do you have one of those fancy pie servers?"

"I suppose you'll make fun of me for using napkins, too?"

"If you pull out utensils, I'm leaving."

"Fine, but we're sitting at the table."

"Whatever."

Cupid shuffled to the table like a waiter with his ankles roped together while the dog ran circles around his heels. The novelty of the unknown visitor obviously wasn't enough to dissuade the dog from sticking to Cupid like glue, not that Pan could blame her.

Pan took his first bite of pizza before his ass hit the seat. Manners were no match for a piping hot slice of meat lover's pie. Besides, hadn't he already shown enormous restraint tonight? Both pizza and alcohol had arrived unopened, and Cupid remained unmauled though the thought had occurred more than once.

If Cupid entertained similar thoughts, he hadn't let on. He was too busy eyeing the amber liquid in his glass. "Is it ready yet?" How fluidly Cupid moved from caution to curiosity, probably why introducing him to new earthly experiences had quickly become the most entertaining aspect of Pan's job.

"Sure. Just sip it, okay? It's not one of those sweet cocktails you like so much."

Ever the student, Cupid imitated Pan's subtle swirl of the wrist, gentle tip of the glass, and slow, measured swallow. The face Cupid pulled as the alcohol burned its way down his throat was entirely his own. "Ugh."

Pan didn't bother hiding his amusement. "It's a man's drink."

Cupid traded his drink for a slice of pizza, clearly more to his liking. "This is so much better than everything I've reheated in my microwave."

"You have your own microwave?"

Realizing his gaffe, Cupid shrugged, but how could Pan fault him? To the palace born, Cupid had obviously adapted quite easily to his new, luxurious surroundings. Pan, on the other hand, would never feel fully at home in any indoor dwelling, although he couldn't argue with the miracle of modern plumbing.

"So, what happened to the wine I left you?"

"I drank it the night you left."

Cupid's jaw dropped, not a pretty sight with the half-chewed sausage sitting on his tongue. "The whole thing? By yourself?"

"Yep." Pan grimaced, remembering his little pity party and the unpleasant aftermath. Red wine hangovers were among the slowest of earthly wounds to heal.

"Oh, that reminds me . . ." Cupid jumped out of his seat, bolted from the room, and returned a few minutes later with a wad of cash, which he tossed onto the table.

"What's this?" Pan asked.

"I wanted to buy that wine for you, but I didn't have any money at the time. Ruthie paid me with a check before she left. I cashed it at the grocery store. This is for you."

Pan eyeballed at least three twenties. "Wow. That was an expensive bottle."

"I didn't want to skimp."

"So, how's that heart situation going right now with your Worthy so far away?"

"Fine. Nothing's happening."

Grinning around his pizza, Pan said, "I guess that means you're meant to be right here with me?"

"Or Pookie."

"*Ouch*. Just for that, more bourbon."

Pan snagged the pizza while he was up and slapped the box onto the table. To hell with decorum. Maybe the gods were watching, but Ruthie sure as shit wasn't. He refilled both glasses. If all went well, they'd finish off the bottle together tonight; if not, Pan would finish it off himself after his best friend disappeared.

Cupid sped through the pre-drink routine, braced himself, and tossed back a swig as if taking medicine. "It's getting better," he declared.

"Yeah, your tongue is numb."

"That helps." Cupid took a thoughtful sip, and Pan tried not to smile when Cupid swiftly downed his pizza chaser. "Have you spoken to Cheri since . . . y'know?"

"No. Are you trying to start a fight?"

"No, Pan. I don't want to start anything." The room quieted, the only sound the *swa-swish, swa-swish* of Pookie's tail skimming along the wood floor. "Speaking of fighting . . ."

Pan looked up wearily. "Yes?" If Cupid was about to press this thing with Cheri . . . *goddammit*, way to kill a good buzz.

"I was hoping you would teach me how to fight–with my hands, I mean."

"*Why?*"

"At one point, I thought Zach might punch me, and I realized I have no idea how to fight back."

"You don't need to fight back. You have supernatural reflexes. All you need to do is dodge the good punches."

"That sounds unpleasant."

"It's not ideal. Your goal would be to not get into a fight to begin with."

"You never fight with mortals?"

"I didn't say that."

Cupid narrowed his eyes at Pan. The poor guy had yet to embrace the concept of customized rules.

"Look, I'm the god of the hunt. Fighting is my nature. Who the hell needs to punch Cupid?"

"The guy who thinks Cupid is sleeping with his wife."

"Aha! I see the problem."

"Very funny. Does this mean you won't teach me?"

Pan wiped his mouth and wadded up the elegant dinner napkin. "I suppose I could show you how to throw a punch. If nothing else, it's a great workout." *And I'd get to watch.*

"I guess that'd work. If I'm still here tomorrow." Cupid took a sad sip of his drink.

If Pan had momentarily forgotten they weren't just two buddies sharing a pizza in some McMansion across town, Cupid's grimace reminded him otherwise. His friend was in a significant amount of pain, and it was only going to get worse—the release, the heartbreak, and whatever the gods chose to do to him after that.

"Also, I've been thinking," Cupid said, drifting off into that faraway place where his deep thoughts lived, "if I don't ascend tonight, as much as I'd really like to come back and stay with you, I don't think I can bear to see you with all those other guys. And you shouldn't have to *not* walk around in your underwear in your own house."

Maybe Pan was cruel, or maybe it was the bourbon, but he couldn't help feeling a jolt of satisfaction. He didn't want Cupid to stay across town either, but with the live-in arousal machine, could Pan really promise not to be fornicating night and day? Was he willing to give all that up? "Let me think about it when I'm not half in the bag, okay?"

"Sure." Another awkward silence followed. Sticking to the business at hand seemed to be the safest approach. "So, in case I need to, uh, tidy up here, how much does Ruthie know about you?"

"Only that I'm new in town. I didn't need to tell her as much as I told Mia."

"Just as well."

"Yes, except I don't want her to think I just ducked out of finishing the job or abandoned her."

"Don't worry, Q. I'll tie up any loose ends with the construction project, take care of little Princess Powderpuff here, and make sure your girlfriend understands you didn't just take off. Okay?"

Cupid's gaze darted around the room. "What about us?"

"You-and-me, us?"

"Yeah. We're okay, right? I mean, if I get pulled away, you're not gonna stay mad at me for the rest of eternity?"

"I'm not mad at you."

"You're not?"

"Nope. I believe you're doing the best you can."

Cupid squared his shoulders. "I am, Pan. I swear it." Surely, there was no more guileless creature roaming earth or sky.

"Then, we're good."

The edges of Cupid's mouth lifted, forming once again that newly fallen, pre-fucked-over, reunited-with-his-bestie grin Pan could not resist. "Thanks for giving me another chance, Pan."

Pan tossed Cupid a casual wink, belying feelings that were anything but casual. "Should we kiss and make up now?"

35

GENEROSITY

Zach ducked into the taxi and scooted next to Ruth. A loud moan escaped her as the seat took the weight off her throbbing feet.

"Did you start without me?" He cracked a smile at his lame joke, and she couldn't help but smile back.

"Apparently, my feet did."

"You hate wearing heels."

"Yep."

His grin widened. "You hate dancing."

"Only when I'm sober."

"Hence, the three cosmos."

"Oh god. Did I really drink three?"

"I think so. I might have lost track after my second scotch."

Ruth tipped her head back against the cool seat, closed her eyes, and waited out the spin. "Good thing we're not driving."

Zach's head landed next to hers, his soft chuckle riffling her hair. "Did you drink enough water?"

"We'll find out."

"Here." A cold water bottle met her hand.

"Thanks," she said, opening her eyes and turning ever so cautiously to meet Zach's gaze. "I hope I didn't embarrass you."

"I could never be embarrassed by you, Ruthie. I do, however, think you made the other husbands jealous."

"Pfft. Right."

Zach arched an eyebrow as if he had something to say, then changed his mind. He wriggled a finger into the fat knot of his bow tie and tugged until the ends fall apart. Screwing his chin up out of the way, he fiddled with the top button, exhaling a loud *ahhhh* when it popped open. "God, I really hate these things."

"Some things never change." Like how the glimpse of a crisp, white undershirt still made her tingle. Every damn time.

He gave her a pointed look. "And some things do." *An apology of sorts?*

"We didn't promise to have and hold and never change."

"No, but that doesn't mean it's always easy."

Considering that Zach thrived on change, Ruth took his comment as a very sweet acknowledgment of how hard this was for her.

"Nothing worthwhile ever is."

"True." He clasped her hand. "The Langstons offered to give us a guided tour of the city tomorrow."

"Oh. That's sweet. They seem very nice."

"I told them no thanks."

"You did?"

"I want us to explore together—alone. Find our own favorite spots."

"Very romantic, Zachary."

"Look who's talking. You dropped everything and flew out here. I'm still blown away."

Yes, you pulled the rug out from under me, but I am ready to step into this adventure with you. "I'm your wife. Of *course* I wanted to be here for your big night."

"Well, I understand it was no small thing for you."

"I would never have forgiven myself if I missed such an important moment. You don't get a second chance at those."

"No."

"I feel like I've already missed so much—"

Zach shifted in his seat to face her. "Ruthie, can I ask you a huge favor? I know we have some difficult talks ahead of us, and both of us will have to say and hear things that might be painful. I promise you, I'm ready to have those conversations. But *more than anything,* I really need to get my very sexy wife to my hotel room and peel off that dress you've been teasing me with all night and remind you how much I love you"—he pressed his lips to the delicate skin behind her ear—"and appreciate you"—traced the shell of her ear with his tongue—"and *want* you"—and nibbled on her earlobe. "Do you think you can trust in us and set all the talking aside until I'm finished ravishing you?"

Yes, she wanted that so much, too. "So, what you're saying is, you want to have make-up sex *first* and make up *afterward*?"

Zach laughed right out loud, a deep, bold belly laugh that filled the back seat with his joy. "Is that what I said?"

"Yep, and the answer is yes."

She took in Zach's grateful smile, burrowed her face into the crook of his neck, and closed her eyes. There Ruth nestled until the taxi slowed to a stop.

Zach chuckled into her hair. "I hate to disturb you, but I need my hand."

Ruth's eyes blinked open to the sight of a uniformed man opening her door. "Welcome back." *Buddy, you have no idea.*

Ruth barely had time to register the pain of standing on her swollen feet before Zach's arm looped around her waist. He leaned in close and said, "Can you walk, or should we find a hot bellboy to roll you upstairs on one of those brass carts?"

"Just help me to the elevator, funny guy."

"Don't say I didn't offer."

She kicked off her pumps inside the elevator, releasing a loud sigh as her toes wiggled free.

Zach eyed her enviously. "I cannot wait to open this cummerbund."

"Do it!"

"Nope."

"Why not? We're alone, and besides, you're unembarrassable."

"Can't." He tipped his head to watch the numbers light up. "I need both hands free when we get to the tenth floor."

"Why?"

Zach reached into his jacket pocket and handed her the card key. "Hold this?"

"Oh lord, Zach. What are you—"

The elevator dinged, and Zach whooshed her off her feet and into his arms. "This feels like an occasion to carry my bride over the threshold."

"*Ohmygod*, Zach! Put me down before you hurt yourself."

"You insult my manhood, woman."

"You underestimate my womanhood, man."

"Don't make me laugh." His footfalls landed like Frankenstein's monster, jouncing her from side to side, but there would be no stopping him now. Nobody could out-stubborn Zachary Miller once he'd made up his mind.

Ruth gave up the fight and rested her cheek against his chest. "At least your heart is still beating."

"Just for you, Ruthie."

"I think scotch makes you mushy."

A crooked smile settled on his face, or was it Ruth's skewed view? She became so enthralled with trying to solve that mystery, she didn't notice when Zach stopped walking.

"*Ahem.* Mind opening the door, dear? I got my hands full here."

Ruth stretched the key card toward the handle but couldn't quite reach. "A little lower, please?"

Zach guffawed. "Your wish is my command."

He dipped lower, angling Ruth toward the door—and the floor. The sway, on top of the alcohol, made her head spin. "Whoa." She gripped him tighter with the hand still wrapped behind his neck.

"Could you maybe work a little faster, darling?"

"Why, am I getting heavy?"

"Not at all." As if he'd ever admit to weakness.

Ruth tapped the card against the sensor—once, twice, and miracle of miracles, the little green light blinked on. She grabbed the handle and shoved.

Zach stumbled inside just as Ruth started to make a very ungraceful exit from his arms. She managed to get one foot beneath her, but foot number two had no such luck. Zach held on valiantly, teetering as Ruth tottered, until they balanced out to a steady whole greater than the sum of its wobbly parts.

Ruth refastened her hands behind his neck and fluttered her eyelids damsel-in-distress style. "My hero."

Zach's smile was crooked after all, Ruth decided, just before he leaned in to kiss her with it. Yep, still a total pushover for Zach's kisses. If he even *looked* at her lips with that hooded *you-are-mine*, she'd feel that certain tug inside, as if he'd pulled a string connected directly to her pleasure center. Zach knew this—how could he not?—and yet, he'd always been stingy with his kisses. Maybe they didn't thrill him the same way, or maybe he worried they'd lose their punch, like the old Dustbuster that could barely suck up a grain of salt even with a full charge.

To be fair, kissing required two people to be in the same place at the same time, ideally awake. They were certainly both here now, and Zach seemed to be in a most generous mood.

His sexy mouth merged with hers, pleading yet demanding. He coaxed her lips apart with a whisper of tongue. Their kiss sealed off a world where only the two of them existed. *Connected.* An intimacy they hadn't shared since . . . Ruth couldn't remember the last time, especially through the cosmo haze.

Zach slipped one hand to the nape of her neck and caught her with the other when her knees went weak. His smile creased her cheek. "Y'okay there, tiger?" He barely broke their kiss and didn't wait for her answer. She didn't want him to.

The delicious tease of tongue-on-tongue made Ruth's head swim. She was a live wire in an electrical storm, but if their long-awaited reunion ended with this kiss, then *dayeinu*—it would have been enough.

Here lies Ruth Margolis Miller.
Killed by her husband's kiss.
Died with a smile on her face.

Oh yeah, she was feeling that third cosmo. And the electrifying friction with her husband's body, hard and excited and ready, the bulge below his cummerbund making its presence known. A giddy sigh escaped her. Zach answered with a needy grunt, setting off a shock wave deep in Ruth's belly. With a tender swirl of his tongue, Zach pulled away, drawing a frustrated growl that sounded more Pookie than Ruthie.

He dropped a soft kiss on her nose and chuckled. "Hold that thought. I'll be right back."

"*Back?*"

Where the hell was he going, leaving her all revved up, not to mention unsteady on her sore feet? Punch-drunk on kisses and for-real-drunk on vodka was a tricky combination at the end of a long, stressful day.

Zach seemed to shift into fast-forward, stepping out of his shoes, shrugging off his jacket, snapping off the cummerbund, whipping the bow tie through the collar and tossing it onto the pile. He dimmed the lights—*ahh, so much better*—and dug his phone out of his pants. Was he scrolling through his messages? Ruth tracked his movement until her eyelids grew too heavy.

Soft guitar strains filtered through Ruth's brain fog. *Oh, Zach.* The rhythm lifted her heels—left, right, left, right. In her mind, she was dancing. Her head lolled back—*whoa.*

A pair of sturdy arms closed around Ruth's waist. Her eyes popped open.

Zach stood there, grinning down at her while his Adam's apple bobbed oh-so-sexily. "You started without me again."

"Well, you keep leaving me." She'd only meant he'd walked away, but sometimes, the darnedest things slipped out.

Zach's grin flattened. "Oh, Ruthie." He pulled her into his chest and hugged her tight. "I'm right here."

She rested her head on his chest. "I'm here, too," Ruth mumbled, the tail end catching on a sob.

His hand moved slowly up and down her back. She leaned on him, and he held her up—just as he'd vowed he'd always do, right before they danced to this song at their wedding.

"I'm sorry, Zach. We said we weren't gonna ruin this."

"We're not ruining. We're dancing." At best, they were rocking, but if a little Billy Joel made Zach feel like Fred Astaire, Ruth wasn't about to burst his bubble.

She sniffle-laughed into his chest. "And now I'm getting your shirt all wet."

Zach ran his finger down the edge of her hair, tucked it behind her ear, and met her tipsy gaze. "I guess you better take it off, then."

First-date butterflies beat at Ruth's chest as she reached for the top stud. Her knuckles brushed Zach's undershirt. His mouth fell open with a soft exhale. She hungered for those lips again, rosy and plump from all their kissing. She trailed two fingernails to the next stud. Zach tipped his chin to watch her pop each stud through its hole. Drag . . . *pop*. Drag . . . *pop*.

His lips quirked into a lazy grin as she fingered the button at his waist. "Looks like you're all out of studs."

It was a layup for any romantic heroine worth her salt, but as drunk and horny as she was, Ruth couldn't bring herself to deliver the cheesy comeback. Besides, Billy Joel's final refrain of "You're My Home" had just melted into the opening twang of "Wicked Game." *Bye-bye, brain cells.*

Zach would have his own version of their first time, but he'd be wrong where his memories deviated from Ruth's. That one precious event had seared itself forevermore onto her brain, providing a library's worth of full-sensory details Ruth had lovingly sprinkled across her stories though she was always careful to distort the facts just enough to keep the original sacred.

Zach shyly closing the door of his tiny single. Heavy breathing, sloppy kisses, the random clang-clang *of the ancient radiator. Kiss-walking together to the orange-crate stereo setup, Zach blindly slapping for the power button of the CD player behind his back,* "Wicked Game" *pouring through the speakers. The shallow rise and fall of Zach's bare chest, quickening when she placed her hand over his heart. Zach's soft trail of kisses from the base of her neck to the shell of her ear. His fingers fumbling at the clasp of her bra, sliding the straps off her shoulders, the soft brush of his thumb, Ruthie's shiver. Zach's eyes blazing with desire, the flick of his wrist at the button of his jeans, the slow unzip as if unearthing buried treasure. Mirror-image slides of panties and boxers down shaky legs. Zach gently drawing her hand to his terrifying, thrilling erection, the weight of his flesh in her palm, the power she wielded over him. His guttural grunts, narrowed eyes, the slow, sexy pump of his hips. The ache between her legs, falling onto the thin mattress together, his first touch. The pinhole of pleasure spreading, deepening, mounting . . . exploding into a burst of impossible bliss behind her eyes. Zach's triumphant grin.*

Zach knee-walking between her legs, sheathed and ready, eager but so, so patient. Hands gliding up the insides of her thighs: "Are you sure you want this, Ruthie?"

"God, I want you, Ruthie." Zach bunched up her dress until he met the backside of his favorite panties. "I knew it," he said with a smirk. His fingers plunged inside the elastic, and he tugged her into his hips with a firm squeeze.

More. Ruth grabbed a handful of Zach's undershirt at each side of his waist and pushed upwards until the material was trapped across his chest. Goose bumps jumped to life under her fingertips.

"Zach . . ." she mumbled with an impatient tug, ". . . *stuck*."

He snickered as the message reached his brain. With a farewell tap, Zach withdrew his hands from her panties, made quick work of his cufflinks, and peeled off both shirts. Holding out his cupped hand, he wriggled his fingers. "Don't want to lose my deposit." Ruth dropped the studs on top of the cufflinks, and Zach turned to set the jewelry and his glasses on the nightstand.

The rear view wasn't half bad—Zach's tush in the snug trousers and those two cute Venus dimples just above his waist—but when he turned around and faced her again, all she could see was the Bermuda Triangle of erotica.

What would Thea do?

Ruth stepped toward Zach . . . and closer yet . . . worked open the clasp and drew down his zipper. Zach grinned with delight and answered her uncharacteristic assertiveness by tugging open the bow behind her neck. The top of her dress flopped forward, baring her breasts to the cool air and Zach's heated gaze. She didn't question his desire; even an old, drunken fool like Ruth could read it in his eyes. Zach bent to kiss her, tender at first, then rougher. Ruth ran her fingers through his hair, lifted his head from her chest, closed her mouth over his.

"Take me to bed," she whispered between hard kisses.

"Mmm." Zach smiled against her mouth. "You know I love it when you talk dirty, Ruthie."

Zach took over his own de-pantsing, followed swiftly by her undressing, both of which suited Ruth fine. Zach was better at it anyway. They kissed, less frantic now that they were almost there.

He tipped Ruth gently onto the turned-down sheets and lowered his head to her belly. She could have enjoyed that right now, buoyed by eighty-proof self-esteem and the magic of their reunion, but there was something urgent about the way she needed Zach tonight. She wanted everything at once—her whole husband: heart, body, and soul.

She reached down and tapped his shoulder. He looked up, puzzled. If only she could have spoken all her emotions out loud. She crooked a finger instead. If any part of him was disappointed, she sure didn't see it. He settled over her, his arms and shoulders bearing his weight as he pushed inside.

In recent years, they'd so rarely made love face-to-face, the position of their passionate youth. How much better Zach and Ruthie knew themselves and each other now than their first breathless joining—what they would stand for, where time would wrinkle their faces and gray their hair, how life could be so much sweeter and so much crueler than two innocent, wide-eyed kids could ever have imagined. How the smallest challenges—or nothing at all, really—could drive a wedge between them, and how hard they'd have to fight for the love they were sure would always come so easily.

She'd never been much for that romance drivel where the character shouted out her partner's name in the throes of passion, but when Zach lifted his head, she *saw* him all the way back to December 19 of 1989, plain as day. There he was, the earnest boy who'd promised she was the love of his life two seconds before he deflowered her. She'd believed him then with her whole heart, and she knew it now with her whole life.

"I love you, Zach." She circled her arms around his neck and collapsed his push-up against her body.

Zach found her lips and kissed Ruth until they couldn't breathe. "*Fuck*, Ruthie"—he gasped for air and kissed her again—"I love you, too."

They spiraled up the steep cliff together, riding that razor's edge between the highest expression of love and the basest form of pleasure. Zach drove into her, again and harder still. Greedy for more, she dug in her heels and forced him deeper. He blinked, surprised, before his eyes pinched shut against the mounting pressure. He crashed into her with all the finesse of a battering ram, spilling groans into Ruth's open mouth.

Zach drew a sharp breath, then snapped like a rubber band pulled too tight. She found her ecstasy a split second before he erupted into wild, erratic thrusts. They panted and quaked together, two bodies fused into one, until the last of the sweet aftershocks finished with them, and then they dozed.

36

RELEASE

Damn Pan's supernatural hearing. Did Cupid really have to beat off at this fucking hour? Pan's bourbon-soaked gut had only stopped churning a half hour ago, finally letting him settle into his much-needed beauty sleep. Judging by the volume, Cupid's one-man show would soon be over.

Pan flipped onto his belly and pulled one of the spare pillows over his head. It was no use.

Was Q *trying* to drive him nuts? Some kind of twisted farewell gift to Pan: a soundtrack permanently etched into his memory or leaving Pan infuriated so he wouldn't miss him. *Fat fucking chance.*

Most likely, Q wasn't thinking about Pan at all, but his precious Ruthie, off banging her husband in some faraway hotel room. Sure, that would make Q sad but wouldn't stop him from pitching a tent. Couldn't blame him there. For all they knew, this was Cupid's last hurrah with the wonder cock. *Jesus*, there was a depressing thought.

Fine, have at it, but couldn't the guy at least have had the decency to keep it quiet instead of filling Pan's throbbing head—actually, both of his throbbing heads—with unwanted arousal? He had half a mind to stalk across the hall and take Cupid's cock into his own damn hand. He'd show his good buddy how to finish the job, and then they could both get some shut-eye. In Pan's state of agitation and exhaustion, half a mind was apparently enough.

Throwing off the covers, he bolted upright, knocking his equilibrium out of whack and nearly pitching headfirst to the floor. A brief but fruitful inner dialogue on the pros and cons of underwear followed. Modesty didn't concern Pan, but self-preservation did—especially in the region in question. Did he really want to test his self-control by popping in, buck naked, on Cupid buttering the corn? No, that seemed like a very poor choice.

He hooked a toe inside his discarded boxers and drew them deliberately up one leg, then the other. Planting his feet flat on the floor, he stood slowly and checked his balance. Vertical, for now. He pulled the underwear over his thighs and paused to marvel at the persistence of his full chub before tucking it under the waistband. *Oh, to be a demigod.*

Sufficiently swaddled, Pan ventured into the hallway. The hullabaloo grew louder, Pan's indignation more righteous. Cupid's pre-orgasmic melody was godawful, really. *Not sexy, bro.* More of a keen than a moan, Pan realized as he lifted his knuckles to knock. In fact, Cupid sounded more like a wounded animal than one in heat.

Oh . . . fuck.

Pan burst into the room and bolted to the bed, where Cupid lay writhing in pain, thrashing at the twisted covers and clutching his heart through his T-shirt with both hands. "Q!"

Cupid turned, his anguished face completely drained of color. Sweat spewed out his pores at an alarming rate.

I am such an asshole.

"Shit, shit, *shit!* Breathe, dammit!"

"Trying," he choked out.

"Talk to me. What's happening?"

Cupid licked his parched lips. "I guess I did it."

"You did what?"

"Ru—*owwww*—Ruthie." A shadow of a smile crossed Cupid's face, then vanished. "Liminal . . . they made it."

So this was the heart release Pan had missed witnessing the first time around. No wonder Mia had thought Cupid was dying of a heart attack.

Pan checked over his shoulder for Mercury. *This could be it, the* exodos, *Cupid's final tragic scene.* The clock was ticking, and there wasn't a damn thing Pan could do about it. His own heart banged around inside his chest like a paddle ball ricocheting off cement walls. Watching his best friend suffer was horrific; watching him leave would be worse.

Taking great care not to jostle Cupid, Pan perched at the edge of the bed, grabbed the water bottle on the nightstand, and twisted off the cap. "Drink. You're dehydrated."

Cupid scowled at him. "Not my . . . biggest . . . problem."

"No," Pan answered, "but it's the only one we can fix."

Cupid lifted his head and made a half-hearted attempt to choke down a few sips of water before another seizure, the harshest yet, wracked his body. A hideous wail escaped him. Pan held his breath until the worst had passed.

Cupid tipped the bottle into his mouth again, taking tentative sips at first, then guzzling down the rest. The empty bottle slipped out of Cupid's hand as he sagged into the pillow and closed his eyes. "I think it's over."

"Well, hallelujah." Pan might have been more relieved if Cupid hadn't looked so damn corpse-like.

"Don't forget, Pookie needs her eye drops in the morning."

"Shut up."

Cupid opened one eye and trained it on Pan. "Just in case."

"Fuck that." Pan clambered next to Cupid and snaked a burly arm under Cupid's sweat-soaked neck and the other across his chest. "I am not gonna keep saying goodbye to you, Q. I can't. Do you understand?"

Cupid turned his head and met Pan's sad gaze with one of his own. "I do."

They lay quietly together, words completely useless. Pan ticked off the seconds in his head. No sign of Mercury, and they were coming up on the outer limit. Holding Cupid tighter wouldn't change anything, but Pan refused to loosen his grip.

"Am I staying?" Cupid whispered after what should have been a safe margin.

"Looks like it," Pan whispered back.

Cupid smiled.

Pan shook his head. "That's nothing to smile about, you poor fucker."

"Yeah," Cupid said, his mouth widening into an even bigger grin. "I know."

Pan dropped his face to Cupid's shoulder so his friend wouldn't see the tears. "Can we *please* get some sleep now?"

37

PILLOW TALK

A siren filtered through Zach's snooze. *I must be dreaming* was Zach's first thought as he eased into the here and now: the rumble of the city streets, the dull ache in his head, soft flesh beneath him.

Microflashes of memory popped into his brain like tiny sunbursts on the black curtain of sleep: *Glover. Hotel. Ruthie.*

His eyes flew open. *She really is here.*

Ruthie slept soundly, pinned on her back by Zach's entire right side. *That happened.* Zach hadn't moved an inch since pulling out.

Why would he? Ruthie had come for him—then come *with* him. They were going to be okay. Better than okay. They were a couple again but not the same couple they'd been in Tarra three days ago—all credit to Ruthie.

Zach didn't yet know this woman who'd stormed the fortress, guns a-blazing, willing to risk it all to save their marriage. She'd made him feel like a rock star, and he had to admit, her rose-colored view was contagious. How could all that adulation not make him feel like a sex god?

How lucky was Zach, straddling the best of both worlds? Reliving the breathless passion of their first time while enjoying all the endearing qualities as familiar to him as the back of his own hand.

I'm having an affair with my own wife.

The adorable pout of her slightly open mouth, dragging in each breath with a soft snore she'd deny if he teased her about it. The uneven line of mascara she always cursed while applying and forgot to remove until it clumped in her eyes the next morning. The soft blond hair that had yet to show any signs of aging, unlike his own "distinguished" temples, scattered in twelve different directions on her pillow.

Ruthie would never have let him get away with such blatant ogling if she'd been awake, especially of the "bowling pin" breasts she'd always found saggy and unattractive, an opinion Zach did not share. He especially loved how, at the lightest caress, her nipples would gather into tight little knots—*well, hello*—yes, just like that.

"Are you taking advantage of me while I sleep?"

Busted.

"Your nipple woke me up."

Ruthie grinned. "You're seriously blaming my nipple?"

"Yes, but I forgive you."

A yawn forced Ruthie's mouth open, rippled through her body, and shook her extremities like the end of a delicious orgasm. Zach needed to give her lots more of those.

"*Mmm.* What time is it?"

Zach twisted to check his phone. "It's 2:18."

Ruthie huffed. "So much for staying up all night."

"Just a brief intermission. We still have another four hours till sunrise."

He grazed his thumb back and forth across her breast, enjoying the hell out of her goose bumps and quickened breaths.

Ruthie's gaze met his, shifted to her nipple, and back; Zach's did the same.

He flexed his hips so she could feel his need against her leg. *You sure are a cheap date tonight, Zach Miller.*

"Wow." She quirked an eyebrow. "Really?"

"Can I help it if I get excited looking at my naked wife?"

"Pfft! Who could possibly blame you?"

"Exactly." He popped his eyebrows a few times to counteract her sarcasm.

She smacked her lips together. "I should probably brush my teeth."

"You're really gonna make me move?" Zach tipped onto his side, spilling a sticky puddle between them. "Good thing you woke me. If we'd stayed like that much longer, we might have been glued together forever."

Ruthie shook her head as she scooted toward the edge of the bed. Zach propped his head in his hand, surprisingly excited to watch her walk away.

"Hey, don't go putting on any clothes while you're up."

"Oh shit!" Ruthie whipped around. "I just realized I left our suitcase at the Hay."

"Whoops. I guess we got a little carried away."

"Might've had something to do with the alcohol."

"And you showing up in a backless dress."

"You didn't have to look so hot in that tux, mister."

"If you're that excited about the tux, I'll take the damn thing home. Screw the deposit."

"It's not really about the tux, Zach."

He returned her warm smile. "Use my toothbrush. We'll arrange for a courier in the morning, *or* we could just stay in the hotel room, naked, all weekend."

Ruthie nailed Zach with a once-over that set his skin on fire.

"Let's see how the rest of the night goes." She was all talk, and they both knew it, but he'd take a flirty, naked Ruthie any day.

He gave her a few minutes of privacy before joining her in the bathroom. Careful not to make her self-conscious, Zach tracked Ruthie out of the corner of his eye as she grimaced at her reflection.

"I look like a raccoon who got into a bar fight."

Zach glanced over and grinned. "Ooh, you're right. I think I'll take you from behind next time."

"Rude!" She slapped him on the arm as she hurried back to bed, giggling.

Zach grabbed a fresh hand towel and made a point of tossing it across the bed onto the nightstand.

"Optimistic, aren't we?" Ruthie said.

"Always." That wasn't exactly true. In fact, it had been a long damn time since Zach had dared assume any action was coming his way, let alone twice in one night.

Ruthie flipped onto her side, her back to Zach. Without a moment's hesitation, Zach burrowed under the covers and snuggled in close. When one's wife writes her sexual fantasies in vivid detail, a wise husband does not let the intel go to waste. It just so happened that Zach had very recently taken a refresher course taught by none other than Henry the handyman.

Zach wouldn't describe himself as a masochist, and yet, how else could he explain Monday night's self-flagellation? Riding high on the board's approval, Zach had taken Joan to dinner, where they'd finished off a bottle of Caymus. The buzz followed him back to his hotel room, where he'd planned to fall into a deep, contented sleep. Unfortunately, the giant wall of loneliness waiting inside his room didn't get the memo. Not only was Ruthie not there to share Zach's success, but he fully expected she'd be upset with him—like, *marriage-rocking* upset—for keeping the move a secret. To top it all off, Ruthie was back home in Indiana playing house with the hot, horny handyman.

Somehow, in the grip of his maudlin, wine-infused mood, Zach had decided a reread of *Fixer Upper* would bring him closer to Ruthie. Two hours later, Zach knew for sure the reread had been a terrible mistake. What had once lived as a mere fictitious flight of fantasy had materialized in flesh and blood as if conjured by Ruthie's words. Pinocchio had become a real boy, and it wasn't Quentin's nose that kept Zach up at night. Perhaps most troubling of all, Zach had sprouted wood from the reread. Despite basically watching his wife have an affair, Zach was turned on. And boy, did that piss him off.

He'd slept poorly and sucked it up for the real estate agent, but his heart wasn't in it. Every showing was a new mistress. The apartment Zach suspected Ruthie would love was the sluttiest of all, splayed open in the light of day, displaying all her treasures for every stranger who walked through the door. Later, he'd cloaked himself in the monkey suit and danced for his new investors. Not that Zach minded; he just missed his dance partner. And then she showed up.

Henry retreated to the realm of the imaginary, where he was not only tolerable but instructive. Thea was all about the slow tease. Zach could manage that, now that they'd gotten the initial, frantic bone-jumping out of the way. He started with a tickle at her neck and moved lower with a whisper-light touch. Ruthie never could resist a back scratch, especially when chased by a trail of soft kisses across her shoulders. She rewarded him with a sigh and wriggled backward against his chest. Slipping an arm across her belly, Zach tucked her to him. The soft pillows of her bottom nestled against his groin, exactly where they belonged.

"So, I have a confession to make," he whispered into her neck.

Ruthie tensed. "Zach, *don't*."

"Don't?"

"I always thought I'd want to know, but now that it's in my face, I really don't think I could handle knowing you slept with another woman."

He bolted up beside her. "*What?*"

"Seriously. Please, don't."

"Ruthie, I didn't sleep with another woman."

She flipped onto her back. "You didn't?"

"You seriously need to ask me that?"

"I don't know. I guess I got a little crazy." What killed Zach was that Ruthie didn't sound angry, just sad.

"You *guess*? Ruthie, do you really think that little of me or our marriage?"

"I feel like I'm holding you back sometimes, and Joan"—she said the name as if sucking on a lemon—"wants to help you soar."

"I can't soar without you."

"You seemed like you were doing pretty well. That email you sent me right after the meeting?"

"Yeah, I was excited, but this whole thing didn't make any sense until you showed up. I was a bit of a wreck last night, worried you'd hate the whole idea."

"Well, you know, Zach, there was a simple way for you to find out how I'd feel."

Zach slumped onto his back beside her and searched the ceiling for wisdom. "I'm sorry, Ruthie. I guess I was afraid you'd discourage me from the expansion, and I felt, with all my heart, this was the right direction for the organization."

Ruthie turned toward Zach. "I get it," she said.

Zach propped his head with his hand and met her gaze. "What do you mean?" He held his breath, praying he wouldn't have to speak the painful truths.

"I'm a homebody. I don't exactly embrace change."

Zach smiled. "No, but I should've given you the benefit of the doubt."

"Yeah. That hurt."

"I'm sorry. By the time I found out Glover wanted to move me to DC, you'd already started work on your study. I know how important this project is for you, and I didn't want you to stop moving forward."

"*Again.*" There was no way not to feel the weight of all of Ruthie's self-recrimination and Zach's disappointment over the years.

Zach shrugged. "I was damned if I told you and damned if I didn't, but this grant wasn't a certainty. I rolled the dice. I'm sorry if not bringing you in earlier was a bad decision."

"Honestly, I understand why you didn't. I guess part of me is glad I finished the room even if I won't be able to use it now. It would have been a lot harder to leave the nursery behind." Her thoughtful expression softened into a misty-eyed smile. "I did it, Zach. I finally let go."

"You did. I am so proud of you."

He linked his fingers with her hand against the bed, leaned in, and kissed her in that way that leads to more. She moaned into his mouth; his groin answered with a pleasant tug.

Things were just getting serious when Ruthie pulled back. "Hey, what was your confession?"

He smiled. "I reread your handyman story last night."

"What? You too?"

"Me, *too?*"

It was too dark for Zach to tell if she was blushing, but he could sure as shit see her eyes darting around the room. Zach wasn't sure how to feel about Ruthie rereading the story with the embodiment of Henry just a few yards away. Not to mention how quickly she'd leapt to the wrong conclusion about Joan. What was that saying—*the cheater always suspects?*

Unlike his delicate wife, Zach needed to hear the truth, no matter what. "Ruthie? Should I be asking if something happened with Quentin?"

"No. *God*, Zach. He's a friend." Ruthie couldn't lie to save her life—or marriage.

Zach let out a rocky breath. "I believe you."

"Good. So, you're not jealous?"

"Of course I'm jealous."

"Oh, Zach. You know I'd never be unfaithful."

His heart was still catching up with his head on that point. Zach trailed his finger down Ruthie's cheek. "He brought your smile back. That was *my* job."

"God knows, you tried. I wasn't ready."

"I shouldn't have given up so easily."

"Easily?" Ruthie chuffed. "Zach, it's been years. Maybe I just needed someone whose heart wasn't also broken to lift me out of my coffin."

"Come on, Ruthie," Zach said as gently as possible, considering his own heart was still feeling a little wobbly. "It doesn't hurt that the guy could be Adonis's twin, and he obviously has a thing for you. He told me as much himself."

"I won't deny it was nice to feel wanted."

"That's my job too," Zach answered. "I never stopped wanting you, but I certainly failed at convincing you."

"You don't get to take the blame for that. I'm the one who packed on the pounds. It's pretty hard to feel sexy when you can't stand the sight of yourself."

"And yet, a total stranger managed to."

"There's no accounting for taste." Ruthie reached out and ran her hand up Zach's bent arm, giving his shoulder a squeeze.

"Lucky for me, or I never would've caught a girl like you."

"Mmhmm." She rolled her eyes, her usual response to anything close to a compliment. "Because you weren't hot at all, Mr. 'Wild Thing.' Speaking of which, when did you make that playlist?"

"Oh, I, uh, made it for our anniversary, but that night didn't exactly go as I'd hoped."

"Wow. You really are so much more romantic than I am."

He drew her hand to his lips and left a soft kiss on her knuckles. "Don't tell anyone, but I'm married to a romance writer." *Wink.*

"I think you've always been a few steps ahead of me. Remember how you used to microwave popcorn to cover up for the vomit smell of those gingko trees that mated outside your dorm room?"

"But we had to keep the windows open because there was no way to turn down the heat?"

"And I thought you were deliberately turning your room into a sauna so I'd take off my clothes."

Zach sighed. "Back in the good old days, when you believed that I loved seeing you naked."

Ruthie skimmed his cheek with her soft palm. "I believe you now."

"That's good." Zach sighed. "We need to be more careful this time, Ruthie. We're not actually invincible."

"No. Even the hardiest tree will die without sunlight and water."

"Don't forget fertilization, baby," Zach added, with a thrust of his hips.

"Such a romantic." Ruthie giggled as Zach rolled between Ruthie's legs and put an end to the discussion.

38

HOMEWARD BOUND

"*Ahhh*. Home, sweet home."

"For now," Ruth answered quietly, staring out the window as the taxi turned onto their street. Normally, coming home was her favorite part of any trip, but this place had an expiration date. The decay had already begun.

Zach pulled her hand into his lap and wriggled his fingers until they settled between hers. "You okay?"

"Yeah, I guess I've been so excited to start our new life, it just hit me what we'll be leaving behind."

"I promise I won't rush you. We'll ease into the transition."

The transition. Packing up their lives into cardboard boxes. Selling the house they'd built from the foundation up. Leaving her kids at the center. Saying goodbye to dear friends who'd shared the good times and held them up through the awful ones.

Change sucked, even good change, but if she were honest, the idea of leaving Tarra scared Ruth far less than returning now to the "scene of the crime," this place where they'd both forgotten who they'd promised to be. Would the magic cocoon of four days alone in their new city—hand-holding and stolen kisses, real conversation, making love like newlyweds—shield them from the dull blade of the familiar or the temptations that had sunk their hooks into each of them?

Sigh.

Adonis's twin, Zach had called Quentin. Ruth certainly wouldn't dispute the resemblance, but his physical being, though spectacular, was only a fraction of the seduction. Quentin oozed a lethal combination of charisma and sincerity, and Ruth had always been a sucker for both. On top of all that, he was unfairly talented with his hands. The guy even loved her dog, for crying out loud.

And, as she'd confessed to Zach, it was nice to be wanted. Would Ruth have fallen for Quentin if there hadn't been such a huge void in her marriage? With the rift now repaired, surely Q's charms would be easier to resist.

Her theory lost steam the closer they drew to Quentin's figure at the top of the driveway. He looked over his shoulder and smiled at their approaching taxi. An unnaturally perfect ray of sunshine filtered through the treetops and bathed Quentin in a supernatural glow, and if that weren't bad enough, he had to go and bend over in his hip-hugging jeans, scoop up Pookie, and jog over to greet their car as if he'd been desperate for Ruth's return.

A sharp squeeze of Ruth's hand startled her. *Oops.*

Zach chuckled and gave her a gentle nudge. "Go. I know how much you missed your . . . little marshmallow."

Only slightly tormented by her own eagerness, Ruth sprang out of the back seat, straight into Quentin's welcome-home hug. So much for resisting. For a split second, Ruth forgot about the dog smooshed between them until Pookie let out a harsh *yip*.

Quentin jumped back. "Sorry, girl."

Not one to easily forgive, Pookie glowered at Quentin, scrambled out of his arms, and flew into Ruth's.

"Aww, I think someone's jealous." Ruth barely had time to close her mouth before Pookie's sandpaper tongue made a swipe at it.

"Ahem." Zach pulled up short behind Ruth and snaked an arm around her waist. His warm breath tickled Ruth's ear. "I think I know how she feels."

Quentin's shell-shocked stare bounced back and forth between them. "But I thought . . . I mean, it *seems* that everything went well."

"It did." Ruth and Zach answered together, looked at each other, and grinned.

Zach's hand shot out toward Quentin, releasing Ruth from his embrace but not from the man sandwich, of which she and Pookie were the filling. "I was just messing with you."

"Oh." Quentin took Zach's offered hand as if testing the shower before stepping inside.

"Ruthie was right about you, Q. All of it. Thank you."

"Sure," Quentin answered, regarding all three Millers as if they hailed from a different planet.

"Okay, then," Zach said with a clap of his hands, "Pookie and I are going inside to unpack." He grabbed both suitcase handles and set off toward the door. "Come on, girl. Let's go."

Pookie kicked her little legs against Ruth's grasp. Zach's attention was a rare treat Pookie wasn't about to miss. Ruth bent to the lawn just as the dog flew out of her arms and scrabbled after the suitcase wheels. Hyperaware of Quentin's presence beside her, Ruth focused on the disappearing husband and overstimulated cockapoo until the door closed behind them.

"Your husband scares me a little," Quentin said, tracking Zach's movement up the stairs and across the picture window.

"He really is very grateful. We both are."

"Honestly, Ruthie, I'm the one who should be thanking you. You took a huge chance hiring me and then offered me a place to live when everything fell apart with Pan."

"How could I not?"

Quentin huffed. "For starters, you could have said this would really put a strain on your marriage."

"My marriage was strained long before you showed up." After miscarriage number two, Ruth had firmly and conclusively rejected that old cliché, "Things happen for a reason." It was entirely too cruel to imagine her God could have any reason that would possibly justify taking the life of a beautiful, innocent soul. Still, she had to marvel at Quentin's auspicious timing. "I don't know how, but you seemed to drop into our lives out of the clear blue sky right when we needed you." She sniffled, and Quentin lunged forward to comfort her, which made her sniffle harder.

His arms closed gently around her back, and she melted into his embrace. She wasn't tempted to kiss him this time, but boy, did that hug feel nice.

His words floated across the top of her head. "Did you ever think that maybe someone up there knew you deserved to be happy and sent me to help?"

"Please, don't make me cry again. I'm running out of tears."

"As long as they're happy tears, Ruthie."

"Yes," she said, composing herself enough to pull back from his arms. "*Now* they are."

"That's great, Ruthie. I'm really happy for you." She believed him, but his words were tinged with pain.

Loss. Ruth knew it well.

"Zach and I still have a lot to work out, but I found my husband again, and we're gonna be okay."

"I know you are. I knew as soon as you bought that dress."

The dress. *Mmm*, the heat of Zach's palm on her back. "You really think one little dress can save a marriage?"

The dress had served its purpose well, but *still*, it was just a piece of cloth. Quentin seemed so adorably sure of himself though. As if a mere human could actually unravel the mysteries of love.

"It was your moment of commitment. You realized your marriage could actually fall apart, and you set your priorities on winning your husband back."

"Yeah, that was a bit of a shock." Marriages failed all the time, but not Ruthie-&-Zach.

"Ruthie . . ." Quentin reached for her arm, thought better of it, and stuffed his hands inside his jeans. "I don't think any couple believes it can happen to them, until it does."

What an insensitive fool she'd been not to see it sooner. "You've been through a bad breakup. Not a divorce, I hope?"

His lips flattened into a grim line. "No, but a, uh, close friend of mine went through a terrible one."

"I'm sorry. That's awful. I watched Gail go through it. What a miserable process."

He nodded, forcing a smile. "But that's not you. You didn't let that happen."

"Thanks to you."

"You're the one who got on that plane, Ruthie."

She'd never have another chance to speak about this with Quentin, and he deserved to know the truth. "You know, you really shook me with that kiss."

Quentin froze, doe-eyes caught in the headlights. "Ruthie, I'm sor—"

"You were right, though. *Not* kissing you was probably the most proactive feat of my entire relationship with Zach. Up to that point, I never faced any difficult choices. And then you came along, and for the first time, I had to actively resist temptation."

"And you did," Quentin said, managing to look both hurt and proud of Ruth at the same time.

"*Barely*," she shot back, "but knowing our marriage will hold up under pressure is better than never encountering the challenge."

Quentin's right hand escaped his pocket and drifted to his chest like a schoolboy about to say the Pledge of Allegiance. "You enjoy being tested?"

"'Enjoy' isn't quite the right word, but this whole experience made me appreciate that I would, and *did*, choose Zach all over again."

This time, when Quentin met her gaze, his pain pierced her like an arrow through the heart. Why on earth did affirming her love for her own husband feel like the worst breakup ever? It seemed too cliché to voice that Quentin would meet someone far better suited for him than Ruth—someone younger, prettier, single, and fertile.

Every instinct cried out to touch him, but Quentin had imposed the physical distance between them. Respecting his boundaries was the least she could do. "I feel like I need to apologize to you," she said.

"No, Ruthie. Please, don't."

Tears pooled. "You're very, very special to me."

Quentin turned his head as tears streamed down his cheeks. The hand clawed at his chest as if he would gladly rip his heart right out of his body.

"Quentin, I need to tell you something else."

He turned back, a wounded, trapped animal staring down the barrel of the hunter. "What is it?"

"It turns out Zach and I are going to be selling this house and moving to Washington, DC."

"But your sanctuary—?"

"I suppose the next owners are really going to enjoy it."

His shoulders slumped. He shrank three inches. Ruth died a little.

It was foolish and romantic and selfish as hell, but she couldn't help the fantasy that popped into her head and exited her mouth. "You might just have to come out to DC and build me a new one."

Quentin barked out a dark chuckle. "Oh, Ruthie. If I could, I gladly would."

Every syllable of Quentin's body language reinforced his statement: the downward curl of those beautiful lips, the pain at the corner of his once-brilliant blue eyes, the tense line of his posture, as if he were straining forward against a wall he couldn't break through. To belabor the point would be torture for them both.

"If you need a place to live for a while, I can talk to Zach about letting you stay—"

"No, but thank you. I'm actually all packed up and ready to go." He tipped his chin toward the car. Ruth fought back her tears. "Pan and I have worked things out."

"That's wonderful. I'm happy for you, Quentin."

"Thanks. He even came over to help me set up your computer and hang the new lights. I'm not so great with electrical yet." Quentin cheered a bit, and Ruth could breathe again.

"Oh. So, everything is finished, then?" The news would have made her deliriously happy if not for, well, everyone leaving.

"Yes. Did you want to go take a look before I go?" He turned as if to accompany her inside.

"No." She didn't mean it to come out so sharp, but how could either of them handle standing in that space again together?

He whirled around, new hurt sketched across his forehead. *Shit.*

"Quentin," she said gently, "I trust you. I'm sure it's perfect."

One of Quentin's trying-too-hard smiles settled on his face. "Okay."

"I owe you the last payment for your work."

"No, please, Ruthie. You've already paid me more than I would have asked for the whole job."

"But you gave up your whole weekend to stay with Pookie. At least let me—"

"You know I loved taking care of her." He huffed. "I might even have to get a dog of my own now."

"That will be one lucky dog."

He met her gentle smile with a shrug. They were quickly sliding from sad and awkward to downright morose. The meter was running now that he had no reason to stay. The kindest thing to do now was to let him go.

"I really wish there was something more I could do for you, Quentin."

"There is, Ruthie. Be happy."

39

OPEN MIC NIGHT

Pan slapped a glass onto the pockmarked table in front of Cupid. "I strongly suggest you drink this before Euphrosyne comes out to perform."

"What is that?" Cupid asked. The clear liquid looked harmless enough, but the odor was gamier than the comedian-hopefuls waiting their turn for the stage. "Smells like someone set a loaf of moldy bread on fire."

The flimsy wood chair beside Cupid squealed against the floor as Pan dropped onto the seat. "That is a double shot of tequila to help loosen your funny bone."

"Or dissolve it," Cupid grumbled.

"Don't worry. It'll grow back." Pan chuckled at his own dumb fallen god joke and tipped back his beer.

"Maybe you should get in line so you can share your gift with the rest of the audience."

"Nah, that's my secret stash just for you, bro."

"Gee, thanks. So, this comedy club is supposed to be the antidote to my depression?"

"Should be good for a laugh or two."

"Are you sure?"

"Nope," Pan said, grinning.

"I cannot imagine why you are in such a cheerful mood. My ass is going numb in this chair, my boots are stuck to the floor, the air in here tastes like terror, and there's a very unfortunate soul vomiting up what's left of her insides in the ladies' room."

"Oh, that would be Euphrosyne. She's a bit nervous." Pan's smile widened.

"Glad you're so entertained by other people's misery."

Pan rolled his eyes but refused to lose his smile. "Why else would I drag a broken-down, half-starved ghost with a death wish out for a drink?"

Okay, so Cupid hadn't eaten solid food in three days. Would've just come right back up like whatever the pathetic Grace had put in her belly earlier today.

"I don't have a death wish." Cupid pouted as hard as he could, swirled his glass on the table, and lifted the sour drink to his tongue. "But if I did, I wouldn't waste my last swallows on this poison."

Pan's glass met the tabletop with a bang. He plucked the lime wedge from the side of Cupid's glass and shoved it into one of Cupid's hands. "Hold this."

"Hey!"

"Give me your other hand."

Cupid jerked his arm away. "Why?"

Pan's eyes turned a dangerous shade of green. He snapped his fingers. Cupid's heart skipped two beats. In his weakened state, Cupid could not have fought off a sea nymph with two broken arms. Cupid placed his palm on the table and ever so slowly slid his hand toward Pan, who watched it cross the table the way a cat watches the mouse he's about to eat for dinner:

still, silent, focused. Without warning, Pan pounced, pinning Cupid's wrist against the table.

"Ow!"

Pan bent forward and licked a sloppy arc between Cupid's trapped thumb and forefinger.

"What are you doing?" This was not Versailles. There were no boys in go-go shorts. And Cupid was in no mood for . . . for being in that kind of mood.

"Shut it," Pan warned, reaching for the salt and shaking a crescent-moon onto Cupid's slick skin. "Here's what you're going to do. Lick that salt off your hand, down that drink—all of it, because we're only doing this once—shove that lime between your lips, and suck. Got it?"

Cupid nodded. "Lick, drink, suck."

Pan chuckled. "Such a fast learner. I love that about you." He released Cupid's wrist but stayed right there, a breath away. "Do it, Q."

Gulp. Cupid tried not to focus on his tongue meeting Pan's saliva but instead on swooping up each tiny grain of salt. He fought back a gag and the memory of his first time in the sea. Leucothea had tried to teach him to swim and nearly lost her legs when Aphrodite learned that Cupid had been toppled by a wave. With a deliberate shake of his head, Cupid erased the vision and reached for the tequila. At least the alcohol would rid his mouth of the salt.

The yeasty odor crowded his nostrils. *Don't breathe.* He tipped the glass between his lips. The foul drink met his tongue like a fireball issued straight from Typhon's throat. *Swallow.* Fluid leaked from Cupid's eyes and nostrils. *Swallow.* Liquid flames burned the back of his throat. The glass slipped from his mouth.

Pan shifted in his seat, moved to reach for Cupid's drink. He'd force-fed Cupid before, and the results were not pretty. Pan was one tenacious son-of-a-nanny. No, Cupid was getting this tequila down by his own hand.

He poured the rest of the swill into his mouth and swallowed in painful, labored glugs. The fire scalded a path down his gullet and crash-landed in his empty belly. This drink was, by far, the worst of Pan's Earth atrocities, and Cupid was just forming the words to tell him so when the lime was forced between his lips and held there.

"You forgot to suck."

Cupid mustered an angry glare but did as he was told and worked the juice down to counteract the swamp water burning a path to his extremities.

"Attaboy," Pan said with a grin. "That wasn't so bad, was it?"

"Nnnn!" Cupid batted away Pan's hand and spat the lime at his chest.

"Ho-*ho*. I think someone's been out of touch with his table manners for too long. We're going to have to recivilize you when we get home."

As much as he hated to admit it just then, the concept of home warmed Cupid's downtrodden heart, not as violently as the shot of tequila but in a different, nicer way. Certainly, Pan's methods of administering TLC held all the finesse of a cyclops on tiptoes, especially compared to Ruthie's gracious hospitality and many kindnesses. But Aphrodite had set the bar low enough—the goddess didn't exactly ooze maternal instincts—that Pan's tireless efforts made their impression. The least Cupid could do was try to pretend he wouldn't rather be back in bed with the covers pulled over his head.

"Excuse me? Are these seats taken?"

The two pretty girls probably hadn't seen the flying fruit. Or perhaps they had and decided Cupid and Pan were worth enduring a few shenanigans.

Pan hopped right out of his seat, pulled out two chairs, and switched on the charm. "They are now."

Wonderful. Pan could do as he pleased, but Cupid wasn't fit to charm anyone tonight.

The girl next to Pan slid her elbow along the table till it met his. "Are you guys performing tonight?"

Pan leaned in. "Normally, my friend Quentin, here, would have them rolling in the aisles, but we're just here to support a friend."

Two pairs of eyes shifted to Cupid, waiting for him to say something hilarious. If only he'd shoved that lime wedge in Pan's mouth.

"Ladies and gentlemen, let's give a warm Episode welcome to Grace."

Thank the gods, everyone's attention turned toward the first performer, a frail, young woman dragging her feet to the middle of the stage. Grace, *my donkey.* That was Euphrosyne, barely recognizable with the dark circles under her eyes and the drawn, parched lips.

She blinked into the spotlight like a bug squinting into the sun. With shaky hands, she plucked the microphone from its stand and cleared her throat. "I told my friend I was a little nervous about coming out here tonight. He asked me if I had stage fright. I said, 'No, I'm not afraid of the stage. It's the audience that scares me.'"

Pan tensed, squared his shoulders against the back of the chair.

"So, I thought I would try to sit down and write out my jokes with a pencil, but then I realized there was no point."

Ghastly silence.

"The other day, I went to see my gynecologist."

Some guy at the back of the room yelled out, "I hear there are several openings in the field."

Pan's jaw clamped shut so violently, he could've cracked a walnut.

"The doctor crouched between my legs—" Euphrosyne's joke was cut off again by whistles and animal howls, but she pressed on. "While he was down there, he said, 'My, what a big vagina . . . *What a big vagina.*'"

The *woo-woos* and whistles grew louder, drowning out the microphone, but Euphrosyne shouted above the noise. "Naturally, I was a little upset, so I said, 'That's kind of rude, Doc. You didn't have to say it twice.' and he said, 'I didn't . . . *didn't . . . didn't.*'"

A communal groan rose from the audience. Pan leaned in closer to Cupid and whispered, "That joke is so much funnier when Echo tells it."

The boos started in full force. Euphrosyne bolted from the stage.

"I thought she'd never leave," said the girl next to Cupid, with a sneer that turned her pretty face ugly.

Pan shot out of his chair so hard it clattered to the floor behind him. "I better go."

The three of them watched Pan jog after Euphrosyne. The two girls blinked at each other. "Crap. That girl that bombed is your friend?"

How could this unworthy mortal ever understand that without Euphrosyne, there would be no laughter, no comedy clubs, no joy at all in the cosmos? That if Euphrosyne didn't return to Olympus soon, humor would be a distant memory for the human race? A footnote found in the history books but no longer felt in the soul.

At least that nasty smirk on the girl's face would be impossible, so there was that.

"If you ladies will excuse me . . ."

Their apologies reached Cupid's ears, but he couldn't be bothered. He found Pan outside the ladies' room, his head tipped back against the wall.

"Is she sick again?" The awful retching penetrated the door. "Oh. Never mind." Deep inside Cupid's stomach, the tequila rumbled and rolled.

"This was a terrible idea," Pan said. "Euphrosyne is wasting away down here. Mercury tells me her sisters are a mess. They haven't held a single banquet on the Mount since Euphrosyne fell six weeks ago."

"Wow. What are you going to do?"

Pan let out a sigh laced with despair. "I haven't a clue."

Cupid lined up next to Pan against the wall and gave him a gentle nudge. "You'll figure it out."

"Mmhmm, because I'm doing such a bang-up job with you?"

On top of the Ruthie-ache, Cupid's heart could not bear Pan's defeat. "We should get a dog."

"What?" Pan pushed off the wall and rounded on Cupid. "Like I need another creature to care for. All you fallens aren't already a full-time job?"

"I'll take care of it."

"Oh, you will, huh? What happens when you ascend? I'll be stuck with the little shit."

"Don't pretend you didn't like her, Pan."

"Her, *who*? Oh, you mean that little portable poop factory with claws?"

"They're *paws*, not—"

The bathroom door opened. At close range, the scent of spent stomach innards nearly knocked Cupid off his feet. He could hardly believe this misery of a woman was the same goddess who'd danced in the palace not three months ago, back when Cupid was a mischief-making mama's boy, trapped in a useless preteen body, with a heart that had neither exulted nor suffered from love. Before Cupid was reunited with his best friend, before he fell in love with Mia, then Ruthie. A lifetime ago.

"Hey, Euph." Cupid started toward her with arms spread wide despite her offensive odor.

She looked at him oddly. "Who are you?"

"Who *am* I?"

They both turned to Pan, who burst out laughing. "Euphrosyne, meet Earth-Cupid."

Her sunken eyes nearly popped out of her face. "You're *Cupid*?" She stepped back and took a long, hard look. "Wow."

Pan snorted. "Basically."

"Where are your wings?" She peered over his shoulder.

"Gone . . . for now."

"I heard about your fall."

"What are they saying about me?" *Is Mother feeling wretched about punishing me?*

Euphrosyne rolled her eyes toward Olympus. "Just that you picked the wrong goddess to inflame."

Right.

She gathered steam and bravado. "We both know if Hera had even the slightest sense of humor, neither one of us would be down here."

Pan jumped first, pressing his palm to Euphrosyne's lips as gently as he probably could under the dire circumstances. Pan shook his head, and a second later, Euphrosyne nodded.

Pan released his grip. "If you ever want to get home, don't do that again."

"Got it. Speaking of getting home"—she turned to Cupid—"what are they making you do down here?"

"It's kind of a long, complicated story."

"Apparently, I have time." Reminded of her pathetic performance, Euphrosyne frowned at Pan. "I was awful."

Pan opened his mouth to agree, and Cupid stepped in front of him. "I thought your Echo joke was funny."

"You did?"

"Yes. If my heart weren't completely shattered, I would still be laughing."

As if on cue, Cupid's heart jolted awake like a horse bitten by an asp, just when he'd begun to hope the worst was behind him. He clutched his chest, waiting for the blade of lost love to slice him open once again.

"I agree," Pan was saying, "there's gotta be a better way than stand-up. We'll put our heads together in the morning . . ."

Their conversation floated in and out while Cupid battled the force building inside his chest. The Ruthie-pain cleared out, leaving space for the next agony. New love. He didn't know whether to rejoice or cry.

". . . should probably get some food in Cupid's stomach. Q?"

Pan took one look at Cupid's face, and he knew. "Oh shit."

"Yeah."

"*Now?*"

"I'm sorry, Pan. I can't exactly control it."

"Control what?" Euphrosyne asked.

"Are you sure it's not just the tequila burning a hole in your stomach lining?"

"Dammit, Pan, I think I know the difference between my belly and my heart."

"Sorry. Wishful thinking on my part."

"Can someone please tell me what's happening?"

Pan half turned to Euphrosyne, but his eyes never left Cupid. "This is his punishment. We hoped he might have a little break, but the gods have decided otherwise. His heart is pulling him somewhere, and he needs to follow his signal to the next Worthy."

"Worthy, as in Aphrodite's chosen?"

"Um, excuse me," Cupid said, "I hate to interrupt, but—"

"Right. We need to get tracking. Lead on, Q."

"The thing is—"

"Don't even try to tell me you're doing this alone."

"But—"

Pan's bushy ginger eyebrows slanted toward his nose. If he was angry now, wait till he heard what Cupid had to tell him. "*What?*"

"I'm here."

"Yes, I see that. You're here. We're all here. Now, move!"

"I mean, I'm where I'm going. I'm done. I have arrived at my destination," to quote his car.

"*What?*" Pan's jaw dropped as his gaze passed back and forth between Cupid and Euphrosyne. Yep, angrier. "Please tell me there's a person about to come out of this bathroom, some human who didn't fall from a mountaintop in the sky?"

Cupid shook his head. "There well might be, but—"

"Shut it. I need to think." Pan started pacing, followed quickly by muttering. "This is absurd. Seriously? This job isn't challenging enough? How do they expect me to sort this out, huh?"

Euphrosyne clutched Cupid's sleeve, leaned in close. "Should he be, you know . . ." She pointed toward the sky.

"Definitely not." Cupid took a deep breath and stepped into the path of the wild, red-faced beast that had swallowed his friend. "*Pan.*"

Pan pulled up short, folded his arms across his massive chest, and scowled as if bullying Cupid might change the will of the gods. "I know, I know. I shouldn't lose my cool, but *fffuck*! I've never had two fallens tangled together like this before. How in the—"

"It's not Euphrosyne."

Pan's head tilted so far, his ear touched down on his shoulder. "Say what, now?"

"My heart is vibrating for *you*."

COMING FALL 2021
FROM ISOTOPIA PUBLISHING:

QUITE THE PAIR

BOOK 3 OF THE *CUPID'S FALL* SERIES

VISIT
CUPIDSFALLSERIES.COM
FOR A PREVIEW AND
ORDERING INFO

CAST OF DIVINE CHARACTERS

AUTHOR'S NOTE: The primary name (all uppercase) for each divine is consistent with the narrative of the "Great Syncretism," an invented departure from Greco-Roman mythology. The character snippets offered here are based on canon; where multiple stories exist within the classical sources, I have chosen my favorite version.

ADONIS: Aphrodite's young, beautiful lover.

AGLAIA: One of the three Graces (sister-nymphs), Aglaia is the goddess of splendor.

APHRODITE (Venus): Goddess of love, beauty, and fertility. Married to Hephaestus, bore four children to Ares, including Cupid.

APOLLO: God of light, music, prophecy, and medicine.

ARES (Mars): God of War. Son of Zeus, brother of Hephaestus, father of Cupid.

ARTEMIS (Diana): Goddess of the hunt, protector of new brides. Twin sister of Apollo.

ATHENA (Minerva): Goddess of wisdom and war arts. Sprang from Zeus's head fully formed.

ATROPOS: One of the three Fates ("allotters") responsible for spinning men's fate like thread. Clotho spins the thread of life, Lachesis determines its length, and Atropos cuts the thread with her shears.

CERBERUS: The vicious three-headed hound of Hades who guards the gates of the Underworld to prevent the dead from leaving.

CLOTHO: One of the three Fates, Clotho spins the thread of life.

CUPID (Eros): God of erotic love. Illegitimate son of Aphrodite and Ares. The winged archer of Mount Olympus.

DAEDALUS: Inventor, architect, and sculptor famous for building the Labyrinth for King Minos of Crete to imprison the Minotaur.

DIKE: Goddess of justice and the spirit of moral order and fair judgment.

DIONYSUS (Bacchus): God of wine and ecstasy. Son of Zeus.

ECHO: Mountain nymph deprived of speech by HERA, except for the ability to repeat the last words of another.

EUPHROSYNE: One of the three Graces, Euphrosyne is the goddess of good cheer, joy, and mirth.

HADES (Pluto): Ruler of the Underworld. Brother of Zeus and Poseidon.

HELIOS: God of the sun.

HEPHAESTUS (Vulcan): God of fire and forge, blacksmith and divine craftsman. Son of Zeus, married to Aphrodite, stepfather to Cupid.

HERA (Juno): Queen of the Gods, sister and wife of Zeus. Famous for her ill temper.

HYPNOS: God of sleep. Father of MORPHEUS.

IRIS: Goddess of the rainbow.

LACHESIS: One of the three Fates, Lachesis determines the length of the thread of life.

MERCURY (Hermes): Messenger of the gods, father of Pan.

MORPHEUS: God responsible for sending human shapes to mortals' dreams. Son of HYPNOS.

PAN (Faunus): Demigod of the wild, protector of the herd. Satyr (half man, half goat). One of the only gods thought to have died. Son of Mercury.

POSEIDON (Neptune): Ruler of the seas. Brother of Zeus and Hades.

SYRINX: Nymph who begged the river nymphs to turn her into a marsh reed to escape Pan's unwanted advances.

THALIA: One of the three Graces, Thalia is the goddess of youth and beauty.

THEMIS: Goddess of divine law and order, a prophetic goddess who presides over the most ancient oracles.

ZEUS (Jupiter): Ruler of the gods. Father of many, *by* many—divines and mortals alike.

To get your free, full-color, downloadable guide to the mythology of the Cupid's Fall series, visit: www.bethcgreenberg.com/mythology-guide

ACKNOWLEDGMENTS

Thank you to the readers of *First Quiver*, who took Cupid into your hearts and demanded to know what the gods put him through next. Without your curiosity, who would read Q2?

To my pre-readers of *Into the Quiet*—Shelley, Lisa, and Larry—thank you for your wisdom and generosity with your time and advice. To Maria, thank you for helping my characters find just the right Greek expressions for every situation. To Karen and Sally, thank you for your positivity and support and terrific ideas for spreading the Cupid love.

To my editor, Susan Atlas, thank you for spoiling me with limericks in the margins and for being a true partner in my writing process. Welcome to the editorial team, Lisa Hollett. So great to have your eagle eyes on the final draft. Much gratitude to Domini Dragoone for the lovely page layouts and unending patience.

To the extraordinarily talented cover artist, Betti Gefecht, thank you for reworking Ruthie's slippers and hair style until they were perfect—and for drawing Cupid just right in the very first draft! Mostly, thank you for teaming up with me and making this design process such sheer joy.

To my family and friends who have supported my publishing journey, thank you . . . and don't go anywhere! To my daughter Lindsay, thank you for sharing your talent and experience and teaching me all kinds of things I never imagined I'd need to know.

To my one and only husband Larry, my Right Love and life partner through thick and thin, thank you for being unembarrassable.

ABOUT THE AUTHOR

BETH C. GREENBERG is a former CPA who stepped through the portal of flash (1000-word) fiction into the magical world of creative writing and never looked back. She lives outside of Boston, where she and her husband are occasionally visited by their daughter and grand-dog Slim. *Into the Quiet* is book two of the Cupid's Fall series.

To sign up for Beth's email newsletter and get all the news first, visit www.bethcgreenberg.com/newsletter

If you enjoyed *Into the Quiet,* please consider leaving a review wherever you go to find your next read. Just a line or two really means a lot, especially to an indie author.

FOLLOW:
Website: www.bethcgreenberg.com
Facebook: facebook.com/bethcgreenberg

Made in the USA
Coppell, TX
10 May 2021

55399259R00178